RANDOM

About the author

During his 20-year career in Glasgow with a Scottish Sunday newspaper, Craig Robertson has interviewed three recent Prime Ministers, attended major stories including 9/11, Dunblane, the Omagh bombing and the disappearance of Madeleine McCann, been pilloried on breakfast television, beaten Oprah Winfrey to a major scoop, been among the first to interview Susan Boyle, spent time on Death Row in the USA and dispensed polio drops in the backstreets of India. *Random* is his first novel.

CRAIG ROBERTSON
RANDOM

SIMON &
SCHUSTER

London · New York · Sydney · Toronto

First published in Great Britain by Simon & Schuster UK Ltd, 2010

First published in paperback, 2011

7 9 10 8

Simon & Schuster UK Ltd
1st Floor
222 Gray's Inn Road
London
WC1X 8HB

www.simonandschuster.co.uk

Simon & Schuster Australia
Sydney

A CIP catalogue for this book is available
from the British Library.

A Format ISBN: 978-1-84983-275-5
B Format ISBN: 978-1-84739-881-9

Typeset by Ellipsis Books Limited, Glasgow
Printed and bound by CPI Group (UK) Ltd, Croydon, CR0 4YY

For Jacquie

RANDOM

CHAPTER 1

She was talking but I couldn't take anything in. Her words bounced off me.

Would it be the loud guy with the fair, slicked-back hair? Part of me hoped it would. Maybe he was a regular. He'd need to have been there before if it was to be him.

She and I had only ever been once before, six months earlier, and never would again.

The loud guy would definitely be my choice if I had a choice to make. He had this grating, braying laugh that said listen to me. I looked at him over her shoulder, dodging the words that she threw at me. Let it be him. There was a smugness about him, a loud irritating brashness that rankled. I would gladly, happily, willingly make it him. It couldn't be forced though.

Her words continued to rebound until I caught a few. Something about work. I let them bounce on.

The restaurant was busy with a lunchtime crowd, mainly business types. Any one of them would do just fine. Overstuffed suits and expense accounts, conceited wankers feeding at the corporate trough. Any of them would do. I considered eating slower, delaying the meal until some of the suits left before me so that there would be a chance that it could be one of them.

Maybe that fat guy spraying soup over anyone near him, talking with mouthfuls of bread and broth, splattering the air. He'd do. His shirt was stretched over his paunch and the wing of one collar stuck out of his jacket. He was a scruffy git in a good suit. He was a greedy bastard too, the way he'd wolfed down that soup and was now attacking more bread, tearing at it. He'd do just fine but it couldn't be that way, not contrived. Anyway, his executive heart attack would do the job before long.

I caught some more of her words. She was moaning about the neighbours, the usual dance about their attitude. I switched off again. More rebounds.

There was a sleazy looking prick in a flash suit, staring into the eyes of the girl opposite. She was much younger and much better-looking but was hanging on every word that he dropped on her. He smiled at her like a fucking wolf and I just knew that he was already convinced he'd be boning her before long. And he was probably right. He'd probably fucked every secretary, office junior and brainless bimbo that he'd brought here, impressing his way into their knickers with his wallet and his well-practised lines. Oh he'd do. I wouldn't, couldn't force it but if it were him then that would do me. Chance would indeed be a fine thing.

I batted words back at her with nothing more than nods and shakes of the head, the odd yes and no. She didn't need much from me to make what she thought was a conversation. Just as well. I could think of nothing but the possibilities. Anyone could have passed through that restaurant and left their mark. Anyone. Anyone that I'd never met. That was the beauty of it, the scope of the potential. A world of possibilities, well, a city at least. A city plus a world of visitors.

The tagliatelle arrived. There is something about it that interests me. Strands coming together and running in different directions. Something about the random nature of it. You can pick up any one end and just have no idea where the other end is, no idea which one will move.

I looked at my plate and set my sights on a single end of tagliatelle. I tried to follow it with my eye but lost it quickly. I tried to imagine where it might go, twisting and snaking around and under other strands. An arrabiata maze, a tagliatelle tangle.

Her words barely fazed me. She couldn't lay a syllable on me. My concentration was total.

I had to find the other end of that strand.

I picked one out that looked a definite possibility. I caught the near end of the strand with my fork and pulled it. It slithered, it moved. It wasn't the one I'd thought. I wasn't happy.

There was an older man, maybe sixtyish, giving a waitress a hard time. She'd been too long with the bill for his liking. The miserable old bastard was making her apologize for the third time and you just knew her tip was gone. He'd do too. If he'd been before then maybe he'd be the one. That would do fine.

She had tiramisu after saying that she shouldn't. It looked good.

I had an espresso.

The time was getting nearer and the anticipation grew. My heart raced, my mind wandered and wondered. An accountant? An estate agent would be fine. Perhaps a salesman. Butcher, baker, candlestick maker. Whatever.

She was on the last crumbs of dessert. I would soon know.

A final few words deflected off my shield and I called for the bill. The poor girl who had been bullied by the old guy brought it over and I gave her my warmest smile. We weren't all bad.

I paid, cash obviously, and left a tip. Not too big, not too small.

At the desk at the door were two glass bowls. One held mints, the other business cards. A small paper sign sat beside the cards. *Leave your business card here for a chance to win a free meal for two in our monthly draw.*

What were the chances of that? I wondered. Anyway, I hated tautology.

I put my left hand into the mints and took two out. I reached into the business cards with my right hand. I didn't leave a card. I delved deep into them and took one out.

Jonathan Carr. Salter, Fyfe and Bryce Solicitors. 1024 Bath Street.

Perfect. It wouldn't have mattered who he was or what he did. But it was perfect.

We left.

4

CHAPTER 2

He waved his hands around theatrically as he spoke, seeking attention, drawing glances. The fat man that was with him stroked his ego and laughed with him.

I watched him in the mirror if I looked at him at all. Reflected on him. I listened.

He laughed about clients he had overcharged. He sneered about the idiots he represented. He talked about the girl behind the bar and what he'd do to her. He boasted about a redhead named Amanda and what she'd done to him.

By then I knew his wife was named Rebecca and was blonde. They had no children. I knew a lot about him.

His secretary was Pippa. He drove an Audi TT and a Range Rover. The plaques on the intercom told me that his neighbours were Morrison, Kemper/Astle, Wightman and Moore.

He drank either champagne or imported beer. He liked tapas. He always ignored *Big Issue* sellers. He said 'cool' a lot. One night a week he went to a lap-dancing club in the

Merchant City called Hot Legs. Twice I saw him go into a massage parlour near St Enoch's.

Lunchtime usually meant here, the Corinthian. Evenings meant Tiger Tiger. Nights meant home to the trendy flat on the Clyde. It all meant very little to me.

All style no substance, that was Jonathan Carr. Expensive pinstripe suit. Spectacles that I took to be 'designer'. Shoes that were too young for him. His hair was tinted and gelled. Carr was late thirties trying to be early twenties. I didn't like him.

I'd followed him. To the Corinthian or from it. From his office to Tiger Tiger. From Glassford Street to the Clyde at Scotstoun.

I didn't like him at all but that didn't make any difference. I didn't dislike him in order to serve my own ends or to short-circuit any potential guilt. The reason I didn't like him was that he was a prick.

He seemed at home in the Corinthian, sunning himself in the vast main bar, puffing up his ego under that ridiculously ornate domed ceiling and the elaborate cornices of seraphim and cherubim.

The Corinthian annoyed me. It was a bank until the late 1920s when it became the city's high court for nearly seventy years until it was then turned into this monument to bad taste. It is debatable at which time it was more criminal. It was a magnificent Victorian building but it had been plastered with so much gold leaf and crystal that it reminded me of an old whore with far too much make-up. It tried for plush refinement and it managed classy brothel.

Carr and the fat man he was with, the man he called Alastair, were fitting clients. It flattered them to be somewhere so cheap and yet so expensive. The cost of the drink was intended to keep the riff-raff at bay. They were drinking champagne at £60 a bottle. It was Glasgow and it was lunchtime. Drinking champagne was ridiculous.

A young woman walked past and Carr fixed his eyes on her bottom. He raised his eyebrows and licked his lips. Alastair laughed and leered with him. I loathed them.

They finished. Good, we could go. I was out of place here and I didn't like that.

Carr made a show of holding the champagne bottle upside down to check it was empty then slipped a fiver under it to leave as a tip. He slapped Alastair noisily on the back and they made for the door.

I didn't turn to see them leave but finished my beer and gave them a head start. I knew where they were going.

I caught sight of them again walking down Ingram Street, maybe sixty yards in front of me, in a direct line to the Duke of Wellington with the traffic cone on his head. I wouldn't get too close. Not yet.

CCTV cameras. They were everywhere. On me now for sure. On Carr. On Alastair. Following every step, every twitch of the head, every thought. The cameras made life difficult but not impossible. There was always a way.

At the Gallery of Modern Art they separated. Alastair waddling towards Queen Street, Carr going on towards Buchanan Street. I stayed with Carr, crowds between us, protecting him, protecting me.

7

He had a swagger that was ridiculous on a man that was just five foot five. It was a strut. He swayed along Buchanan Street as if he owned it.

He turned onto Bath Street and made for his offices. It was 2.30. I watched him spring up the stairs to number 1024 and disappear behind mahogany doors. That would be him for the afternoon and I'd return at 4.30 and sit in the cafe across the road. It was Wednesday and he would most probably leave sharp and head for Milngavie. Milngavie was where the redhead lived.

Three Wednesdays I had watched him and three times he had gone there. What did he tell the blonde wife? Bridge club, business, a snooker match, Rotary? It didn't matter to me.

When I returned, I had to sit in the cafe for just fifteen minutes before the doors to his office opened and Carr scampered back down the steps onto Bath Street. A man on a mission. He would go to the NCP on Renfield Street and get his TT. He would take Port Dundas Road to the A879 and then Auchenhowie Road to Milngavie. He'd park in the next street to the one where the redhead lived on the edge of the village. He'd leave around 11.00 and be intending to be back at his flat by 11.30. A creature of habit.

I followed him from a distance until I was certain where he was going. I then turned, went home and waited.

I drove to Milngavie, stopping just once, then on through to the other side of the village. The stop took just a few minutes and I was earlier than I'd intended. I had to drive on for fully ten minutes then turn back towards Glasgow.

My eyes were all over the clock, my speed and the road in front. I was a bit scared. My heart raced. So many things could have gone wrong. He might have noticed before he began driving. Someone else might have stopped for him. Someone might drive by. He might have left earlier. Or later.

My plan was full of holes. I'd need to do better.

Then there it was stopped in front of me. The TT. He'd not got quite as far as I'd thought but close enough. I could just pick out the silver Audi in the dark. He was standing by the back wheel with a mobile phone in his hand. I prayed he hadn't used it yet.

I pulled up behind him and got out. He had a flat tyre, of course he did. He seemed to have driven over a nail. Unlucky, I said.

He didn't look twice at my false numberplate, paid no attention to the baseball cap that covered my face to anyone driving past and couldn't possibly be aware of the spare tyres that I had put on the car before I set off to ensure I left no discernible, traceable pattern from my own.

Of course Carr didn't know how to change a tyre. I did and could help. He was really grateful about that. He had been just about to call someone.

The road was too narrow where he had stopped, I told him. There was a lay-by half a mile up the road that he could pull into. It wouldn't do the tyre or the car any more harm.

He did so.

The lay-by was hidden from the main road by a row of slim trees. It was perfect.

I told him I would get a jack out of the boot of my car and asked him to have a look at the wheel so he'd get an idea of how it came off in case it ever happened again.

I saw the look on Carr's face. He had no intention of ever changing a tyre. He'd buy a new car before he did that. Still he'd bend down and pretend he was looking at something if it kept me happy.

That's how he was when I closed the boot and walked to his car. That's how he was when I swung the jack and smashed the back of his head.

I felt the impact reverberate through my arms. I hadn't expected that. I readied myself to swing again but there was no need.

His face crashed into the car's side with a bang and when he slumped back soundlessly I saw that his face was almost as bloodied as the back of his head. He fell to the ground unconscious.

I took the duct tape from my pocket and stuck it firmly across his mouth, sealing it shut. I then took out the tube of superglue and dabbed spots of it on the inside of his nostrils.

Satisfied that there was enough of it, I then held the sides of his nose and squeezed. A few drops of the glue leaked out onto my surgical gloves but the rest soon locked his nostrils tight.

Carr stirred. Maybe the initial blow had worn off, more likely the fact that he couldn't breathe had alerted his inner emergency alarm.

He looked puzzled. He fought for air but there was none

to be had. His head rolled, his jaws tried to work the tape free, his eyes pleaded. I watched his chest heave as his lungs searched for oxygen and hurled themselves against his chest. He looked up at me. I looked down at him. Looked him in the eyes.

He didn't seem quite so full of himself now. *Jonathan Carr. Salter, Fyfe and Bryce Solicitors. 1024 Bath Street.* Didn't look quite so cocky at all.

Air hunger kicked in. An interesting condition. Strangely, it isn't diminishing oxygen levels that cause it but rising levels of carbon dioxide in the blood. This is detected by sensors in the carotid sinus and causes all hell to break loose in the body. It triggers respiratory distress, provoking the body to find any way it can to get air into the lungs. It is irrational and desperate. Carr's body thrashed at the air around it.

The hunger didn't pass but was overtaken by hypoxia. His head hurt. His skin took on a faint blue tinge. He shook. Brain damage was already in motion. Heart failure was minutes away.

His eyes closed over. He still shook, still kicked for oxygen that wasn't coming.

A few more minutes and he was dead. Suffocated. Asphyxiated. Comprehensively and fatally deprived of oxygen.

Finally, I took the pair of secateurs from my pocket and cut.

Strange. I had expected more blood.

CHAPTER 3

I'd come up with the idea of cutting off his finger after a bit of thought. I wanted something to make sure they knew it was me, something to remember me by. The finger was easy, straightforward and not too messy. It would make me look crazy enough but not a complete psycho. Didn't want them to think that.

Of course there was a risk in posting it to the cops but I was certain I had covered myself. I bought enough padded envelopes in one go so that I wouldn't have to go back for more. I bought them long before I began. They were cheap, mass-produced and bought from three separate chain-store stationers.

The postage was correct, a tricky matter given the Royal Mail's introduction of Pricing in Proportion. Anything thicker than 5mm or heavier than 100g has to be in a large letter rather than a letter and is priced accordingly. Anything thicker than 25mm or above 750g has to be classed as a packet. 25mm could take most pinkies quite easily and the weight was clearly not an issue. I posted two clothes pegs to myself as a trial run.

I wore surgical gloves from start to finish. There wouldn't be so much as a ridge or a spiral, far less an identifiable fingerprint.

I printed the address labels off on my bog-standard, thousands-sold-every-month PC printer rather than take any risk of handwriting analysis. The labels were self-adhesive. *CID, Strathclyde Police, Stewart Street, Glasgow G4 0HY.*

I didn't lick the envelope to seal it, I used water. Life must have been so much easier for those of us with things to hide before the advancements in DNA.

I would use a different postbox each time, each of them nowhere near the prying eyes of CCTV cameras. Each posting would be done at a busy time, a baseball cap tight to my face, the package hidden away till the last moment.

The secateurs were bought from B&Q months before. Sharp enough for the job, sold by the thousand, small enough to slip into a pocket.

Above all, the finger meant nothing. They would think it had some other significance, some hidden meaning. It didn't.

It was my signature but it wasn't my hand. That made me laugh.

The finger might point them in the wrong direction. Funny.

The little finger is the strongest on the hand. Because it has a dedicated muscle and is the shortest, it gets the most leverage.

The finger hadn't been mentioned in any of the newspaper reports though. It had probably arrived at the cop shop too late for it to make the morning editions. Maybe tomorrow, maybe next time.

I'd read every one, scoured every line. Watched every news bulletin too. I wasn't glorying in it though. It wasn't my fifteen minutes. Not yet.

I wanted to know what they knew. Getting caught was not part of my plan.

They all carried the story. Some had it tucked away, some splashed it. Some just reported the facts as they knew them, others made wild guesses about criminal links, revenge and bitter clients. Mostly it was just bollocks.

The *Herald*. Wednesday, 11 February 2009. Page 2.
Solicitor found murdered.
by Andrea Faulds.

The body of a solicitor was found in a lay-by outside Milngavie yesterday morning. It is believed he was murdered. Jonathan Carr, a 37-year-old solicitor in the firm of Salter, Fyfe and Bryce, was found around 6.30 a.m. by a man walking his dog. Police have not revealed the cause of Mr Carr's death but it is thought that he received severe injuries in an apparent attack.

Detective Chief Inspector Lewis Robertson of Strathclyde Police said, 'Mr Jonathan Carr, a solicitor in a Glasgow firm of solicitors, was found dead this morning. Strathclyde Police are treating the investigation of his death as a murder inquiry.

'We will not, at this moment in time, release details of the injuries perpetrated on Mr Carr. However we can say that they were violent and severe. We would urge anyone who was in the vicinity of the lay-by on Glasgow Road between 11.00 p.m. and 1.00 a.m. or anyone who has knowledge of Mr Carr's

last movements to come forward and help in this investigation. All information will be treated in the strictest confidence. Members of the public can contact the CID room at Stewart Street or telephone Crimestoppers on 0800 555 111.'

DCI Robertson would not be drawn on any possible motives for the attack on Mr Carr. The man who found Mr Carr's body, Mr Stephen Costello, said that his pet springer spaniel Asterix had become agitated and pulled him to the spot where he discovered the lawyer. Mr Costello immediately called the police.

Jonathan Carr was a married man with no children. His wife Rebecca was said to be extremely distressed last night and was being comforted by her family. Mr Carr had been in the firm of Salter, Fyfe and Bryce for five years. He was said by friends to enjoy playing golf and snooker and was a prominent member of his local Rotarians club.

Neither the police nor Mrs Carr knew why the solicitor was on that road, whether he had been visiting friends or clients in Milngavie or was just driving through. The victim's car, a silver Audi TT, was found near his body. The car's keys were still in the ignition and it was believed to have a flat tyre. The police would not speculate on whether it was a chance killing but did concede that robbery did not appear to be a motive as the car had not been taken.

That was day one. Day two it got less room in most. By day three there was no mention at all in a couple of them. Still nothing about the finger being cut off. Nothing about it being posted to the cops. There was no way the papers wouldn't write about that if they knew so it could only be that the police hadn't told them.

Why?

Procedural reasons. Operational. That was what they always said when they didn't release information. What the fuck did it mean though? They didn't want people to know about the finger being cut. Wanted to stay a step ahead. Of me? Yeah, right. OK, I'd watched enough TV programmes. Read enough books. They would get crazies down the station, confessing to the killing. My killing.

The cops would ask them about the finger. Ask them to prove they'd done it. The crazies wouldn't know about the finger and would be thrown back on the street in two minutes. And the police would worry about copycats. Some real crazy would murder someone and slice off their finger to claim credit for the first one. Fuck that for a laugh.

Day two in the papers had seen a new name. Detective Sergeant Rachel Narey. Robertson was still quoted and he was obviously the main man. But two of the papers quoted this Narey. I liked her.

The *Herald*. Thursday, 12 February 2009. Page 5.
Carr speculation dismissed.
by Andrea Faulds.

Strathclyde Police yesterday rejected claims about the murder of Glasgow lawyer Jonathan Carr as 'wild speculation'. Detective Sergeant Rachel Narey said that they were still keeping an open mind on the investigation but branded some press conjecture as 'extremely unhelpful'. DS Narey said, 'Our investigation into the murder of Mr Carr is still at a very early stage and we will explore every avenue in our determination to find the person or people responsible.

'However, there has been some wild speculation about both Mr Carr and the reasons for his killing which have been little more than guesswork or gossip. There is no reason to think that any of the theories put forward

in certain sections of the written media have any foundation whatsoever.

'At best this is extremely unhelpful and at worst it is irresponsible. Some of the people that have written this rubbish should

think of the implications before they do so. It gets in the way of a police investigation and is distressing to Mr Carr's family. When there is something concrete to report then you can be sure that we will let you know.'

Yes, I liked her. Feisty bitch. She was on television as well. Robertson spoke and she stood by his shoulder in most of the clips. The camera liked her too.

CHAPTER 4

Four years I'd driven a taxi. Still didn't feel like a proper job. Still just something to see me through.

Nine years I had worn a suit and pushed numbers round spreadsheets. Nine years of balancing budgets, making projections, income and expenditure. Accounting for this, accounting for that. No accounting for eventualities.

After it happened, I was in and out of the office for a few months. Compassionate leave, then back, signed off ill, then back.

Drinking too much, thinking too much, arguing too much, threatening to beat people up too much. Sent home to think again. Then paid off. All very sorry that it had to come to this. Nobody's fault. Sure. Fuck you.

After that I had eight months at home, looking at walls and going up them. Then I went to work for Cammy Strang driving a taxi. It worked for me, I guess. They called me mate. Or driver. Sometimes they'd call me pal or buddy. When the booze or the pills or the anger or just the sheer fact of living in Glasgow got to them, they'd call me things that really weren't very nice at all.

People flit in and out of your life when you are a taxi driver. Few of them ever register on your consciousness, they are just shapes and voices and half-arsed directions. They are demands for receipts and hands reaching out for change. They are threats to your upholstery and assaults on your opinions.

It suited me. They weren't real people so you didn't have to have real conversations with them. If pushed you had the traditional taxi conversation and all you had to give were the traditional taxi answers. It was an old game.

'Been busy the night, driver?'

'What time you been on since?'

'Time you on to?'

'Long shift that, eh?'

'You into the fitba?'

'Who do you support?'

'Aye, but who do you support?'

'Aye? Very good. But who do you really support though?'

'Aye, fair enough. Rather no say, eh? Nae worries. I'm a Rangers man maself.'

'Been busy the night, driver?'

Aye, I've been busy. Busy driving drunken wastes of space like yourself home. Busy shipping deadwood out to dead-town. Busy listening to shite. Busy thinking. Busy gliding through neon and never wondering about the creatures passed in the night. The only thing that could conceivably interest me about anyone I drive is that they might be next. Any one of them.

Glasgow seems a much smaller city at night. Smaller and

deader, brighter and greyer, emptier and scarier. Streetlight tunnels to nowhere and bogey men that go stab in the night.

Drive a taxi in Glasgow and you see its people at their worst. Never, ever, at their best. Dead men drinking. Drunk men barely walking. Drunk girls barely capable of talking. Every cliché you can think about this city you see in the back of a cab. 'Been busy the night, driver?'

Sometimes, just sometimes, the shapes in the back of the car said things that made me listen.

Late as it was, he was still in a suit, tie yanked to the side and down. His eyes were booze red in the rear-view mirror and he was howling of the stuff. He could more or less stand still in front of Central Station and was capable of walking to the door so that was something.

'Awrite, mate. How you daein? Springburn. Croftbank Street. Been busy the night?'

'Not too bad.'

'It's fucking jumping in the toon. Must be keeping you gawn.'

'Aye, busy enough.'

'Time you been on since, driver?'

'Just a couple of hours.'

'Cool. Bit wasted masel. Gid night though.'

'Aye, good.'

'Workin' in the morning in aw. Ah fuckit, ah'll be fine. Here, d'ye read aboot that lawyer that got kilt?'

Just a slight pause.

'Aye.'

'Fucksake. Killin lawyers, what's it comin tae? Ah well, wan's a start, eh?'

Silence.

'Ah said like wan's a start, know what ah mean?'

'Aye.'

'Fuckin' lawyers, shower a bastards, man. Screw you for every penny you've got. Here it'd be good if the cunt that kilt this wan's gonnae start knocking them aw aff. Know what ah mean?'

'Aye.'

'Wan's a start. What d'ye think? Gangsters that did it? Fund oot in the middle uh naewhere like that.'

'No idea.'

'Stands tae reason, man. What the fuck was he daein oot there onyways? Shady if ye ask me. Got gangsters written aw o'er it.'

'Aye, maybe.'

'Makes a change fae some stupid wee ned getting hiself stabbed ah suppose. An they say a change is as good as a rest. Gae the cunt a medal that's what ah say. See the fitba last night?'

'No.'

'Guid game, man. Never a penalty though. No way, no how. Who'dye support yersel?'

'No really into football.'

'Aye bit who dae you support?'

'Partick Thistle.'

'Aye? Who dae you really support? Bet you just say Thistle to any drunk that asks you, eh?'

No shit, Sherlock.

Another night a couple got in. Middle-class types, middle-aged. Picked up at the Theatre Royal on Hope Street and heading for Milngavie. Take a pound out of the cliché bank. They were both half cut and squabbling, none of it any interest or business of mine until I heard the name. Tuned right in then.

Him. 'But Jonathan was a good guy.'

Her. 'Jonathan was a prick.'

'Oh, come on, the guy is dead.'

'Doesn't change the fact that he was a little shit. Treated Becca something terrible. I am sure he was cheating on her for years.'

'He's been murdered for Christ's sake.'

'Yes, and I'm sorry about that. Actually, I'm not sure I am.'

'Gillian!'

'Oh, come on, David. He would have sold his grand-mother for a tenner and he would have probably fucked her as well.'

'Christ sake! Look keep it down, and anyway you don't know he cheated on Becca.'

'Ha. No? Your precious friend Jonathan would have shagged a barber-shop floor. You know that full well. Don't think he didn't try it on with me.'

'What?'

'Oh grow up, David. Of course he did. The way he was I'd have been insulted if he hadn't.'

'You didn't . . .?'

23

'Oh, fuck off.'

'That's a no?'

'You shouldn't have to ask.'

'No, of course not.'

'It's a no.'

'OK.'

'Do you think that maybe . . .?'

'What?'

'Do you think maybe Becca did it?'

'What!'

'Or had it done? It makes sense. If you were doing what he was doing then I'd have you killed too.'

'Jesus Christ, Gillian!'

'I'm just saying, and take that by way of a warning. I never did like the number of times you two went to Rotary together.'

'Gill . . .'

'Oh, shut up. It's the next on the left, driver.'

Something about the night makes people open up. Alcohol probably. Driving through the city with a complete stranger at the wheel. It's like talking into the mirror. But sometimes, sometimes I wished they would just shut the fuck up.

It is like the city is whispering at you. All babbling away at once, the way crazy people hear voices.

'When you on till? Working again tomorrow? Been doing this long? My wife left me. I hate my job. Read about that murder? What team do you support? Been busy the night? I've been waiting an hour for a fucking taxi. See what happened to that lawyer? Terrible night, eh? What time you been on since? I hate this weather. This traffic is murder, isn't it? Did you read about that murder? Did you read about that murder? Did you read about that murder?'

'Been busy the night, driver?'

CHAPTER 5

There was a girl from school. Jill Hutchison.

My first love.

So corny but nothing truer. First time I'd felt it and it threw me big time. I couldn't understand what was going on. Every time I saw her, my stomach turned over and my thinking went wonky. Stammer, stutter, smile, sweat and scarlet. I couldn't put sentences together properly. I talked complete and utter shite when I most wanted to talk sense.

Didn't know what it was at first and when I worked it out, I wasn't impressed. If this was love they could keep it. Couldn't help myself though. For all I couldn't understand what was happening to me, it wasn't hard to work out why.

She was amazing. Beautiful. Smart too. Sweet and funny. She made my head spin. Long, lush black hair and fiery brown eyes. Her smile killed me.

It was three years before I had the guts to ask her out. Could barely believe it when she said yes. On the way out of a physics class, I bumped into her accidentally on purpose and we got talking. For once, the words came out more or less as I meant them. By the end of a three-minute conversation, I had asked her to see *Top Gun*. I'd had a plan to suggest going to see *Nine and a Half Weeks* but chickened out. It seemed for the best. Mickey Rourke and Kim Basinger would have given the wrong impression. Tom Cruise was a safe bet.

I kept my hands to myself and my verbal diarrhoea under control. It went well. It must have, she kissed me and said we should go out again.

I was fifteen and the happiest guy in the world. Pictures. Parties. Walks. Her room or occasionally mine. Listening to Prince, the Thompson Twins and the Jets. Touching each other. Never more than a snog and a grope. That was fine by me.

Of course I wanted to do more. I strangled myself three times a night thinking about doing more. The thought of it burned me up every time I looked at her. But that's not the way it was. I loved her. I respected her. If she wanted to wait then I'd wait. God knows she was worth waiting for.

She had this thing where she would look right in my eyes as if I was the greatest thing since I don't know what. It was a kind of shy thing, looking up as if I wouldn't notice. Sometimes she would put a hand on either side of my face and touch me really gently. Then she'd kiss me really slowly, full on the mouth. Sensuous, that's the word for it. Sensuous.

So sensuous that one time I actually came in my pants by her just holding my face and kissing me like that.

Of course I wanted to do more. Guys would ask me if I was doing her and I'd say no. They'd laugh but I didn't care. They said that they definitely would and I didn't doubt it but there was more to it and they just wouldn't understand.

I told them I respected her and they laughed some more.

Then, four months into it, we were to go to a party that I couldn't make it to on time. I was playing football and we'd agreed she would go along first then I'd get there as soon as I could after getting changed. 119 Clelland Avenue. I remember the address even though I don't remember whose house it was.

It sat on the sweep of the bend and had two large conifers either side of the door. The path was gravel. I can still hear its crunch. I knocked on the door although the music banging through the windows should have told me it was a waste of time. Madonna. Full blast. Funny the things you remember.

After a couple of minutes I just pushed the door and went in. There were kids everywhere, most of them I knew by sight or name.

Couldn't find her at first and tried the kitchen and the various groups that stood around in huddles. I dragged a couple of kids from their drinks and asked if they knew where she was. A girl shook her head, a guy smiled and shrugged. Then one told me she was upstairs.

I made my way through the folk on the stairs. Talking, snogging, drinking. I missed the sniggering though or else I might not have opened that door as I did.

There she was.

Naked and impaled on top of an eighteen-year-old bastard named Tony Di Rossi.

Not sure what was worse. Seeing her. Writhing. Her head back, hair flying. Listening to her beg him for more. Beg him for it harder. Or knowing that I'd have to walk back out of that house, my ears burning, my face scarlet, my mouth hanging open and salty with my own hot tears. Every dickhead in the place laughing at me.

Fucking bitch.

Maybe I'd opened the door quietly, maybe she just wasn't listening. Either way she didn't know I was there.

He did though. He saw me and looked. He kept on thrusting at her. His bastard grin said, 'Enjoying the show?' His bastard grin said 'Oh she's good.' 'Oh she's loving it.'

I couldn't move. I watched. Watched her drive herself down on him. Talking dirty to him.

No, the worst thing was that I was turned on by seeing her naked. First time. I was being humiliated beyond my worst nightmares. The girl I loved was betraying me in front of my eyes and all I could think of right then was how amazing her breasts were. I was hard. Maybe if she'd seen me earlier, she'd have stopped but by the time she did, it was way too late. She came all over him as she saw me.

There was a flicker of surprise and maybe some guilt on her face. Not much. Certainly no remorse. Right then, she wasn't regretting anything.

He saw her look and knew it for what it was. He loved it. He was laughing. Laughing loud. At me.

As I found my legs and my senses and lost my hard-on, I left the room, left the house, left Clelland Avenue.

I knew everyone was laughing at me.

Fucking bitch.

Fucking dirty bitch.

I got over it a long time ago though. It's not the thing, not the reason. I moved on, met someone, got married, had a beautiful daughter. I left Jill Hutchison and that house in Clelland Avenue behind me.

Some scars never quite heal though and sometimes I remembered. Sometimes I was fifteen again and it stung and I hated Jill Hutchison.

First love, first hate. Never forget them.

That was why I was sitting with the Glasgow South phone book and working my way through the Hs. Not looking for her, not that stupid. If you are going to pick a name from the phone book at random then you need somewhere to start. Hutchison was as good a name for my purpose as any. Better than most. She'd be ruled out, so would anyone related to her. Anyone else would have to take their chances with fate.

There were Hutchesons, Hutchiesons, Hutchinsons, Hutchisons and one solitary Huntchinson. More Hutchisons than anything though – maybe 200 of them on the south side. It would be one of them.

I paused a moment and considered what I was doing. And what I would do. There was anticipation, fear and excitement. There was an uneasiness crawling deep in my stomach. Uncertainty. Possibilities. Power. An unmistakable

31

feeling that there would be no turning back. Once picked it couldn't be unpicked. No matter what.

I realized I was breathing heavily. I could sense the very ends of the hairs on the back of my arms. Maybe this was how a wolf felt before it attacked. The heart sending blood surging to every vessel it needs. It was pounding.

I closed my eyes and stuck my finger on the page. Simple as.

Hutchison, Wm. 16 Portland Street, Whiteinch.

I read his name five times and savoured it, turned it over. *Hutchison, Wm. William Hutchison. Billy Hutchison. Bill Hutchison. Willie. Will.*

Poor old William Hutchison, whoever he was, was going to pay an awful price for the behaviour of a fifteen-year-old slut twenty-odd years earlier.

Fucking bitch.

Don't analyse it. It's too obvious, doesn't need it. I wanted to hurt her, punish her, make her regret humiliating me. Even though she would never know, this was my way of doing it.

Fate's a funny thing. *Hutchison, W* from Rutherglen and *Hutchison, W.G.* from Barrhead were a fingernail away from theirs and knew nothing about it. Sitting either side of *Hutchison, Wm*, they were blissful in their ignorance. Best way for them.

I couldn't help wondering who they were. Walter? Wilma? Wendy? Young or old, good or bad? Butcher, baker or mover and shaker? Would they have been difficult or easy, fought or succumbed? Would it have mattered?

Of course, I knew nothing about the man in Whiteinch either but that would change soon enough. Me and William Hutchison would become acquainted. I'd get to know him pretty well before I killed him. That was the way it had to be.

CHAPTER 6

It turned out Billy was a bookie. An accountant of the turf variety with his own shop on Maryhill Road, one of the handful of independents left in the city. Places like his relied on regulars. Offering slightly better prices than the big high street guys to keep the punters coming back. He'd know them all by name, know whose wife not to talk to, know whose secrets to keep, know who'd be good for credit and who wouldn't.

He'd be a bit shady, bound to be, but legit enough. There would be a good few bets never chalked up for the taxman. He'd maybe be paying a bit of insurance to keep his shop from going up in flames, protection money to ensure a safe trip to the bank with a bag of takings.

Billy the bookie was in his late fifties, a cheery, grey-haired man of about five foot six with steel glasses, a belly and a purple face. His stomach, face and nose told me he liked his beer and whisky. So did his lunchtime visits to the Imperial Bar.

He lived an easy fifteen-minute drive from his shop, a

big semi in Whiteinch with garden front and back. His wife was a faded woman with hard-worked hair, nicotine skin and 1980s clothes. I twice saw two guys who were probably grown-up kids that had flown the coop.

I watched him get into his car to drive to the shop.

I watched him walk from his shop to the bank and saw him stop fully five times to chat with this person or that.

Billy Hutchison knew everyone in the street and they all knew him. He had a joke for most, a quiet word for others. For every one of them he had a breezy smile. He tousled kids' hair, he patted dogs and he waved at passing cars. Chances are he would have helped old ladies across the road if any of them needed it. He was Santa, offering 2–1 the field.

It didn't make any difference. His was the name at the end of my finger and that was all that mattered. Carr had made it easy for me by being a total fanny but that wasn't the point. Random is random.

I slipped into the pub and watched Billy. I was much more comfortable in the Imperial than I had been in the Corinthian. The beer, bunnets and bandits hid me better than champagne and chandeliers. No one looked twice.

Billy held court at a table in the corner. He sat with cronies and there was a lot of laughing and waving of hands. They all enjoyed the craic but Billy was king. No doubt about it.

The bunnets – whether they wore them or not – knew their place. They could have a pop at Billy, make a joke at his expense, didn't matter. When Billy spoke they listened and laughed. He was the money man and that bought him stature.

I watched him knock back a pint of special and a large whisky. He wolfed down a plate of lasagne and chips. Chips with lasagne? Christ, the 'chef' deserved killing.

He had another pint and two more double whiskies. He chased the lasagne and chips salad down with apple pie and cream.

He had lasagne on his shirt, spots of cream on his collar and a mix of the whole mess on his face. To celebrate, he wiped his mouth with the back of his hand and burped. It was more than a rift. It was an open-mouth belch that he exaggerated by making it roar from his belly.

Billy the bookie sat back to let everyone marvel at his talent and his mates duly paid homage by all laughing with him.

I guess you can find a reason to kill anyone if you look hard enough. Billy Hutchison – nice old guy, burping slob – had just signed his warrant. I finished my drink, left the pub and went home.

It was fully two weeks until I went back to Maryhill and went into Billy's shop. I'd seen him go into the Imperial just after twelve and the first race was the 2.00 at Sandown. Billy would be back in the bookies by 1.30 so that gave him nearly an hour and a half to fill his belly and display his manners.

I walked and waited – I didn't need to watch him eat again. Walking when you have nowhere to go and no wish to be noticed is a strange thing. You can't just look aimless, there has to be a direction about you. Pick a spot in front of you and walk quick enough, not too quick. No eye contact, keep in the shadows, be casual. Walk as if you are whistling without actually doing so.

I got far enough, checked my watch, looked around as if I was a bit lost and making my mind up. No idea if anyone was actually watching me. Checked my watch again, puffed out my cheeks and turned around.

Back to Billy's.

It was ten past two, the first race was over and the place should have filled up a bit. More customers, more cover.

I had one worry though and there was no way I could think of to test it except by going in. Suck it and see, no other way to go. CCTV. The bane of my frigging life. Well, my new life.

I had spent a lot of time thinking about it. Pros. Cons. There were no pros. I would say that I lost sleep over it but I didn't sleep much anyway. However the thought of them definitely made me anxious. If there were cameras in there then it could only be bad news. The only question was the degree of trouble.

My only protection was the baseball cap on my head and while that would help, it was hardly a disguise. One shot of me in the shop meant a link could be proven. No getting away from that. It would be a while yet before anything happened to Billy and it would mean someone checking through a lot of film but it could be done.

Maybe Billy didn't keep the film more than a day or two.

Maybe Billy had cameras with no film in them. Maybe Billy had no camera. I didn't like maybes. I needed certainties. Random only gets you so far.

What was my take on Billy boy? He had money but not that much. The house was reasonably expensive but not that much. Semi. Semi-detached, semi-expensive. I'd looked at his shoes – a hundred quid a time with worn heels. He ate lasagne and chips but wore a watch that was either worth five hundred pounds or a tenner depending on whether it was legit or a snidey. He had a two quid haircut and two twenty-grand cars in his drive. He walked to the bank. Mrs nicotine skin and hard-worked hair carried Louis Vuitton handbags and went to bingo twice a week.

My money was on Billy not having a camera. It was a big bet. Bigger than anything placed in Hutchison's Independent Bookmakers. I figured that he wouldn't want to spend the money. Figured he'd not want everything that happened in his shop to be recorded either. Figured he'd have a dummy camera at best.

For figured, read hoped. For hoped, read prayed. Except I didn't pray to God any more.

I had finished my return walk and was outside the bookies. I didn't hesitate even though I wanted to. I breathed deep and approached the door. Let there be no cameras. No cameras. No cameras. Keep saying it, make it so.

I pushed through the frosted-glass door and went in, knowing that the last thing I should do was look for the last thing I wanted to see. Scanning the little shop for cameras would be like holding my hands up.

There were newspapers pinned up on the far wall and I headed over to hide myself against them until I got my bearings. I made as if I was poring over the Sandown form. Made as if I knew what I was doing. Checked out the floor. Worn carpet. Rolled-up betting slips. Rogue ash showed someone was ignoring the smoking ban.

The walls behind the pinned-up racing pages could have done with a lick of paint. There were chips out of the Formica tabletops and a loose wire sticking out below a light switch. Thoughts of electrocution strayed across my mind.

I found a betting slip and wrote out a line. Fiver on the favourite in the second.

Billy took the bet himself. There was just him and a slightly chubby twenty-something girl with dark hair behind the counter. He gave the slip the once-over before giving me some cheesy 'last of the big spenders' grin and clocked in my bet. He'd barely seen me although it didn't matter if he did. Only mattered who else saw me. Billy wouldn't be talking.

He gave me my copy of the slip and turned to the next punter.

I looked at him just a moment longer than I should have done. Imagining all kinds of things and thinking it odd that I was standing so close to him. I was stalling and it was stupid and yet I didn't, couldn't, pull away. The chubby girl was looking at me, her eyebrows knitted, about to ask if there was anything wrong. Sure, I thought, I am going to kill your boss and I'm having a good gawk at him first.

You got a problem with that? Instead I made a show of checking my betting slip and nodding my head before sliding back into the cover of the punters.

They were the usual mixed betting-shop crowd. Old guys shuffling a quid a day around Lucky 15s and Yankees at a few pence a line. Loud younger guys in football tops banging in single bets and claiming it is all fixed when they lose. Quiet types who slide their slips over the counter and never let on whether they've won or not.

I stood with them and faced the two TV screens just like they did. Difference was I was the only guy in there hoping that his horse wouldn't win. And I wasn't looking at the television but looking for cameras. I saw none. Thank fuck for that.

Diamond Mick, the favourite that I'd put my fiver on, came in fourth. Thank fuck for that too. I wouldn't have to go back to the counter and give Billy or the assistant another look at me or another reason to remember me.

I scrunched up my betting slip and made as if to let it fall at my feet with all the others. Instead I slipped it into my pocket. No one was paying any attention. If they looked at anything other than the form for the next race it was at a skinny ginger guy in a Celtic shirt who was telling anyone that would listen that the entire sport was fixed.

I had my back to the counter and was walking out when I heard Billy laughing, telling everyone that their luck would change in the next race. A beaten favourite was a good result for him. Or it should have been. Billy's luck wasn't as good as he thought.

'Come on, boys,' he was telling them. 'Can't win them all, but things can only get better, as Tony Blair used to say.

'Tell you what. I'll give you a quarter point on the next favourite above whatever the SP is. Can't say fairer than that, now can I? This is going to cost me money, I can feel it in my bones.'

Billy's bones. The bones of Billy the bookie. A single shiver passed through me.

It was three full weeks before I went anywhere near Billy's shop again. Three weeks of thinking, planning, waiting.

Patience, patience.

Means and opportunity. Method. Detail and more detail. Devil in the detail. Pitfalls, escape routes, eventualities. Everything had to be considered.

A part of me hankered to go back there and to get on with it but the majority of me – the cold, dead part of me – knew better.

The hot, living part, the last traces of the old me, was getting ahead of himself. Thinking of Billy's bones, his last sound, his death rattle. Dead me reined it back in.

There was no rush, things had to be done properly or not done at all. Billy could wait. Billy the bookie wasn't going anywhere. Not yet.

Three weeks of reading, researching, deliberating, rejecting, debating. Do it this way, do it that. But never a moment to think not to do it. Never that.

Even when I went back to the bookies, even then I was

there for an hour, no more. Then not there again for another two weeks. No rush.

In between, I went past his house in the middle of the night. I got out of the car and walked. I timed myself.

I practised. I worked through things in my head. My cold head. My dead head. Billy Hutchison. Billy the burping bookie. I thought about him a lot.

The rear of his shop backed onto the Forth and Clyde Canal. The bookies was Billy's castle and his moat gave shelter to shopping trolleys, beer cans and condoms. The canal steals through Glasgow unseen and unheralded. At Maryhill it almost separates the city from the country as if it were the present from the past. One bank holds back the bams of Maryhill Road and the other protects rabbits, mink and roe deer. Never the twain shall meet unless a wild child of the Wyndford is particularly hungry.

I sometimes used to play around the canal when I was wee and knew the basin well enough. I hadn't been down there since the days it ran dirty and a lungful of canal water would have had you dicing with death. It has been cleaned up in recent years though and fish have a better chance of survival in the water than the locals do on the land. No chance of the fish ending up as junkies.

It had been a while since I'd been on the canal but you don't forget your way. It was an easy job to climb down the bank a hundred yards along and then hit the back of the building without being seen by anyone other than a passing fish. Billy's moat was also his back door and he'd have been as well leaving it open. A two-tick fiddle with a thin rasp and a latch was lifted and I was in.

The bookie wasn't too hot on security, emptied the safe every night so nothing to steal. But I didn't want to steal, I had another commandment to break.

I knew Billy was in the Imperial and I knew he'd be at least an hour, much more likely two. It was Thursday night and that meant Billy would come back to the bookies alone after the pub. He always did. I reckoned he crashed out for a few hours before sobering up a bit and driving home to the wife with nicotine skin.

I knew I had time to work.

My brother was an electrician and I'd helped him out a few times when he took on big jobs and needed a hand. We'd rewired a few houses together and although my expertise was heavy lifting, fetching and carrying, I knew one end of a screwdriver from the other. He'd shown me a few dos and don'ts. I was about to put some of the don'ts into practice. I rewired, closed the back door behind me, taking care to leave it off the latch and got out. I hid in the shadows of the canal bank, waiting and thinking.

The human body is a great conductor of electricity because it is so full of water. Throw in dissolved salts in the form of blood and other various bodily fluids and you have a ready-made superconductor. Electricity can go from top to toe in the blink of an eye or at the flick of a switch.

The amount of damage done by electrocution depends on the size of the current and the length of the time it is in contact with the body. Ohm's law says that the voltage of the source is equal to the current passing through the circuit – in this case the body – and the resistance to the flow of current it offers . . .

Whatever way you look at it, a fat old man with a dodgy ticker makes for a lovely conductor. But only once.

You don't get taught that kind of stuff when you help your brother out on rewiring jobs but you can pick up a hell of a lot from Google. Said it before, the Internet is a great thing.

Two hours and ten minutes I waited on that canal bank. Two hours and ten minutes until I saw a light go on in the bookies. It went on very briefly.

I wasn't there when they found him of course but I could picture the scene. The staff would turn up in the morning and be surprised the place was still locked up. One of the wee wummin would produce her spare key. The door would be opened and they'd see there was no one in the shop. They'd go through the back where the stairs led to the small flat above. At the foot of the stairs they would find Billy, dead as the deadest doornail, at the foot of the light switch he'd tried to put on.

It would be obvious enough that he'd been electrocuted. Grey hair frazzled and on end, burns black on his hands, lips charred, eyes wide. Hardly a surprise either given the state of the place. One of the wee wummin would probably mutter that they'd warned him often enough that someone would get fried. Chances are it would have killed anyone but with the condition of Billy's heart he'd not have stood a chance in hell.

45

They'd call an ambulance although they knew it would do no good. They'd call the police too. They'd all look at Billy and at the dodgy wiring in the bookies and it would be obvious to every one of them what had happened.

Obvious that is until they saw his right hand. Until they saw that he was missing a finger. A pinkie. Neatly chopped off. Severed.

CHAPTER 7

I bought every Scottish daily newspaper but found mention of it in only three of them. It didn't please me.

The *Herald*. Saturday, 9 May 2009. Page 6. No byline.
Tragic accident

A Glasgow bookmaker has been found dead in his office in Maryhill. William Hutchison (58) was discovered by staff yesterday morning when they opened the premises in Maryhill Road. It is believed that Mr Hutchison was electrocuted as a result of faulty wiring. A post mortem has been ordered by the Procurator Fiscal's office. Mr Hutchison is survived by a wife and two grown-up children.

The *Daily Record*. Saturday, 9 May 2009. Page 7.
By Collin Docherty.
A photograph of Billy taken when some footballer
put on a charity bet in his shop.
Bookie burned

The body of well-known Glasgow bookie Billy Hutchison was found in his Maryhill shop yesterday. Horrified staff came across the electrocuted and badly charred body of Mr Hutchison when they opened up the bookies at 10 a.m. One distraught cleaner had to be treated by ambulance staff after finding her boss.

Mr Hutchison was a well-known figure in Maryhill and had owned the bookmakers there for 22 years. He was well respected in the local community and held regular charity events that attracted the support of players from Celtic, Rangers and Partick Thistle in aid of Multiple Sclerosis. In 1998 he was named Maryhill Citizen of the Year for his fundraising efforts.

Police would not speculate on the cause of death but it is believed that faulty wiring in the premises contributed to a horrendous accident. A post mortem will be carried out. Yesterday, Mrs Agnes Hutchison was too distraught to speak about her husband's death. A neighbour, who did not wish to be named, said, 'This is terrible. Agnes will be devastated. Billy was such a nice guy and they were devoted to each other. It's a tragedy.'

Around five o'clock, I bought the final edition of the *Evening Times*. It was slightly more promising.

The *Evening Times*. Saturday, 9 May 2009. Page 3.
By Martine Blake.

Police have refused to confirm or deny suggestions that the death yesterday morning of Maryhill bookmaker Billy Hutchison is being treated as suspicious. The body of Mr Hutchison was found in his Maryhill Road premises by staff and it was believed that he had been electrocuted. Staff who discovered Mr Hutchison confirmed that his body showed signs of extreme electric shock. It was thought that faulty wiring was to blame and staff confirmed that the shop's wiring system was in dire need of an overhaul.

However, it has since emerged that the officer originally in charge of the incident, Sergeant Alex McElhone, has been replaced by Detective Chief Inspector Lewis Robertson. DCI Robertson is a senior detective based at Stewart Street. Strathclyde Police today refused to comment on the involvement of a murder squad detective in

what was seemingly a tragic accident, saying it was merely procedural and that they would not comment further on an ongoing investigation.

This has inevitably led to speculation that police now doubt whether Mr Hutchison's death was the accident it initially appeared to be. No one at Hutchison's bookmakers or at Mr Hutchison's Whiteinch home was prepared to comment on a possible change of direction in the investigation into his death.

CHAPTER 8

I'd decided to make DS Rachel Narey my new best friend. Whether she liked it or not.

That was why Billy Hutchison's finger did not go in an envelope addressed to the CID at Stewart Street as the first one had been. It was sent directly to her.

DS RACHEL NAREY
CID
50 STEWART STREET
GLASGOW
G4 0HY

Same kind of plain brown padded envelope, same printed label amended to suit, same process, same level of caution and self-protection. Different postbox. Different recipient. I just wished I could have seen her face as she opened the envelope and Hutchison's pinkie slid onto her desk. A picture I'm sure.

She would have worn gloves of course. Assiduously careful

not to contaminate the evidence. She would have known what was inside, they would all have known. There would have been a crowd of them around her desk. Waiting, wondering. As soon as they saw the envelope, the place would have been buzzing. They'd have come running, shouting people in from fag breaks, excusing them from interview rooms, all bursting to know for sure.

As soon as they saw the finger it would confirm what they had all thought from the minute they heard about Hutchison's missing digit. Two words. Serial killer.

One word. Nutter.

Another word. Overtime.

The cops would have been loving it and hating it all at once. A psycho killer on their patch. Good and bad all in the one package.

A stubby, nicotine-stained finger lying there on an evidence bag on a standard-issue desk. Hard and white. Rigid edges of skin where the blades of the secateurs had ripped it away from the hand.

Sharp intakes of breath. Shouts. Swearing. Jokes. More swearing. Every pair of eyes in the place on that finger but the prize was Rachel's.

She'd have been thinking the same as them. Why her? I hoped a little bit of her would have run scared at the knowledge that she had been picked out by a double murderer. I was certain that a bigger bit of her would have been pleased.

The other cops would have hated her for getting the finger. Some – the lazy, the old and the unambitious –

would have been pleased it wasn't them but hated her all the same. That's the way people are.

The young ones, those with a hungry eye on quick promotion through the ranks, would have fucking despised her for getting it. They'd have killed to be the name on that label on that envelope with that finger. Why that fucking bitch? Her boss, Robertson, was probably more pissed off than most.

Too bad, it was hers. And it was hers because it was in my power to make it hers.

Billy was dispatched on the Thursday night, the finger posted the next day. Rachel Narey got it on the Saturday, no weekends off for her or me.

Early on Saturday evening, perfectly timed to catch the Sunday papers and the evening news, Rachel did another news conference. This time DCI Robertson stood at her shoulder rather than the other way about, probably trying to appear supportive but only managing to look vexed. It was her show now and everyone knew it.

She wore a dark suit with a white blouse underneath. She looked a bit nervous at first but soon hit her stride. She said she would be making a short statement but would not be taking any questions.

'Yesterday morning, the body of William Hutchison was found in the premises of his bookmakers on Maryhill Road. We have good reason to believe that there were suspicious circumstances relating to Mr Hutchison's death but are not prepared to go into the details of those at present.

'We would ask anyone who was in the vicinity of 670 Maryhill Road on the evening of March the 8th to contact us. All information will be treated in confidence.' She was looking directly at the camera now. Into the camera. She was looking straight at me.

'There is someone out there who knows what happened to Mr Hutchison and I am asking that person to go to his local police station. It is very important that you speak to officers now before things get worse.'

She must have been screaming inside. Desperate to tell everything. Two murders, one killer. Two severed fingers, one maniac.

'You have information which may ease the suffering felt by Mr Hutchison's widow, Agnes, and their family. I am asking you now to come forward with that information.

'Ladies and gentlemen, thank you for coming along this evening. We will provide you with any further information when it becomes appropriate to do so. Thanks for your help on this matter.'

Immediately there was a clamour among the reporters who were standing off camera. One shout came through the hubbub. 'DS Narey, is this a murder investigation?'

She levelled the questioner with a stare that put the brakes on every other reporter's attempt to talk to her.

She held his gaze long enough that he must have been squirming. The contempt was dripping from her.

'I said I wouldn't take any questions.'

She clearly wouldn't take any shit either.

* * *

A big, black dog appeared on our street. An overweight Labrador cross, with red eyes. Didn't seem to belong to anyone. But it looked at me.

It didn't bark or growl. Didn't run towards me or turn away. Just looked. Looked at me as if it knew something.

I asked if anyone knew whose dog it was but no one did. No one even seemed to have seen it around.

Must have, I told them. Big, black thing. Red eyes. Heavy with a belly on it. Must have seen it.

No.

Sat on the corner outside the McKechnies'. Or opposite ours.

No.

Big, black dug. Surely?

No.

I remembered my granddad had a dog like it. Not as heavy maybe. Name of Mick. Looked just like this dog on our street, except not so heavy.

This dog that nobody knew who it belonged to. This dog that nobody else had seen. Four days in a row I saw this dog. This big, black Labrador cross.

Four days I saw it and then it disappeared. Strangest thing.

CHAPTER 9

Nobody talked much about Billy Hutchison from the back of my cab. Glasgow went on being Glasgow. City centre. West end. South side. Rat runs. Drunks. Businessmen. Drunk businessmen. Airport dashes. Rain shine and rain. East end. North side. Big tips, no tips.

Pollokshields. Carntyne. Barmulloch. Ibrox. Parkhead. Carling Academy. Queen Street Station. More drunks. Traffic jams.

So much city. Maybe it was no surprise that no one seemed to notice a single soul slipping from it. Single because no one connected Billy the bookie to Jonathan Carr. No one talked about the double killing that nobody knew about. No one talked about the double killer that walked unknown among them.

To the people in the back of my taxi I was just mate or driver. I was just a pair of eyes in the rear-view mirror.

To me, they were just yawning, jabbering, disconnected mouths. I listened for mention of Billy but there was none. But for a single day when Radio Clyde news carried a fifteen-second report as part of their twice-hourly news bulletin, there was nothing. Even that day it disappeared when some ned got himself stabbed in Possil and the sports news was extended because a Rangers defender had a knee injury.

Billy had come and gone in a flash and people either didn't notice or didn't give a fuck. That wasn't what was bothering me though. I didn't give a fuck about Billy either. I didn't care that they weren't talking about him but I did want them to talk about me. Or rather, about the man that dispatched Carr and Hutchison. The man that cut off the little fingers of their right hand and posted them to the police. I wanted them to talk about that man.

But Glasgow just went on being Glasgow.

Gallus. That was the word that summed up the city best. A Glasgow word. It meant bold and cool, it meant great, it meant cheeky and brash, it meant fearless and cocky. It meant self-confident and stylish. It meant all that and more. Hard to explain if you hadn't used it since you were old enough to talk. Glasgow was certainly gallus though.

Time was I revelled in that gallusness. I was part of it. As gallus as the next guy. But that was before, before it was all taken away. Now I was on the outside looking in through a rear-view mirror as Glasgow spilled in and out of my taxi on their way to or from a drink or an airport.

Busy the night, driver?

Sometimes I just looked at them through that mirror. Held their gaze and let them try to guess. Do you know who I am, what happened to me, what I have done? Do you know what I am going to do? They never did. They never even came close.

Instead they bleated about the weather. Moaned about rain as if it was important. A little rain never killed anybody.

Football, money, traffic, football, rain and football. What I had done hadn't dented the consciousness of this place, hadn't touched the sides. That would change, I knew that. I needed to be patient.

Sometimes though, when they moaned on and on about such trivial nonsense, about nothing at all, I wanted to slap them, to tell them what real troubles were. To let them know what real suffering was. Mostly though I just wanted them to shut the fuck up. I needed to let them drift in and out through the taxi, blissful in their stupidity and their ignorance. The eyes were supposed to be the window to the soul but they saw nothing in mine. They looked but they did not see. All the time I was thinking, planning, waiting, wondering. Inside it was all there but they just couldn't see it.

The SECC. Central Station. Wee wifies with bags of messages. Hyndland. Pick-ups at the ranks. Flagged down in the street. Mount Florida. Early starts. Late finishes.

Garthamlock. Celtic Park. Kids to school. No smoking. No drinking. No eating. No throwing up. Cathcart. Johnstone.

I drove them. Drove by them. Drove through them. Picked them up and laid them down. I took their money. Gave them their change. I was right there and they did not see me. They did not know that I existed.

Suited me fine. For now.

I'd drop the flag and set the meter going, ferrying the sleepers and the talkers, the happy and the sad to wherever it was they wanted to go. Sometimes of course I'd get duffed for the hire and some chancer would do a runner into the night leaving me out of pocket.

I'd been sixth on the rank at Central on a slow Wednesday evening, one of those long waits that can happen when you time it wrong in between trains. Sitting watching the to and fro, flicking the wipers on and off to keep the wind-screen clear, moving forward every few minutes till all at once a train has come in and there is a queue desperate to get moving.

When I got to the front, a hard-looking sort in a black leather jacket and a bag slung over his shoulder was the next in line. Wouldn't have been my choice but it wasn't mine to make. He got in the back, gave me an address in Barrhead then got on his mobile to tell someone that his train was in and that he was in a taxi, would be there in twenty.

You get a feeling for people. Even when you couldn't care less about 99 per cent of them, even when they only existed on the very edge of your world, sometimes they set off alarm bells. This guy stank of trouble.

I caught him in the rear-view. He had finished his call and was staring out of the window. Scar just in front of his ear that ran onto his jaw line. Eyes set hard. Permanent scowl on his lips. Don't know if he sensed me looking but he turned and stared at the mirror. My eyes switched back to the road.

I turned the cab onto Waterloo Street and made for the motorway. Ten miles to deepest Barrhead, past the airport and off. Silence all the way. Quiet the night, driver. Through the lights on Main Street, first right at the roundabout then deep into the warren of crescents. He was on the phone again. Nearly there. One minute.

Next left and into a narrow street with three-storey flats either side. Snipers alley.

'Stop there on the left,' he said.

I stopped.

'You're no getting paid for this so fuck off.'

I held his eyes in the mirror but he stared me down, daring me to argue. He didn't take his eyes from mine as he pointed up to the left. I followed his arm and saw two figures on the balcony, one holding what looked like a rifle.

The door was locked and would stay that way till I unlocked it. I could have driven off with him in the back seat but that didn't seem a great idea. I didn't know what was in that bag that had been over his shoulder. Anyway, he'd read my mind.

'You'll no reach the end of the street. Like I said you're getting fuck all money. Now piss off.'

I released the lock, the red light disappeared and he opened the door. It slammed shut and I watched the back of the black leather jacket as its wearer slipped into the close without once looking back.

I was raging and out of pocket but something deep inside my dead soul found it funny. A runner had just taken me for a mug and I'd let him. The hard man had decided he'd get a free ride home and that I could do nothing about it. He thought I was nothing and maybe he was right. He thought I was no one. A nobody.

I laughed quietly to myself as I put the taxi back into gear and drove slowly out of that street in search of the motorway. I wasn't a nobody. I was somebody that they hadn't heard of yet.

I'd killed. Carr and Hutchison. More would follow. I was going to be known. And yet here was some gallus bastard with the bare-faced cheek to leave me without a fare. I laughed.

It happened. Door lock was supposed to stop it but you weren't always ready. Money is coming out of the pocket, handle is released and before you know it they are out the suicide door and off into traffic with your money in their hand. Comes with the territory. But there is no way they'd have had the nerve to try it if they knew what I was capable of. There wouldn't even be a bare hire if they knew that. There'd be a tip every time.

CHAPTER 10

Life used to have a rhythm. Maybe it still did but while it used to be a constant, understandable, workable, bearable thing now it wasn't. Hadn't been for six years. If there was a new rhythm then it wasn't one I could live with. It jarred. It messed with my head. Clanging noises fucking with my ears and my mind. Even though it was now supposed to be dancing to my tune, it still rang raw and rattling and upsetting.

A long time six years. Where there had been order there was discord. Like Thatcher lying before television cameras, whimpering about harmony as she bastardized the words of St Francis of Assisi yet whipped up more conflict than ever before. What was the norm had quickly become something very different and much worse.

I knew it was the same for her, my wife, but that didn't make it any easier for me to accept the way she chose to deal with it. Each to their own is all very well but she was way off the mark. Wrong.

It was her rhythm, her solution. But wrong just the same.

She filled her days with her campaign; using it to shut out everything else, blot out the world. She would leaflet, she would petition, she would persuade and harangue. She would sit on committees and chair discussion groups. She would carry placards and stand outside Parliament. She was on first-name terms with MPs, MSPs and councillors.

Every fucking minute of it a complete waste of time.

She complained, she moaned, she whined. She grumbled, criticized and bleated. She had achieved absolutely nothing and would achieve absolutely nothing. After all, the one thing that she really wanted to accomplish was impossible.

That morning was just typical of it. It was just after seven and I was slumped over the breakfast table, drowning in a mug of coffee and sinking lower after a long night shift. She had charged into the kitchen, her hair tied back, businesslike. Just a few stray strands of the fair hair that had caught my eye all those years ago managed to escape the clutches of the hairband. She had a waterproof on over a suit jacket. Ready for all weathers and all circumstances.

She had aged maybe fifteen years in the past six. Lines where there had been none. Her green eyes deeper and darker. Her mouth set harder. I think she was smaller too. Not that she had ever been much over five foot but I think it had all beaten her down another half inch.

Not that morning though. She was ready for the day. She was bustling around the house full of the joys of a day ahead, believing all the false promises that it held. She even sang a bit. I caught her humming a few bars of something under her breath, a rarity in our house these days. I bridled at it. Half-witted optimism was not something likely to cheer me up after a long night at the wheel. Glasgow had been enough for me without this too.

I knew I was supposed to ask where she was going, I knew I didn't care and I knew she would tell me anyway. I just stared into the murky depths of the coffee and stayed silent.

'Going to the Scottish Parliament today,' she breezed at me eventually. 'Train through to Edinburgh then to Holyrood.'

I gave her just a nod in response. Any more would have signalled interest, even encouragement. Any less might have kicked off another row.

She looked back at me for a bit longer. More in hope than anticipation I was sure. Something in her eyes made me cave.

'What's happening there?'

She brightened. She enthused. 'A protest outside the main entrance. Should be a couple of dozen of us and I'm really hopeful there will be press coverage. Maybe television too. BBC Scotland didn't say they'd definitely be there but it is in their diary. Fingers crossed.'

Uh huh. Fingers crossed right enough. Couple of dozen meant there would be five or six. Hopeful meant very unlikely. In their diary meant no fucking chance. We had been there so many times before.

With that, she swept up whatever it was she felt she needed and deposited them in a selection of bags and pockets. A last mouthful of tea was knocked back in an exaggerated haste and the cup placed down with the hurried air of a woman on a mission.

A last look round, a wave of her hand as if she didn't even have time to speak, and she was out and off to catch the eight o'clock train to Edinburgh. I watched the door bang shut and could only shake my head at the shudder that was left behind. It wasn't just the eight-hour shift that had left me tired.

I tried to listen to her footsteps as they faded away, tried to capture the final, faint smack of heel on concrete, strained to hear the very last sound that I could. With each wilting, softening step I spiralled into sleep until my head was on the table and my mind had drifted to another time, another place.

I sat like that for an hour before waking sore and stiff and dragging myself off to a cold bed for a further four uneasy hours of sleep. As ever, slumber offered no escape from a waking nightmare. It just brought memories and distorted versions of an already disturbed reality. I'd long since given up any hope of finding some sanctuary with my eyes shut.

It was nearly five before she returned, as deflated and self-righteous as I'd expected. She dropped her bags and coat as if throwing off armour. The weary warrior returned from the front.

The same dance as the morning. I was to ask how it had gone. I didn't care. She would tell me anyway. The truth was found between the lines. She had stood in the rain outside the Parliament for three hours along with eight other well-intentioned, misguided halfwits. Every one of them holding a sign and wasting their time. This wasn't how it was told to me.

Few MSPs even noticed the dripping bodies littering the entrance to their talking shop and those that did paid little attention. Eventually one made a token gesture and invited three of them in out of the rain for a cup of tea and a five-minute head-nodding session. A cursory chat forgotten as soon as they were back on the Royal Mile.

Suitably patronized, the would-be revolutionaries had trotted off again, overflowing with self-praise and having achieved the square root of fuck all. Oh how pleased with themselves they were on the train back to Glasgow. Making notes, eating sandwiches and taking it in turn to pat each other on the back.

Nor was that the end of her day of busy non-achieve-ment. In the afternoon, she was back in Glasgow pushing for a meeting with members of the education committee. I hated to think what they made of her. Probably filed under nutter or nuisance.

She maybe even knew that but it wouldn't stop her. Nothing would. She had her mission, just as I had mine. She had tried to get me involved, of course she did, but it was another battle she could never win. At first I made excuses, couldn't be here, couldn't make it there. I was working, I was tired. But she kept pushing till I just had to tell her straight that I didn't want to get involved.

I had stopped short of telling her why. Spared her that added pain and she inevitably responded by resenting me, shutting me out even further. She grudged my lack of involvement, hated my disinterest. Thought I was just sitting back and taking it, doing nothing.

I let her think it. To do otherwise would have meant opening up a deep can of worms we were both desperately trying to keep a lid on.

So she had done her duty, another day of active inaction and now she was home signalling the start of the collapse, the sinking into oblivion.

The first pill was taken within ten minutes of her being through the door. She halted her deluded monologue just long enough to sip water and bite tablet. Lockdown had begun for the night.

She was still talking as I sat a plate and cutlery in front of her. She was still telling her self-serving lies when I dropped a breast of chicken, new potatoes and green beans onto the plate. The food was no more than a minor barrier to her. The one-sided conversation was her justifying her existence and it would have been cruel to interrupt.

Finally the food was gone and the talk began to fade. She was dropping deeper.

The television propped her up for a few hours. Staring at the box in the corner, the spirit going and the flesh weakening. Images playing back across her increasingly glassy eyes, soap operas and situation comedies sending her deeper and deeper.

I sat too, in a growing conspiracy of silence. Not watching, not caring, my own plans playing out in the theatre of my mind.

By nine all the pills were rattling around inside her as she made her way upstairs to bed. I knew that in minutes she would be fast asleep.

By day a misdirected human dynamo. By night a spent force. By day the accidental campaigner. By night a locked-down impenetrable cell. The day was the fuel and the night the hunger.

Day and night shutting out demons that were hurling themselves at her door, battering to be let in. Better to let them inside. Welcome them with open arms and use them to your ends. Better by far.

With her gone I still sat and gazed at the television. No more or less lonely now that I was alone. The night was mine and there was work to be done. I'd drive the streets and see what the morning was to bring.

CHAPTER 11

Sauchiehall Street is now a straight, mile-long broadway but it used to be completely different. It was once a winding, narrow lane with villas each standing in an acre of garden. I liked that. The idea of random, winding roads turned into a direct route. The name came from two old Scots words that have since been bastardized into English, much like the entire country. *Saugh* is the Scots word for a willow tree and *haugh* means meadow. That's why I started counting at Miss Cranston's old place near the corner of Blythswood Street, the Willow Tea Rooms. Good a reason as any.

I'd begun walking at the Donald Dewar statue in front of the Royal Concert Hall but didn't begin a countdown until I got to the tea rooms and the windows full of the Mockintosh stuff that would have had Charles Rennie spinning in his art nouveau grave. The tea rooms were Glasgow history though, a tourist's favourite.

The Room De Luxe had silver furniture and leaded glass work, a genuine thing of beauty produced in a city of sweat and ugly temper. Mackintosh's genius was to harness

Glasgow's contrasts, mixing right angles and curves, traditional and modernist, poverty and prosperous, beauty and beaten brow.

A good place to start.

The place you begin is always important. Not as vital as where you finish but important all the same. There is logic and logic. Some would have considered me crazy but I had my own reasoning.

I counted as best I could.

One. A youngish guy in a Rangers away top. Cap pushed back on his head, tracksuit trousers and trainers. Classic ned look. Crappy chain round his neck. Lovebites and at least one tattoo.

Two. His mate. Same uniform except with the addition of a scar from ear to mouth. His hands thrust in his pockets, his mouth going at a hundred miles an hour, man.

Three. A girl. Just a bit older than Sarah would have been. Perhaps nineteen or twenty. Knee-length boots and a short skirt. Way too much make-up. She looked at me. I didn't like that. She was someone's daughter. Some father waiting to be hurt.

Four. A jaikie bouncing from bin to bin. That special Scottish pallor on his face; white skin gone grey, red nose and battered cheeks. He was smiling all over his face and just for a second I envied him. He most probably didn't have any more than a couple of quid in his pocket and his brain was fried with Bucky but he was happy. Remember happy?

He stopped me, cut across my path and stood there so

I couldn't pass. He started singing to me with his hand held out in front of him. This wasn't good, not good at all. It was changing things and it would make people look at us. At me.

I could smell him. Dampness on his clothes, foul BO and rancid breath. He was murdering 'Danny Boy' with this stupid grin on him. I wanted away, wanted past, wanted to keep counting. People were flooding by and I wasn't counting them.

I scrambled into my pocket and pulled out a couple of pound coins, thrusting them at him to buy freedom. I needed past him, had to get on. But instead of getting away, it made him thank me, grasping at my hands, his breath hammering at me.

Panic took a hold. I wanted to shake him off, throw him to the ground. People were passing by and everything was changing. The dirty, drunken old bastard didn't know what he was doing. I couldn't have this.

He treated me to another verse of 'Danny Boy'. I was his new best friend but I wanted to be anywhere else but there.

I tore my hand out of his, breathing hard and dancing round him. He was shouting at me as I moved. I ignored him and prayed everyone else was doing the same.

I marched on, counting and walking. Ticking them off as they passed me, then and not before. Walking. Counting. Waiting.

Five and six passed in a blur. Seven, eight, nine rushed by and I felt as if a flood was going over me. Business suits and green school uniforms, ladies doing lunch and builders' bums. I was drowning in possibilities and realities.

I was spinning, reeling out of control and had to regain it. Ten, eleven, twelve, they kept coming. I was counting, trying to slow my breathing and calm my nerves all at once.

It was eighteen before I was remotely settled. A balding businessman with a briefcase stuffed under his arm. He caught me looking at him and glared. That was OK. He'd never think anything of it.

Nineteen and twenty were a young couple hand-in-hand. I was composed now. He was tall and fair, she was short and bottle-blonde. I was fine again. They were giggling and whispering.

I slowed, I breathed out. I kept counting. Walking and counting. I had crossed Blythswood Street and had already counted past thirty.

So many people. It wouldn't be long.

There was a rush through the mid-forties and a lull before a few more crossed my path. Not for the first time it struck me how many of the population of the dear green place came in only two colours, ash grey or sunbed orange. The brow-beaten and UV beaten. Glasgow was all-sorts. All races, shapes and sizes and they kept coming past me. I tried to paint quick pen pictures of them in my mind but how could you tell the reasonably well-off from the struggling, the Protestant from the Catholic, the asylum seeker from Jock Tamson's bairn, the Pole from the Partick boy? How did you differentiate the oppressed from the oppressor, the trodden down and those that trod on them, the deserving and those that deserved it?

I didn't know and it didn't matter. Maybe better that I didn't know.

Past the queue at Greggs and past Paperino's. Three to go and I had a definite feeling of how close it was. I itched for it. I wanted to look ahead but stopped myself.

Fifty-four, near the corner of Douglas Street, was a young bearded guy with a bag over his shoulder and a look of superior stupidity on his face. A student. A member of the most feckless, pampered bunch of idiots on the planet. Time was he'd have been planning a revolution or protesting against the occupation of Iraq. At the very least he'd have been tending his cannabis harvest. This guy was probably going to see his financial adviser or going home to watch *Neighbours*. Oh he'd have done.

Still he was only number fifty-four.

My heart was pounding. I told myself to be calm. Fifty-six would be here and nothing could stop it any more than worrying would hasten it.

Fifty-five was an old Chinese woman. She was maybe about 120 and seemed less than five foot but then she was bent near double, forced over by time and rain. Something about her reminded me of an old neighbour. I couldn't think of her name but then I couldn't think of much else but the next person that would walk past me. It could be anyone at all. It excited me, sickened me, slightly scared me. My pulse galloped.

I dragged my eyes along the pavement but saw no feet. There was no one in the three or four yards of me. Then I saw a pair of shoes. Small shoes.

I raised my eyes and saw a boy of about eleven or twelve. Fuck.

He had a mop of fair hair and a squint grin, scuffing his feet along Sauchiehall Street as he gazed half-heartedly into shop windows. Oh fuck.

Fuck. Fuck. Fuck.

He seemed in a bit of a daydream, this kid without a care in the world. The tail of his shirt was hanging below his jumper in the way that boys liked to wear it. Faded jeans. That silly, quirky grin.

Rules. Number fifty-six.

I felt sick to my stomach. Rules. My rules.

The boy glanced up, curious. I must have been staring right at him. Of course I was. He was still walking and I willed him to stop. He wasn't going to. He was nearly in front of me. Stop, you have to stop.

Two more steps and he would be number fifty-six.

Then, from somewhere off my radar, a shape pushed past the boy, barging into his shoulder and knocking him over. The shape charged past me.

I watched the boy pick himself up and offer a dirty look to the person that had shoved him.

I followed his gaze and saw a short, stocky guy in his mid-twenties barrelling back up the street, not mindful in the least of anyone around him. I was looking at the back of number fifty-six.

Or number three depending on how you looked at it.

CHAPTER 12

I followed him, this little guy who liked to push wee boys out of his way. Not just kids either. The squat, weaselly man didn't have much care for anyone in his path. He barged past women, he got in the way of men bigger than him. He walked with the disregard of a bully and the confidence of someone twice his size.

I stayed ten and twenty feet back. I watched.

He was maybe five foot six, with short, spiky hair, weighing twelve stone or so. He turned a couple of times and I caught a bashed face that looked as if it had been in the wars. He looked like a dog with a bad temper.

He cut a path back up Sauchiehall Street. He had a strange confidence for such a wee guy. No fears. His strut reminded me of Carr. Little men, big egos, yet completely different.

I didn't have time to think about Carr. This man was in front of me now. I might never see him again. The time was here and now. However risky, however long it took. If the chance came it would have to be taken or be lost. I knew it.

The little man passed people who recognized him. Two young guys in near-ned uniforms. They got close and they talked fast. Little Man looked around before shaking his head. He nodded towards the concert hall end of the street. They looked at each other and then they nodded too. They walked away from him.

Little Man had talked a lot with his hands. His eyes were going right and left, his mouth was tight and fast but his hands were working overtime. He moved on.

He hit the pedestrianized area and kept walking. When the road crossed with Renfield Street he jinked to the right, causing two girls to move out of his way, and entered a pub, Lauders.

This wasn't good. I didn't mean it to be like this. I chose Sauchiehall Street for my own reasons, but only to identify him. Or her. Not to do this.

Still . . .

I walked on past Lauders without breaking stride or looking back. I walked on to the shops under the concert hall, looked in the window of one and pretended to study whatever was there. I stood. A minute. A long minute. I shrugged and turned away. I walked back where I'd come from. I walked into Lauders.

I knew Little Man would be in there but I didn't look for him. I went to the bar and asked for a pint of heavy.

The barman didn't say anything but poured it. I didn't say anything but paid him.

I looked in the mirror and caught myself. Me. Still me.

I sipped at my pint. I sipped again before I looked round.

Fat guy. Drunk guy. Old guy. Another drunk guy. Little Man. I gulped my pint and looked away.

He was sitting on a stool with the two near-neds standing beside him. They were still talking close, fast and quiet. Little Man's hands were signing for the deaf. There were nods and shakes of the three heads. Little Man jumped off his stool. I was ready to move but he only went as far as the toilet.

One minute later, one of the near-neds followed him. The other stood looking around, standing guard from outside. I watched in the mirror.

Two minutes later, the near-ned and Little Man came out. I saw Little Man had a moustache of sorts. A streaky fair line above his lips. He looked like a ferret. A ferret that had eaten a mouse. I didn't like Little Man.

I know, I know. I didn't like Carr. Now I didn't like Little Man. It didn't matter. Coincidence. I wasn't trying to convince myself or make it easier. I just didn't like them. Little Man had a beaten dog face. Beaten and ready to bite. He had something funny about one of his eyes, a squint or something. He looked like someone you wouldn't turn your back on but that was OK because I had no intention of doing so.

He was grinning all over his face, his mouse-eating grin. Little Man knocked back the last of his drink, a vodka and Red Bull, and called for another. He necked it in two seconds flat.

The near-neds disappeared, huddling close, leaving Little Man to look around the pub as voddie and RB number three or four arrived in front of him.

It was swallowed slower than the one before but was ended with a shrug and a final slug of vodka. Little Man was finished.

He got off his stool. Said his goodbyes to the barman and left.

I sat. Unsure. Unprepared. I needed to wait. I needed to follow. Couldn't do both.

Shit.

I felt my heart racing again. I hated the indecision, the not knowing, the hesitancy of choice. Shit.

My teeth were clenched. Damn. I could almost feel the beads of sweat start to form. I felt panic and hated myself for it. Every second wasted was a second lost, every second lost was a waste. Make a fucking choice. If I let him get a start then he had umpteen choices of which way to go. If I rushed after him it might look odd. People might look.

Shit. I was going. I turned and left by the door he had.

I looked left to the concert hall. I looked right back up the street. I looked up and down Renfield Street.

There. Was it? Maybe a hundred yards down Renfield. Yes. Was it? I was sure of it. A short, spiky head bobbed and pushed among those next to it. Little Man.

I started to rush after him but slowed myself. Fucking CCTV. I made sure I was quicker than him but no more than I needed.

Thirty yards. Yes. Twenty yards. Definitely. Him. Number thirty-six. Number three. Little Man. My man.

He went into two other pubs. Five vodka RBs. One more

toilet visit. Lots of hand speak, lots of mouse-eating grins. I hated Little Man.

He pushed his way out of what turned out to be his last pub and made his way back up towards the bus stop on Hope Street across from Molly Malones. He went into the chip shop there and came back out, supper in hand, swaying a bit waiting for his bus.

I was behind him, clinging to the wall of the Savoy Centre and hoping for shadow. I'd wait. Unprepared but ready.

Bus came. Destination Baillieston. Little Man got on. So did three old women, two old men, two kids. And me.

I sat and watched the back of his head. His scratchy, weaselly head. His cocky, smart-arse head. His bullying, strangely confident, ugly head.

Out of the city centre. Some people got on that he knew. Some got on that knew him. I could see that.

He nodded at some, waved at others, sneered at some more.

Give me one chance. It had to be a safe chance. I wouldn't take unnecessary risks but I would take a chance. Oh I would.

It was dark now. Not very dark but dark enough and getting darker.

Edge of Baillieston. Little Man got out of his seat and stood. He shouted.

'Next stop, big man.' Little Man wanted off the bus.

The bus slowed, three others got off and at the last minute I got up too and jumped off. It wasn't the way I wanted it but who would notice or care?

He walked one way, I walked the other. Not far obviously. First chance I got, I turned and headed back. There was

Little Man, cock of the walk, arrogant little bastard, maybe a hundred yards ahead but clear in view.

Some kids ran to him. Slowed him. From where I was, the boys looked no more than fourteen or fifteen. Little Man stuck his hands in his pockets, he brought something out and acted the Big Man. They disappeared.

So did Little Man shortly. Into a pub. The Brig Tavern. I didn't go in. There was no way I could go into somewhere like that and not be noticed. Alarm bells would go off as soon as I entered and I couldn't have that. I walked in large circles, hunched and hopefully unseen.

On turn three I saw him emerge from the pub. He was staggering and that pleased me.

He turned a sharp right from the pub onto a bit of scrub ground behind it. A short cut. There was rough ash, broken glass, rogue shopping trolleys, dog shit and trees. Fifty yards of darker darkness before the near light.

Chance.

I shouted. The voice came out of me before I knew it.

'Hey, wee man.'

He slowed then stopped. He looked over his shoulder, wondering who had the cheek to call him wee, obvious as it was. He looked me up and down and saw no threat. He also looked curious. I guess I wasn't what he expected.

I took money out of my pocket. A hunch. Little Man looked around and came closer. He wanted to be much closer.

I held it nearer to me as if hiding it. He liked that. He came on. He came to me.

82

I walked to the edge of the scrub, seeking the shadows. Little Man liked that too. He was within five feet of me. I could see his eyes and he could see mine. He grinned. That mouse-eating grin.

I looked around. He thought it was me being safe and it was. He was warmed by that but he was wrong.

He reached for the money. I smiled and shook my head. I beckoned him closer. I put the cash in my inside pocket. He came closer. So close.

He grinned. I smiled.

I reached inside and pulled out the knife. I reached in and drove it into him. Again. Again. Again. I pulled him right onto me and plunged it in deep. Little Man wasn't so big now. He did look at me though. Surprised.

Dead.

I pushed him off me and watched him fall back flat.

I slashed at his neck twice and then wiped the bloody blade across his face. His eyes were open and so was his mouth. That was strange. Well, unexpected anyway.

I reached into my pocket and took out the secateurs. I cut off his finger and pocketed it.

Job done.

I was cold and breathing hard but not sweaty. I didn't like that.

I cleaned the blade of the knife on Little Man's jacket, then did the same with the secateurs. I took a plastic bag from my inside pocket and slipped them both in there before putting it back in my jacket.

My shirt was splattered in his blood. It would be

incinerated later but for now zipping my jacket to the neck would cover it.

I took off the clear surgical gloves from my hands and slipped them away. They too would be burned. So would the jacket.

It was time to go home.

CHAPTER 13

Daily Record. 28 September 2009. Page 2.
By Keith Imrie. A photograph of the crime scene.

Police have launched a murder hunt after the body of a known criminal was found in wasteland in the Baillieston area of Glasgow after a suspected gangland slaying. Thomas Tierney was brutally stabbed to death shortly before midnight last night just minutes from his home in Rhindmuir Drive. A full-scale search of the area was being conducted into the early hours and was due to restart this morning.

Tierney, known locally as Spud, was stabbed several times in what police are calling a vicious attack. As well as multiple wounds to his stomach, chest and abdomen, Tierney was slashed around the face and neck. His body was discovered soaked in blood by regulars from the nearby Brig Tavern on Easterhouse Road.

One local man, who did not wish to be named, told the Daily Record *that he came across Tierney's body at closing time.*

'I'd just left the pub and was heading home. Me and a couple of the guys had only gone about 50 yards when we saw Spud lying there. We almost fell over him. He was covered in blood. Absolutely drenched in it. Somebody's obviously shanked him.'

The witness was reluctant to speculate on a motive for Tierney's murder but it is believed he was the victim of a gangland hit.

'The wee man never did anybody any harm,' said the witness. 'OK he was maybe a bit shady but that was it. This is bad. Someone will pay for it.'

The man who found Tierney confirmed that he had been drinking for around half an hour in the Brig Tavern before leaving around 11.30. The other drinkers left the pub at midnight and it was then that they discovered Spud Tierney's cut-up corpse.

Murder squad detectives were on the scene within minutes and a security cordon was set up around the body. A detailed search of the area and door-to-door inquiries were carried out last night. Detective Sergeant Rachel Narey said that investi-

gations were at an early stage but that she urged anyone with information to come forward.

'Strathclyde Police were alerted at 00.10 that a body had been found on land adjoining Easterhouse Road in Baillieston. Detectives were quickly on the scene and found the body later identified as 26-year-old Thomas Tierney.'

Police are appealing for anyone with information to the killing or Thomas Tierney's whereabouts earlier that day to contact Baillieston police station or Crimestoppers on 0800 555 111. All calls will be treated in confidence and there may be a reward. Police sources last night confirmed that Spud Tierney was known to them and was thought to have been a drug dealer. He is said to have been an associate of well-known Glasgow businessman Alexander Kirkwood.

I carefully placed the pinkie of the man I now knew to be Thomas Tierney in a padded envelope. I drove to the east end and posted it in a pillar box in Bridgeton.

With that it was winging its way directly to the desk of

Rachel Narey who was doubtless already waiting for the postman with bated breath and forensic scientist.

Package posted, I turned around and drove to work.

I did all that with the utmost certainty that things had just begun to go wrong.

CHAPTER 14

I had a problem. Potentially a rather serious problem. The little man with the mouse-eating grin was named Thomas Tierney. Known, apparently, as Spud. The papers said so. They said he had been stabbed just minutes from his home. They said police were seeking witnesses to his last movements. They said he had been drinking in the Brig Tavern. They said he had been brutally murdered. They said it may have been a gangland killing.

Yes. Gangland.

They said Tierney was a known associate of Alexander Kirkwood. That was the problem. The papers said Kirkwood was a well-known Glasgow businessman. That meant gangster. That meant trouble. In Alec Kirkwood's case, it meant trouble with a capital F.

Glasgow is a village with a city within it. Everyone who lives and breathes in the other city plays by different rules, speaks a different language, lives by different laws. The world is woven inside, under and around the official Glasgow.

The other city has its own police, its own civic leaders,

its own lawmakers. It has its own code of conduct and it all runs perfectly smoothly as long as everyone plays the game. Some people live entirely within the other city and couldn't leave it if they tried. Some live on the fringes, others make day trips in and out. Some of us can speak the language and know lots of people who live there but try to keep our distance all the same. Except when it suits us.

Right then, it suited me to trade chat with people who lived closer to the other city than I did. They heard things that I wanted to hear. Things I needed to know. Alec Kirkwood was police, councillor and lawmaker in the other city. Big cheese. Bad man.

He wasn't strictly A-list. The very fact that he was even known to the likes of me made him B-list. Big and bad but B-list all the same. No one knew who the A-list guys were but chances are, these days, they were not even in Glasgow at all. Strings pulled from Liverpool and London.

I knew of Kirkwood but I knew people who knew people who knew him. Guys like Ally McFarland. He knew people but thought he *was* people. Ally was in his late twenties and not as bad as he liked to make out. He'd sell some dodgy gear and get in a fight when he'd had a swally but that was about it. He was mates with some of the heavies in the Star Bar over in Royston and liked to drop their names in to impress. He also liked the sound of his own voice. And best of all, he liked me.

I think there was a bit of him that felt sorry for me after what happened. Normally I'd hate that but it suited my purpose. Let him think what he likes as long as he talks. And he talked about Kirkwood when I asked. Kirky was not a happy bunny. He had taken the killing of Spud Tierney as a personal insult.

Image is a funny thing in the other city. The likes of Alec Kirkwood need to keep a low profile for the public and the press but needs his name in lights as far as the scumbags go. They need to be shit-scared of crossing him. Even the thought of thinking about messing with him should make them pish their pants.

He made sure everyone knew that if you touched one of Alec Kirkwood's boys then you were a dead man. Simple as that. I'd touched one, big time. Serious problem.

The people that knew people said that Kirky had this thing about having a quiet life. He believed that if everybody did as they should then everybody would be all right. Everybody would have money in their pockets and an easy life. Everybody knew the cops wanted a quiet time of it too. They didn't need to come around stirring up dirt to see what shit was lying beneath it, they already knew. Everybody was happy.

Kirky had this line he liked to put about. Everyone behaves and everyone's fine. But if some muppet shits in the ice cream then the party is over.

I'd killed Spud Tierney. I'd put the keech in the Häagen-Dazs. Now Alec Kirkwood wanted revenge. He wanted me. He just didn't know it yet.

The strange thing is that I'd actually met him once. I was drinking in the Comet in Ruchill, a pub with a certain reputation. I hadn't been that comfortable even going into the place. It was only the fact that the two guys I was with were locals that I could even be in there without getting my head kicked in. A quick pint and away.

Then the door opened. In walked this guy and the entire place froze. Got the distinct feeling guys would have jumped through windows if there weren't bars on them. I didn't know who he was but there was no doubting that he was somebody. He was no more than five foot ten but gave the impression of being bigger. And that was despite being followed in by four gorillas who were all well over six feet. He reminded me of a game show host. Weird but he did.

Smart, tailored suit. Corporate hair cut. Always adjusting his cuffs or the knot in his tie. Grinning like a man who knew all the answers. I guess he was good-looking. Ask a woman.

I'd say he was about thirty-two. Face unmarked, which surprised me even before I knew who he was. There was something about him reminded me of George W. Bush. That wasn't a compliment.

Game show host. Businessman. Politician. It was as if he had been on some correspondence course for charisma. He was glad-handing everyone around him. He even shook mine. He would hold people's gaze with this grin and nod at whatever they were saying as if they were saying the most interesting thing he'd ever heard. Above all, there was a supreme confidence about him. It was an arrogance, a sureness that was almost surreal. It was as if he was running for election but had already got every vote locked away.

The guys I was with were lapping it up. The man's pure class, they said. Got five jacuzzis in his house, they said. See that suit? Bought me a drink. Great guy.

Aye, right. He nodded and grinned at me just the way he did with everyone else. I don't think he heard a single word I said. When I found out who he was, that suited me fine. Alec Kirkwood had fought his way out of Asher Street in Baillieston, a mental bampot who was as handy with his head as he was with a baseball bat. He hurt a lot of people and won the kind of reputation you need to separate yourself from the herd.

Those that tried to stop him found their houses firebombed. Those with asbestos homes had their pets poisoned. Some even went to their kids' school to find that Uncle Alec had already picked them up and looked after them for a couple of hours. He never touched them. It was a message.

A mental case. Psycho. Mad, bad and deadly to know.

He worked his way up. Swapped his bovver boots for an Armani suit and his knuckleduster for a chartered accountant. Too smart to get his hands dirty these days. Still plenty of blood on them though.

He now had one of those knock-through council house rows where three homes had been turned into a ranch. He was established. He was establishment. Other city establishment. He thought himself a cut above the rest, a smart guy among smartarses. A game show host among mongrels.

Those who knew said that Spud Tierney was a dealer for

Kirkwood. He was an irritating wee shite by all accounts. It was only being Kirky's boy that had kept him alive for as long as it did. People knew he was Kirkwood's and that was his passport through closes and schemes, it was his shield of invincibility. Right up till when I killed him.

They said he was a yappy wee dick who was always winding folk up. He'd needle guys twice his size and the only wonder was that he'd never been killed sooner.

Spud was low life and low rent. He'd bang out wraps to wasters. A few quid here, a dirty tenner there. He'd shank out smokes and snifters, pills and pokes to any hoodie or Burberry bam that had scraped the necessary from their giro.

He wouldn't be missed but there was something else. I'd worked it out. I just hadn't worked out if it would be a good thing or not. I had sawn off Spud Tierney's finger for my own purposes. Kirkwood obviously wouldn't know that. So what would he think? Easy peasy, he'd take it as a sign. Tierney had been killed because he was Kirkwood's and that finger was someone's way of telling him so.

There was probably a hundred ways that a wee nyaff like Spud could get himself stabbed. World he lived in, it was obvious. But being found minus one digit would be sure to have Kirkwood thinking it was more than just a deal gone wrong, more than just someone taking a dislike to his mouse-eating face. He'd see that single missing finger being stuck right up in front of his face. He'd think rivals. He'd see threat.

You'd maybe think that for someone like Kirkwood,

there'd be a hundred possibles who'd have done Spud Tierney to get at him. Maybe you'd think thousands. The people who know people say the truth is quite different. There'd maybe be thousands who'd like to, hundreds who'd like to think they had what it takes. There would be a handful who'd actually have the balls.

They spoke of candidates. Could be sure Kirky would be doing the same.

There was the Gilmartin brothers from Easterhouse. Two up-and-comers who had been throwing their weight about. Supposedly a big jump up in class for them to look at Kirky but you couldn't rule it out. Men get greedy.

Tookie Cochrane. Big bastard. Kirky's counterpart on the south side. Word was it was unlikely to be Tookie, he'd know a full-on turf war was a waste of everybody's time.

Mick Docherty. Medium-sized dealer who thought he was big league. He thought he was Huggy McBear, all flash gear and a big, big mouth. The suggestion was that Kirkwood liked Docherty for it because it would take someone stupid or crazy to do Spud Tierney. Docherty didn't just deal it, he used it. He was way fucking unpredictable.

Seemed Kirky was sure that the sawn-off finger was a message from one of them. Don't shoot the messenger? Aye right, he wouldn't just shoot him, he'd rip his balls off and nail them to the gates of Ibrox. He'd shoot the messenger and whoever sent him.

Word was already out that Kirkwood wanted to know every second of Spud Tierney's whereabouts for the day he was killed. He wanted to know everyone that he sold to, everyone that said boo to him, everyone that stood next to him while he pished. He wanted to know everything he ate, everything he drank, he wanted to know which side of the bed he'd got out of in the morning. If anyone so much as looked at Spud the wrong way – or the right way – then he'd know.

He also made sure that the people knew exactly what he had said to his right-hand man, a maniac by the name of Davie Stewart. 'Five o'clock,' he'd said. 'If no one turns up the fucker who did Spud by five o'clock then we pull in bodies and hurt them.'

They say Davie Stewart had smiled. They say that Davie would have been hoping that five o'clock saw nothing but silence. He liked hurting people and that was why Kirkwood had him around. Davie didn't give a flying fuck about Spud Tierney but he would gladly break fingers or fry someone's bollocks to find out who did him in. And Kirky would gladly let him.

Five o'clock? It came and went. It was showtime. Davie Stewart's show.

There was a guy worked for Mick Docherty who ran drugs out of the Victory on the edge of Baillieston. They say it was strictly Kirkwood's turf but it was borderline and small beer and so it had been let go a long time ago as long as Docherty's boy, name of Jimmy McIntyre, behaved himself. Everyone behaves and everyone's fine.

Davie Stewart and two others hauled Jimmy Mac out of the Victory, kicking and screaming in front of a pub full of punters, and tossed him into the back of a white van.

The fact that he didn't go quietly would have been perfect for Kirkwood. If you make a point, you want everyone to hear it.

In no time, Jimmy was sitting in a chair in front of Kirky. He was a lanky sort with red hair and way too many freckles. He was still talking tough and making out how he wasn't worried. He talked the talk but he looked about ready to shit himself.

They say Davie Stewart didn't look all that pleased at that, thinking that if Jimmy Mac gave it up too easy then he would miss out on his fun. Maniacs are like that.

Alec Kirkwood pulled up a chair and sat right in front of Jimmy, looking him hard in the eyes, saying nothing. Davie Stewart took up a position to Jimmy's left. Jimmy knew he was there and was dying to glance at him but was shit-scared to defy Kirkwood by looking away. Davie was boring his eyes into him, no doubt thinking all kinds of bad thoughts and trying to force them into Jimmy's skull.

Five minutes Kirkwood looked at him without a word.

Jimmy spoke. Jimmy was joking, Jimmy was giving off casual, Jimmy was trying real hard for cool. He got nowhere near it. He had nothing to say but he spilled his guts anyway.

He asked if it was about Spud Tierney. He asked it twice. He said if it was then he knew nothing. If he knew anything then he'd say it.

Kirkwood just sat and looked at him.

Jimmy kept saying he knew nothing. Kept saying he would tell him anything if he had anything to tell.

Davie Stewart got out of his chair. Jimmy heard him move but couldn't look. Kirky wouldn't let his eyes go. Jimmy's left eye strained like fuck. He could feel Davie Stewart's breath on him and he wondered if every story he'd heard about this mad bastard were true. They were.

Jimmy Mac sweated. He began to pish himself. He was near to crying.

At last Jimmy couldn't take it any longer and turned his head to Davie. Big mistake. As soon as he turned, Davie Stewart stuck a screwdriver in his eye.

Jimmy screamed for a long time. Blood and tissue spurted from his eyes and he opened his lungs and roared.

Davie hadn't thrust the screwdriver all the way home of course. Too high a chance that would have killed him. He just forced it in enough to burst the eyeball and let Jimmy Mac know that he was serious. It was a message. Kirkwood's message to the other city.

They let Jimmy scream for a bit then sob for a bit. Then Davie grabbed his hair and yanked it back hard on his head. He asked him what he knew about Spud Tierney's death.

Jimmy Mac found a voice and burbled that he didn't know nothing. If the Tierney killing had anything to do with Mick Docherty then he knew nothing about it.

They knew he was telling the truth then. He was too shit-scared to do otherwise.

All of that was bad enough and all down to me, but it got worse.

Before they bundled Jimmy Mac into the white van and before they drove him back to the Victory and before they threw him out of the van's back door onto the street in front of the pub. Before they did all that, Alec Kirkwood told Davie Stewart to bring out a pair of pliers and clip off Jimmy Mac's pinkie.

Shit.

CHAPTER 15

They talked about Spud Tierney from the back seat of my taxi. It was all over the papers, talk of turf wars, tit-for-tat violence, contract killings and gangsters. Mostly it was shit.

Sometimes they talked to me, sometimes they were on mobile phones. Acting tough, talking gallus, playing the big man, playing the big so what. Nobody in Glasgow was scared of a bit of organized criminal bloodshed.

They might have been outraged or shocked, disgusted or interested but not frightened. Most of them were way too cool and street smart for that. Scared was for Edinburgh or teuchters. They lived in Glasgow, therefore they were duty-bound to be hard about such things. Curious indifference was the most they were allowed to muster.

'Aye, stabbed. That's right. A dealer. Know Alec Kirkwood? Aye, one of his guys. Bodies going to be piling up, way I got told. See the game last night? Terrible, wasn't it? Ref was hopeless.'

Or else they were on their high horse about it. A disgrace. Police should be doing something about that kind of thing. More bobbies on the beat. If those people had proper jobs then they wouldn't have the time to go round stabbing each other.

Others relished it because if they were killing each other then they were leaving normal folk alone. Let the fuckers stab each other all they want. Every one deid is one less bampot on the streets. Give them more fucking knives and guns and let them get on with it.

They still didn't talk about me because they didn't know I existed. If anything I had slipped further into the shadows because they thought Thomas Tierney was a gangland killing. Glasgow had no idea who I was. Outside the ranks of Strathclyde Police I was nothing. They knew me, they wanted me but no one else gave a damn.

A cop got into the back of the cab just days after Tierney. Saw him for polis right off. The clothes, the hair, the way he carried himself, all off-job casual but couldn't have been anything else. Polite enough but no chat, which obviously suited me just fine. Gave me an address in Millerston, couple of streets back from Hogganfield Loch, and settled back in the seat. We had driven maybe five minutes when his mobile rang.

'All right, Gavin? How you doing?'

Pause.

'No, heard nothing. She's keeping it all to herself. Asked around but no one knows what's going on.'

Pause.

'Aye, I know. Place is going mental.'

Pause and a narrowed glance at my eyes in the rear-view. I watched the road.

'I don't know how she expects to keep a lid on this for much longer. Three of them for fuck's sake. One was bad enough but three? Shit's going to hit the fan big time when this comes out.'

Long pause.

'She doesn't have a clue. Not a Scooby. Neither of them do. Miles out her depth. Fucking drowning in it she is. Serves the bitch right.'

Pause.

'No, no way. Sorry but all she has to do is hold her hands up and admit she's not up to it. Should have it taken off her. Fucking three of them. Fucking unbelievable.'

Pause.

'No, I don't.'

Pause.

'That's no the point. Nothing to do with it.'

Pause.

'No, I don't know either. No idea. Some sick joke. But it shouldn't matter. Nothing to do with it, certainly no reason for her to run with this.'

Pause.

'Aye well, we'll see soon enough. Fuck knows what's going to happen if there's a fourth.'

Very short pause.

'Well, you can hardly rule it out.'

Pause.

'I'm just saying. This is out of hand already, Gav. Way out of hand. Three of the fuckers.'

Long pause.

'Yeah, but he doesn't know that, does he? So he'll think what he wants, do what he wants.'

Pause.

'Oh no. No chance. That's her call. No one talks about it, she says. Her call.'

Pause.

'Not our problem. Our problem is what happens when this comes out. We'll all be right in it then. Way she's going it's her mess. Let her lie in it.'

A long pause then a laugh. A harsh, crude laugh.

'Aye, course I would. Am no denying that. So would you. Not the point though. Like I said, it's way out of hand already. Fuck knows how this is going to pan out but I can't see how it's going to be good.'

Short pause.

'Aye. Too right. A fucking nightmare. Shit! We should be all over this. Blasting it from the rooftops, not this softly, softly pish.'

He breathed out hard.

'No, nor me, mate. All right. Speak to you tomorrow. Cheers.'

He snapped his phone shut with an angry click. At the sound of it shutting, I looked in the mirror and caught him glancing at me. He glared back, challenging me. My eyes went back to the road. Nothing to do with me, guv.

Maybe it *was* nothing to do with me. Maybe I was paranoid but it didn't seem likely. I made him for a cop and was sure that every cop in Glasgow was talking about me.

As much as no one else knew I existed, I must have been number one topic of conversation for the police.

I knew I was gripping the steering wheel a bit harder than I should have been the whole way through his chat. The chat that might have had nothing to do with me. I was cool. I was detached. I was compartmentalizing. But I knew it was having an effect. My heart was beating just a bit faster. My blood was hotter. The he and the she of his talk with the Gavin guy were reverberating round my head. I was thinking, calculating, considering. I think I might even have been sweating just a bit more than I should. I was aware of my pulse.

Suddenly I was aware of traffic lights changing above me as I drove along Cumbernauld Road into Stepps. Fuck, fuck fuck. I slammed on my brakes just after amber had become red. Fuck. Streets and windows and signs jolted into my head and it was like my ears had popped on an aeroplane. I slid to a halt a few feet beyond the line and realized I hadn't noticed much except his voice since some time back when we were on the bypass.

He shot forward a bit in his seat and swore.

'Fuck's sake.'

'Sorry. Sorry about that. Changed on me.'

'Aye. So I saw.'

He glared at me again in the rear-view.

I tore my eyes from his before I could glare back at him. So tempting but that would have achieved nothing and might have done a whole lot of harm. Heart beating fast. Pulse throbbing. I had a long game to play.

I breathed and I waited. Tried to make a point of not holding the steering wheel too hard. Long game. Big move still to come. Cool your blood.

The red ticked away like a stopped clock. Tick, tick, tick. Changed. Red. Red and amber. Green. Took my time. Eased away.

He glared at me again. I looked back blankly.

'Fuck's sake.'

Like it was all my fault.

He was just one cop. One polis man among eight thousand. One man among a million in Greater Glasgow. What the fuck did his opinion matter? He obviously didn't know what he was talking about. Didn't know anything about anything.

I was on edge. Didn't realize it until then. Had wanted people to talk about me, about it, about them, but as soon as one did I got edgy. Not good. There were big things about to happen. The most important thing. Not the time to get anxious.

I didn't look in the rear-view mirror again. Eyes front. Didn't look at him again, didn't breathe until we had gone onto Royston Road and it was time for the turn onto Mossbank Drive.

'This one?'

'Aye. Then first left.'

I turned right. I turned left. He said twenty yards. I stopped. He got out. He left a shit tip. Closed the door behind him without a word.

He was nothing. I breathed. Big city, small village. He

knocked on the door of a house which opened and closed behind him.

I breathed and drove off. I drove on.

His conversation might have had nothing to do with me. I didn't care. I knew what I had to do. I knew what was going to happen.

CHAPTER 16

I'd read about serial killers. I would look in bookshops and in the local library. Never bought a book, never borrowed one. I've a very good memory. Some I read on the Internet but kept that to an absolute minimum. I knew everything was logged, everything monitored, everything watched.

I watched documentaries. Bought satellite television just for that. Read magazines, paid for in cash, bought in different places.

Ted Bundy. John Wayne Gacy. Fred West. Jeffrey Dahmer. Dennis Nilsen. Albert DeSalvo. David Berkowitz. Alexander Pichushkin. Pedro Alonso López. I knew them all.

Henry Lee Lucas and Ottis Toole, Charles Ng, Ian Brady and Myra Hindley. Albert Fish. Leopold and Loeb. Aileen Wuornos. Harold Shipman. Andrei Chikatilo. John George Haigh. John Christie. Peter Sutcliffe. Josef Fritzl.

Then there was Jack.

Some said the Ripper was overrated. I always remembered someone saying that to me: 'Jack the Ripper is overrated.' Just like that.

In purely numerical terms he was probably right. But what he forgot, what they all forget, is that Jack got away with it. The single most famous serial killer in history yet still unknown. Outstanding.

Some people think they know who Jack was but they don't. They can't know.

They call themselves Ripperologists, those who study Jack. Those that are into him in a big way. Ask ten Ripperologists who killed those women and you will get eleven different answers.

We know the women's names.

Polly Nichols.

Annie Chapman.

Liz Stride.

Kate Eddowes.

Mary Kelly.

Five prostitutes of Whitechapel. Victims of life. Victims of Jack. Jack killed them, ripped them. But we don't know why and we don't know who.

They say he was Queen Victoria's whoring grandson Eddy, the Duke of Clarence, driven mad by syphilis. They say it was the Queen's physician William Gull. They say it was her obstetrician John Williams.

He was the painter Walter Sickert. He was Carl Feigenbaum, a German sailor. He was an insane Polish Jew, Aaron Kosminski.

It was the Ripper diary confessor James Maybrick or the bogus doctor Francis Tumblety. It was barrister Montague John Druitt, the abortionist Dr Thomas Neill Cream, the

Polish poisoner George Chapman or Mary Kelly's lover Joseph Barnett.

It was them and it was a hundred others but it was none of them. It was Jack. No one knows who he was.

Jack did what Jack had to do then he stopped. Disappeared. Slipped back into the London fog. Untouched.

Know what though? Jack's biggest secret is that maybe he didn't even exist. There is a theory that says there was no psychopath stalking the streets of Whitechapel, no madman hunting down prostitutes to kill and dissect them. Those women died all right but this theory says that there was no Jack.

It goes that three men worked together to do the murders. Their plan, if you believe it, was to cover their true intentions by creating the myth of the Ripper. These men were high establishment, variously connected to the Royal Household and were set on protecting its interests. Whether it was mad Prince Albert Victor that needed protecting or Gull or Williams, you can take your pick.

The bottom line is that one of the five whores, Mary Kelly, knew too much and was prepared to tell. She had to be silenced. But the killing of Mary alone would have left a trail back to the palace. Maybe the police would not have bothered their arses too much about a murdered prostitute but if they had looked into it seriously then motive could eventually have led them to the truth.

So the plan was devised. A story spun. A play performed.

Mary Kelly and her friends were slaughtered and the murders made to look the work of a complete monster.

The silencing of Mary Kelly was hidden amidst the other four. She was the needle. They were the haystack.

The beauty of it was that it was made to look like madness but in reality it was clinical, reasoned and sound.

So was it true, this theory among theories? I didn't know but I understood it. I respected the logic.

Rationale. It was where the others – West, Bundy, Nilsen, Dahmer – messed up. They were wild beyond reason and mostly insane. Jack was sane enough not to get caught. Ever.

Dahmer was a drunken, morbid obsessive. West was a sexual compulsive with a gruesome fascination for mutilation. Brady was power-driven and bitterly resentful. Nilsen was a self-absorbed fantasist, another suffering from an addictive compulsion.

All were off their heads in their own crazy ways even if they had a competent sort of insanity that let them pass for sane. The detective who arrested Nilsen described him as 'frighteningly normal, an ordinary sort of man'. Shipman was mad enough to kill maybe more than 300 old people yet sane enough that none of them suspected him. Dahmer was able to convince cops that a fleeing victim in the street was a liar, a lover scorned.

But they could only play at being sane. And they could only do that for so long. It kept tugging at them. Their addiction, their obsession, their compulsion, it always made them do it one more time. No rationale.

The urge they couldn't resist was what undercut any kind of normal thinking and what drove them to do what they did. Not evil or any such pish, just uncontrollable obsessions.

There is a lot of rubbish talked about evil when it comes to serial killers. Numbers mess with people's moral outrage. The thinking goes that someone who kills twenty people is more evil than someone who kills two. The man who rips his victims apart is more evil than the man who doesn't. The woman who kills is more evil than the man. The man who mutilates one victim is more evil than a politician who sends millions to their death in the name of patriotism or oil. It's all bollocks.

I doubted there was any such thing as evil. I used to think there was but then I used to think there was a God. If God represented good and there was no God then why would there be evil?

Even if there is evil then it is in a man's actions not in his soul. Whatever someone has inside is irrelevant. Only deeds matter.

I knew plenty of absolute bastards who never killed anyone. Harold Shipman, if you believed him, was a nice old man who eased people's pain.

I didn't claim to know anything about evil. I just knew my serial killers.

I knew my ain folk too.

Scotland gave the world television and the telephone, penicillin, the pneumatic tyre, the steam engine and the bicycle, radar, insulin, calculus and Dolly the sheep. But we are also right up there with the best of them when it comes to killing people.

America's first recorded serial killers were ours. Two cousins, pretty much unheard of over here, named Bill and Josh Harpe. Born in Scotland, they changed their names when they moved to America. They became known as Micajah and Wiley, Big and Little Harpe.

In the late 1700s they slaughtered at least forty-one people in a blood spree lasting a year. Their favourite trick was to beat or stab someone to death then gut them, rip out their insides and fill them up with rocks. The body would then be thrown in the river and allowed to sink.

They killed their own children too, poor little bastards born to the three wives they had between the two of them. One eight-month-old wee girl cried once too often and the father grabbed the poor wee thing by its ankle, smashed its head on a tree and threw it dead into the woods.

Then there was old Sawney Bean, the man who washed his hands in the blood of a thousand souls. But just like Jack, all was probably not as it seemed. Alexander Sawney Bean. Said to have been the head of a forty-eight-strong family of cannibals in Ayrshire. An incestuous, murderous bunch who are supposed to have lived in a cave during the day, venturing out at night to slay unwary innocents and drag them into their lair to be dissected and eaten.

Some tales have it that as many as 1,000 were killed and devoured by Bean's incestuous band but more likely the whole thing is just another load of bollocks. Chances are Sawney and his brood were just an invention. A figment of an English imagination determined to damn the reputation of the Scots in the wake of the Jacobite rebellions. Everything is the fault of the English, don't you know.

Then there was Bible John, another one that maybe was and maybe wasn't.

In the late 1960s, the spectre of the scripture-quoting killer in a dark suit haunted Glasgow's dance halls. Three murders, countless sightings, umpteen police interviews and a city living in dread. It sounded vaguely familiar.

Patricia Docker in 1968, Jemima McDonald and Helen Puttock in 1969. All went to dances at the Barrowlands ballroom and all ended up dead. They were said to have last been seen talking to a tall, well-dressed, red-haired fellow. A man named John that liked to quote the Bible.

John was the Scottish Jack in more ways than one.

Now some cops believe that there never was a Bible John, that the killings of Patricia Docker, Jemima McDonald and Helen Puttock were never linked except in people's minds. And in the minds of the cops. They now think that the whole climate of fear, the idea of a serial killer stalking the dance floor, was misplaced and misleading.

The three killers of those three women may even have escaped because Glasgow's finest were looking for one man. One serial killer where none existed. There were three needles alright but the cops were just looking in one haystack.

Even if the Bible-quoting John was not the Scottish serial killer champ, there were plenty others to step forward and stake their own claims.

Robert Black killed at least three little girls, perhaps as many as nine more. Nilsen murdered at least fifteen men.

Brady killed five children and claimed to have killed five more. Peter Manuel was found guilty of seven murders but probably committed fifteen. Angus Sinclair had just two murders on his record but was being investigated for a string of others. Peter Tobin, brutal killer of at least two and probably more besides. Thomas Neill Cream, abortionist, Ripper suspect and poisoner. Born in Glasgow and killer of five. Staff nurse Colin Norris, angel of death and killer of four.

It's hardly what you would call a fine tradition but a precedent nevertheless. A lot of serial killers for such a little place. The best small murdering country in the world. Stick that on your tourist posters.

Wha's like us? Damn few and they're all deid. That's Scottish irony.

But they are not like me. And I am not like them.

CHAPTER 17

He stirred slowly. His head bobbing up and down on his chest as he fought to clear his head.

When his eyes were fully opened and focused he saw me sitting in front of him. He jumped. His eyes spread wide. I was pleased to see that he looked as scared as he was confused.

It was only then that he seemed to realize that he was bound hand and foot. His arms were tied securely to the chair, his legs to the legs. He struggled but got nowhere. He was going nowhere.

He looked around but in the dim light all he could see was me. And that suited me fine. I wanted to make myself smile at him but I couldn't. The best I could muster was a glare. Wallace Ogilvie, his limbs bound, his mouth taped shut, his confusion total, was in front of me. He did not know who I was.

'Pierre Ambroise François Choderlos de Laclos.'

Wallace Ogilvie shrugged as best he could.

'Pierre Ambroise François Choderlos de Laclos,' I

repeated. 'He was the author of *Les Liaisons Dangereuses*. You'll have heard of the film.'

Wallace Ogilvie just looked at me.

'He wrote it in 1782. You know a quote from it though. *La vengeance est un plat qui se mange froid.*'

Wallace Ogilvie continued to look.

'No? I thought you might know a bit of French.'

Wallace Ogilvie shook his head warily.

'Hm. How about Klingon then?'

Wallace Ogilvie's eyebrows knitted tight in bewilderment.

'Stupid but it's often quoted as being a Klingon phrase. You know, from *Star Trek*. *bortaS bIr jablu'DI', reH QaQqu' nay*. It took me ages to learn that.'

I was trying to be glib. Trying to scare him with it. Using it to stop my anger spilling over. Control. I was the one in control.

'No Klingon either then?'

Wallace Ogilvie shook his head. Very scared.

'It is also said to originate in Sicilian. *La vendetta è un piatto che si serve freddo*. Others believe it has its roots in Chinese, Spanish or Pashtun. The Internet is great, isn't it?'

Wallace Ogilvie was talking now behind the tape. I couldn't make out a word. His eyes were talking too. They were telling me that I was mad and he was terrified. Perhaps. There is a fine line between the appearance of madness and insanity itself. Even I didn't know which side of the line I stood on.

'Got it yet?' I asked him.

When Wallace Ogilvie shook his head again I wanted to

slap him or kick him. No touching though. I had kept our contact clean until now and did not want to dirty my hands or feet on him. Control.

'*La vengeance est un plat qui se mange froid.*

'*bortaS bIr jablu'DI', reH QaQqu' nay.*

'*La vendetta è un piatto che si serve freddo.*'

I put my head very close to his. I whispered. 'Revenge is a dish best served cold.'

His eyes opened wider at that. He was trying to speak again. I didn't need to hear the words. Revenge? For what? Who are you? Where do I know you from?

Then there it was. Recognition.

Oh, he knew now all right. I nodded and managed a smile at last.

'Yes. That's right.'

Wallace Ogilvie shook his head furiously. His eyes were pleading, begging with me. No need to beg, I thought. And no point.

'I'm not going to lay a finger on you,' I told him.

I saw hope in his eyes. Faint, short-lived hope. A bit cruel maybe. The hope disappeared when I reached for the switch on the wall and flooded the room with light.

'*La vengeance est un plat qui se mange froid.*'

His eyes took in where he was and it filtered through to his brain.

We were in a freezer room. A huge industrial meat plant room that could house a whole herd of frozen cattle. But for now there was only me and Wallace Ogilvie. The white walls shone brightly under the fluorescent lighting, giving little indication that the meat plant had lain empty for nearly a year. The owners had taken a subsidy offer from Lithuania and upped sticks, leaving behind a workforce and a factory they couldn't sell. Everything was in working order in case a buyer could be found but that hadn't happened.

Security, such as it was, was easily bypassed. There was nothing to steal, nothing to use. No carcasses.

Not yet.

I think Wallace Ogilvie had worked it out by this point. That would explain why he had begun to cry. He shook and sobbed. He wailed in protest deep behind the tape.

I'd often wondered about pity. Wondered how I found it so easy not to give it room. I was supposed to feel it. I knew that. It was the natural, human response and I still clung to my humanity.

But my capacity for pity died the day she did. It disappeared along with hope, dreams and faith. I had no time and no use for pity. I compartmentalized. It's easier than you might think.

Anyway, given that I had no pity for the others then it was never likely I'd have any for Wallace Ogilvie. I'd risen above any temptation to offer compassion to the rest so it was no effort to do the same with the man before me.

Pitiless. Merciless. Hard-hearted. I could do those. But not unfeeling. Right then, I was awash with feelings.

So was Wallace Ogilvie. He had pissed himself, a telltale pool at his feet and a dark stain at his groin. The stench was awful. Urine, fear and sweat swirling together. Disgusting but strangely pleasing in the circumstances. I was glad to know that Wallace Ogilvie was so scared he couldn't control his bladder. That he was so pathetic.

It would have been good to think it was remorse but you don't pish your pants out of guilt or repentance. Fear. Pure, unadulterated fear. He cowered before his Lord out of dread and his Lord was me.

There was plenty I could have said to him but nothing came out. It was all there in my head but unsaid.

I looked at him. Stared at him. His head was on his chest now. It would have been so easy to hit him. Punch him, strangle him, kick him in the head, break his legs. So tempting. But I already knew what I was going to do and so it seemed did Wallace Ogilvie. Or perhaps he simply knew that he was going to die.

I stood over him, waiting until he lifted his head and looked at me with his red, pleading eyes. I nodded at him. It was now.

I turned and walked away, closing the door behind me. There was a window cut into the door so that I could see Wallace Ogilvie and he could see me. I stood for a few moments, looking at him and catching my own reflection in the glass. I looked calm apart from my eyes. They looked strained, wild.

I threw the switch. It was out of Wallace Ogilvie's view but he would soon know that I had done it.

I stood, watched and waited. My eyes were on his, his on me. I wanted to see the reaction, the first sign of realization. I wanted to see him twitch.

Ten minutes and nothing. Maybe the unit had lain idle

too long. I began to wonder if it was working properly.

Fifteen minutes and I was sure it wasn't operational. I began to wonder if I could fix it. I'd no idea where to start. It would be terrible. It was all going wrong.

Then he twitched. It was just a shake of a shoulder. A single shiver. It was enough.

A surge of exhilaration and anticipation ran through me. He shivered with cold and I shivered with excitement.

I spoke to the glass in front of me. I spoke to him knowing that he probably couldn't hear.

'The normal body temperature of an adult human is 98.6 degrees Fahrenheit. Your core temperature is already less. But I guess you know that by now.

'Feel that tightening across your shoulders and neck? That's known as pre-shivering muscle tone. It means your body temperature has hit 97 degrees.'

He began to move more. His legs shook against their bindings, his shoulders trembled, hunched and flexed. He was rubbing himself against the chair, the little that the ties would allow. His feet were shaking and kicking as best they could. His head swaying side to side.

'Colder now,' I told him. 'Perhaps 96 degrees. Your body is shivering so that you generate heat by increasing the chemical reactions required for muscle activity. Amazing but that can actually increase surface heat production by 500 per cent.

'The bad news is that you can only keep that going for so long because your muscle glucose gets depleted and fatigue kicks in.'

He was shivering so much now that the chair was dancing, shuffling an inch here and there as he did anything he could to get warmer. It was hopeless though.

'Your hands are especially cold, aren't they? Your palms will be no more than 60 degrees. Painfully cold. That's because your body is instinctively sending blood coursing away from your skin, deeper inside you. It is deliberately letting your hands chill to keep the vital organs warm. It won't be enough though.'

Now he was really shaking, trembling violently. It was almost as if he was having a fit.

'Your body temperature has dropped to 95 degrees. You have hit mild hypothermia and your body is undergoing its maximum shivering stage. It is contracting your muscles to generate more heat. Don't worry. It won't last long.'

I waited and watched and waited some more.

The shivering was violent and broken by pauses. Then the pauses got longer and the shivering shorter.

Before long he had stopped all attempts at movement, no real efforts to move his legs. All he did was shiver. Then eventually, as I knew it would, the shivering stopped too.

'Oh dear. Heat is draining away fast now. Half of it is disappearing through your head alone. Your ears must be so excruciatingly cold. You are below 95 degrees now. That's bad. Every one degree drop below 95 means that your cerebral metabolic rate falls off by five per cent. You are losing it. When your body temperature hits 93 degrees then amnesia will start to prey on you. Pity that, I don't want you to forget anything. Not just yet.'

He just sat slumped in front of me now, occasionally raising his head to look at me with a half-hearted glare. It was the best he could manage. His skin was turning blue. His pupils were dilated.

'You're in profound hypothermia now. Your temperature has fallen to 88 degrees and your body can't be bothered trying to keep itself warm any more. Your blood is thickening. Feel it? Your oxygen intake has fallen by over a quarter. Your kidneys are working overtime. If you hadn't already pished yourself then you would probably do it anyway. Your body is giving up the ghost.

'In case you are wondering, and you probably are, there is no specifically defined temperature at which the body perishes from extreme cold. Nazi doctors, those sick bastards that experimented with cold-water immersion baths at Dachau, calculated death at around 77 Fahrenheit. Sometimes it's lower, sometimes higher.

'Chilling, isn't it?'

His chest was heaving. His breathing was severely troubled.

I watched him intently.

'You will now be about 88 degrees and your heart is in overdrive. Chilled nerve tissues are blocking the heart's electrical impulses. It is becoming arrhythmic, pumping less than two thirds of the normal amount of blood. There's less oxygen, your brain is slowing. You might be suffering hallucinations.

'It's going to get worse. Two degrees lower and you are going to feel really weird. It's the strange bit. You are going to feel hot. Really hot. It's at this stage that people freezing to death feel so hot that they start ripping their clothes off. Sadly that's not an option open to you. You will just have to suffer.

'No one really knows why but they think it's because constricted blood vessels suddenly open and create a sensation of extreme heat against the skin. It will feel like you are burning up.

'Your body is shutting down. It doesn't want to play any more. That's happening now. You are drifting away. Gone. Bye, bye.

'You're not dead though. They call it a metabolic icebox. You're not blue any more, you've gone grey. If I looked I might not find a pulse or detect breathing. But you're not dead. Not yet.

'If, like the Nazis, I let your temperature plunge further then you would have a pulmonary oedema. There would be cardiac and respiratory failure. That would be fine except that I wouldn't know when. You would be fucking dead and I wouldn't know when. And I want to know when. I want to know the exact point of your fucking death. I want to know to the second. You remember that cardiac arrhythmia that you are having? It is very dangerous. Any sudden shock is likely to set off ventricular fibrillation and result in certain death. You need to watch that.'

I opened the door to the freezer room and walked quietly up to Wallace Ogilvie. Oh it was cold, very cold. But I wouldn't be long.

I stood next to him. His head slumped. His body showing no sign of life.

I leaned into him. Put my mouth close to his ear.

And I screamed. I roared. I fucking bellowed my hate into his ear. I thought my lungs might burst with the effort.

His heart jumped once. Just once and I knew it was done.

I left the room, shivering through more than cold, closing the door behind me. I pulled the switch back to off, shutting down the freezing process, and slumped with my back against the wall. I slid to the floor, crying my eyes out.

I would cry until near morning, until Wallace Ogilvie was warmed just enough that I could saw off the little finger of his right hand and take his body elsewhere. Somewhere it could be found.

'*La vengeance est un plat qui se mange froid.*'

I said it out loud although no one was listening.

CHAPTER 18

Memories are like landmines. You never know which one will blow up in your face. You can be mugged by your memories when you least expect it. I was shaving one time, drawing the blade across my cheek when a memory leapt into my head.

Menorca. 1996. The image of Sarah at a restaurant table with the biggest ice cream you've ever seen matched only by the size of the grin on her face. She thought she was the luckiest girl in the world. She was wearing a bright yellow T-shirt with a vivid orange sunburst on it, her blonde hair pulled behind her in a ponytail. A sliver of ice cream slipped from her mouth and trickled down her chin. She laughed till she nearly wet herself. All three of us laughed so much that people turned to look at us.

I remembered that and stared at myself in the mirror. I had the sudden urge to gouge my face with the razor. To bite it deep into my cheek and twist it till it tore a chunk of skin and cheek. I stood and stared at myself as my hand and my mind battled over the grip of the razor.

I didn't do it.

I did try not to let it linger but sometimes the thought would slip under my guard. To meet up with her again. Not to wait. To make it happen. To catch her up before the smell of her left me. Before I couldn't conjure up her face in an instant.

Movies portray sudden flashbacks of memory with bursts of light and images exploding in your head. I used to think that was just bollocks but it is precisely how it happens. For me at any rate.

You can be driving, talking, walking, in mid sentence or mid bite when you are jumped by your past. The memories are always there, lurking, waiting.

Sometimes I had to shake my head to stop them, to clear them out of my mind. Then there was guilt at doing that. For not enduring them. For not putting up with the pain of the memories the way a proper father would.

I'd hear her voice too. Not voices like killers heard, nothing crazy. Just her voice, finishing sentences for me and sometimes telling me what I should or shouldn't be doing. Her being silly or laughing or saying how she loved this film or that food. I'd find myself nodding and saying, 'I know. I know, sweetheart.'

Guilt came at you just as often as memories did. Just as random, just as unexpected, just as deadly. Guilt at what you had done and what you hadn't. Guilt for breaking the biggest promise of all. The one that every father makes to their child. To look after them. To protect them. No matter what.

Sometimes I lay awake wondering what I wouldn't do to have her back. To have her back for good or for five minutes. To have her back in the world even if she wasn't with us. To have her laughing and running. Growing, working, playing. Smiling or crying. Happy or sad. Good times and bad. Just to have her back.

The answer was anything. Anything and more.

Kill? Obviously so. The question was how many and I didn't have an answer that didn't scare me.

The darkness of the night and the blackness of my soul were strange and dangerous places to consider such things. Maybe that was when I descended into insanity but more likely it was desperation. I would try anything, do anything, think anything, hope for anything.

In the early days, the black, black days, I would hold my breath. I'd convince myself that if I closed my eyes and didn't breathe for a full minute then when I opened them again it would be back to the time when everything was alright. It never worked but I'd try it again and again. I'd screw my eyes so tight it would hurt but it would never work.

I'd make mental pacts. If I did this or that then time would turn.

I'd give up everything I owned. That was easy. Every penny I had or would ever have. My house, my health. I'd give my life, of course I would.

I tried to wish myself dead. I tried to make deals with the God I didn't believe in. With any God, with any Devil. I'd scream within myself, demanding that someone listened. Take me. Bring her back.

129

The things I'd promise would get darker and worse. They had to because the first lot didn't change anything.

If giving up my life wouldn't do it then I'd offer up the lives of others. If wishing someone dead would change things then I'd wish it. Instantly.

One person. Two. Ten. A village. A city. A country.

There wasn't a limit. How could there be? What kind of father could draw a line and say I'd do this or that for my daughter but no more? There is nothing that a father wouldn't do.

I'd imagine a tsunami was summoned up by the God that I didn't recognize and was about to flood the entire eastern seaboard of the United States. The God would say to me that I could halt it with a single word and save the lives of millions. Or I could have five minutes with the girl that was taken away from me. No contest.

In the middle of the night it is easy to wish away the lives of millions of people. You close your eyes as tight as you can and condemn them to death and hope beyond hope that when you open them again everything will be alright. But no matter how many you kill with your mind it is always the same.

You begin to wonder if one actual death would do more than millions of pretend ones. Maybe if it was the middle of the day rather than the depths of night then you'd dismiss the idea. Maybe if you weren't driven to distraction by the unbearable awfulness of being alive. Maybe if you weren't me.

Otherwise you grab at any straw, any hope, any chance.

You know, of course, that it won't change things. Time cannot turn. You are not stupid, you know that. Yet you try, you have no choice, your mind demands it.

One death. It's not much. Not for a life. Not for her life. A bargain.

Then you may wonder about more than one killing. You may wonder about how much revenge would be worth in a pact with the God or the Devil. You offer up the lives of others and you promise retribution. Surely either would do. Both would be a guarantee.

It becomes an easy decision to make. You promise to do something that suddenly seems easy and right in return for the one thing that you want above all else. Who wouldn't do that for the person that means more to them than any other? Not you. Not me. Definitely not me.

What sort of father wouldn't do anything for his daughter?

CHAPTER 19

Same anonymous envelope, same procedure. Once the police found Wallace Ogilvie's body then they'd be expecting it. There would be an expectant queue at Rachel Narey's desk awaiting the post.

But the finger went to Keith Imrie at the *Daily Record*. I was pretty sure he wouldn't be expecting what was going to land on his desk. I just hoped that after shitting himself that he would be able to find out what he needed to know.

I couldn't be sure from his stories if he was up to it or not. Much of the stuff he had written up till then had been crap. But he was getting the scoop of his life dropped in his grubby lap and all he needed to do was make a few phone calls. These guys had contacts, all he had to do was use them. Just in case, I gave him a helping hand as well as the finger. I included a printed slip of paper with five names on it.

DS Rachel Narey.
Jonathan Carr.
Billy Hutchison.
Thomas Tierney.
Wallace Ogilvie.

A finger and five names. Nothing else. I didn't want to join the dots completely for him. Four unsolved murders. One cop. One severed finger. One big fat scoop. Work it out Imrie. Come on. You can do it.

Phone Rachel. Phone the cops that take your backhanders, the cops that let you buy them drinks, the cops that take used cash for information. Get off your lazy arse and do the work.

Imrie didn't let me down. The headline in the *Record* screamed 'Jock the Ripper'. Above it a strapline roared 'Serial killer stalks Glasgow. Four dead'. In full glorious and gory colour, across the front page was a huge picture of the severed right pinkie of Wallace Ogilvie.

The cops would be furious. I was pleased.

Inside there were photos of Carr, Hutchison, Tierney and Ogilvie. There were quotes from anonymous police sources. There was an abrupt quote from Rachel Narey. There was sensationalism all through it.

It was perfect.

CHAPTER 20

SERIAL KILLER STALKS GLASGOW. FOUR DEAD
JOCK THE RIPPER
EXCLUSIVE by Keith Imrie.
Friday, 16 October 2009.

FOUR VICIOUS unsolved murders which have baffled Strathclyde Police were carried out by the same person – a crazed psychopath who mutilates his victims. The Daily Record *has uncovered stunning proof that links the four cases and reveals that a serial killer is stalking Glasgow.*

Scotland's number one newspaper has handed over vital evi-dence to the police which may lead to the capture of the barbaric murderer. The killer of city lawyer Jonathan Carr, book-maker Billy Hutchison, drug dealer Thomas Tierney and busi-nessman Wallace Ogilvie has sparked the biggest murder hunt since the city was terrorised by the Bible John case in the 1960s.

Full story on pages 2 and 3.

FINGERS UP TO COPS

A PSYCHOPATH who has carried out four brutal and seemingly unrelated murders in Glasgow is taunting police by sending them body parts from his victims. The Daily Record *can exclusively reveal that each time Jock the Ripper strikes, he saws off the right little finger from his prey and then posts it to police officers. Detectives are said to be infuriated at being mocked by the sick killer. It has made them even more determined to catch him but it is believed that they have no significant leads.*

The latest sawn-off pinkie was acquired by this reporter. It has been handed over to Strathclyde Police and they are currently carrying out DNA tests to establish identity. However there seems little doubt that it belongs to the Ripper's fourth and most recent victim, businessman Wallace Ogilvie.

Police sources say that they are working on the basis that there is no link between the four murders. While they maintain an open mind on the matter, they believe the killer strikes at random.

Sources close to the investigation say that detectives had deliberately withheld from the public and the press the fact that all four were murdered by the same person. They did so for 'procedural reasons' and to avoid public panic. However, the force was last night blasted by community groups and local politicians for not releasing information which could have helped saved people from the Ripper. Councillor Bill Houston said that Strathclyde Police had been derelict in their duty to the public.

'There is a serial killer in our midst and the people of Glasgow have the right to know that. There is no way that the police should have kept this information to themselves. Someone who is deranged enough to murder four innocent people and cut off their fingers is completely out of control and people need to know that they must take appropriate safety measures.'

Tam Pearson, community councillor for Maryhill, said that there was great unease in the area and people were terrified the

Ripper would strike again.

'People are afraid to leave their homes at night. It is an utter disgrace that the police knew there was a killer like this on the loose and didn't see fit to tell anyone. Somebody should lose their job for this.'

The Ripper first struck on February 10 when he murdered lawyer Jonathan Carr in a lay-by near Milngavie. The killing of the 37-year-old was originally thought to have been a robbery gone wrong or a revenge attack from someone involved in a previous case of Mr Carr's. However the Record's startling revelations now make this look unlikely. Strathclyde Police have consistently refused to reveal the manner of Mr Carr's murder but we have learned that his mouth was sealed and his nostrils glued together until he suffocated.

Victim number two was popular Maryhill bookie Billy Hutchison. The 58-year-old was found electrocuted in May and his death was originally thought to have been a tragic accident. However the subsequent involvement of murder squad detectives gave the first clue that all was not what it seemed.

The Ripper struck for the third time when he murdered small-time Baillieston drug dealer Thomas 'Spud' Tierney. The 26-year-old was stabbed to death in what was viewed as a retaliatory attack by a rival gang on September 27. Tierney was a known associate of Glasgow businessman Alexander Kirkwood.

Victim number four is businessman Wallace Ogilvie (52) who was murdered on Monday. The cause of his death was not made known by officers but they appealed for anyone who had information as to his last-known whereabouts to contact them.

The Record can exclusively reveal that Mr Ogilvie had been frozen to death before dying of a heart attack. As well as a finger being removed from each victim and sent to the police – initially to the CID and then specifically to Detective Sergeant Rachel Narey – the Record can reveal that there is DNA evidence conclusively linking the four deaths.

Although Strathclyde Police refused to confirm it, sources

maintain that on two separate occasions, DNA of one victim was found on the body of another. It is thought that the same implement was used each time to sever the finger of the victim and that blood, skin and tissue was transferred from one to another.

One officer close to the case said, 'It is grisly stuff but it looks like the killer didn't even bother to clean the blade of whatever he used – we think it was a pair of gardening type shears – after he hacked the fingers off these people. The lab guys found bits of skin and tissue belonging to Carr and Hutchison on the finger cut off Spud Tierney. There were then DNA particles of both Carr, Hutchison and Tierney found on Ogilvie.

'No doubt we'll find the same thing once the results come back on the latest victim.'

The Ripper case is being led by Detective Chief Inspector Lewis Robertson and Detective Sergeant Rachel Narey. When the Daily Record contacted DS Narey by telephone she said that she would not comment on operational matters. However when the Record

told her that we were in possession of a severed finger which we knew to belong to one of the Ripper's victims, she could not hide her surprise. She agreed to meet with this reporter and took possession of the severed finger.

DS Narey agreed to make a statement on the unsolved murders but the Record would like to stress that this was not dependent on the provision of the finger. We were happy to hand it over as part of our civic duty and to help the police catch the maniac that is terrorising the city.

'I cannot confirm that these four men were killed by the same person but I can say that Strathclyde Police are looking at all four cases as part of the same investigation. We have ruled nothing either in or out of that investigation.

'There has been contact by someone who may well be the killer of one or more of these men but we would prefer not to comment on the nature of that contact in order to reduce the possibility of imitators.

'The revelation of the nature of any contact between a possible killer and Strathclyde Police would, in this instance, be unhelpful and possibly damage this investigation.'

The Daily Record, its editor, management and owners take the safety of the public very seriously indeed and that is why, after much consideration, we have taken the decision to publish the details we have about this horrendous killing spree. We do not take lightly the possibility of interference into a murder investigation but we believe that public safety is paramount. The people of Glasgow need to be fully informed about the murderous lunatic that has already taken four lives.

We can also reveal that Strathclyde Police have recruited a leading Cracker-style forensic psychologist to work on the case. Well-known profiler Dr Paul Crabtree has been involved with the case since the third murder. He has drawn up a profile of the Ripper and officers are now working within certain parameters in their pursuit of the killer.

Strathclyde Police have always been reluctant to make use of such profiles in recent years so some will see the hiring of Dr Crabtree as an act of desperation. Crabtree himself has previously been openly critical of the force's suspicion of forensic psychology.

The Daily Record will continue to help Strathclyde Police in any way it can in the course of this investigation. In the meantime, we ask all the people of Glasgow, indeed all of Scotland, to be vigilant and to contact this newspaper if they have anything which might help catch Jock the Ripper.

CHAPTER 21

Crazed.
Psychopath.
Barbaric.
Brutal.
Sick.
Deranged.
Maniac.
Murderous.
Lunatic.

Perfect. Say what they want. Think what I want them to think.

CHAPTER 22

I had been on day shift so knew she would be sitting waiting for me when I got home. I was sure she would know by then but apart from that I had no idea what to expect.

I closed the front door behind me and paused for a second or two before going in search of her. I opened the door to the living room but one look inside showed me she wasn't there. I tried the kitchen.

She was sitting at the table with her back to me. Her hair was loose but unruly, as if it had been pulled out of a hairband and just left where it fell. She was wearing a dark cardigan and it was pulled tight to her.

My heart was in my mouth. Maybe for the first time in a very long time, I knew the feeling of fear.

She must have heard me come in to the house. Must have heard the kitchen door open and close. Knew I was standing behind her but she didn't move, didn't speak. I walked round her to the other side of the table, seeing the open newspaper that lay in front of her. Even before I looked at it I knew what it would be. Couldn't be anything else. The photographs of Carr, Hutchison, Tierney and Ogilvie – although she was only looking at one of them. The lurid headlines screaming at her. The words, so many words. All laid out in front of her eyes.

There was no tea or coffee on the table. No kettle on the boil. Just her, the table, the newspaper and the photograph of Wallace Ogilvie.

I pulled back the chair, deliberately scraping it against the floor so it made a noise before I sat down. She didn't flicker. Her eyes, red and wet, stayed fixed on the paper.

My breathing was stilted and I could hear my heart. My eyes went from her to the paper and back again. I tried to will her to look up and say something.

I followed her eyes. She was reading it all, word after word, not for the first time I was sure of that. But after every few paragraphs her gaze switched to the photograph of Wallace Ogilvie for a few moments then back to the text. Few paragraphs, picture, few paragraphs, picture, few paragraphs picture.

I could see she was nearing the end of Imrie's article and hoped that meant she would stop and look at me. Speak to me. Tell me what it meant to her. I almost began to speak as she reached the last few words, ready to ask or answer. But her eyes switched back to the beginning of the story and she read again.

Few paragraphs, picture, few paragraphs, picture, few paragraphs picture. I watched her go through it all again, forcing myself to gulp down a nervous, anxious breath. Her eyes strained over it, every now and again a single tear escaping and trickling down her cheek.

Few paragraphs, picture, few paragraphs, picture, few paragraphs picture until she again neared the end of the article.

This time she suddenly lifted her head and looked at me through her wet screen. She looked at me for an age, help-lessly trying to get words out. Struggling.

'I'm glad,' she said at last.

Just that. No explanation. None needed maybe.

She just kept looking at me and I didn't know what to do. I was sure she didn't want me to go to her and hold her. A bit of me wanted to do just that. A very small part of me wanted to tell her everything. I told that part of me to stay quiet.

'I'm glad,' she said again. Her voice was level, making it hard for me to read as much into it as I'd like. She sounded tired too, even more than she would normally do at that time of night.

She just looked at me. And just for a bit, I wondered if she knew. Or guessed. But she couldn't.

'I am glad that bastard is dead,' she whispered. It wasn't like her to swear. Even when it happened she didn't swear. She shouted and she cried a lot. For maybe a year and a half she cried all day and cried all night. Then the pills started, the crying stopped and she slept at night. After a year and a half of constant grief she gave in and let chem-icals dictate her mood and sleeping habits. Eighteen months after losing my child, I lost my wife as well.

I just looked at her, giving her time to say more, to open up if she wanted. Maybe to say the one thing that I wanted to hear her say. Her mouth opened and closed a couple of times, silent tears slipping down her face and stinging her lips.

I tried to remember how long it had been since I kissed her. Her birthday was July so probably then. How long since I kissed her as if I meant it, how long was that? Did I kiss her after Sarah was killed? Hard as I tried, I couldn't remember. I held her, held her for the longest time, so hard and so close but couldn't remember kissing her on the lips the way a husband and wife should.

Her mouth opened again, words hanging off them but unspoken. She choked them back, swallowed them whole. Then her eyes left mine and dropped to the table. She looked at the swirls of the pine and the lines of the grain as she eventually found some more words that could leave her.

'I am so fucking glad that bastard is dead. I am so fucking glad he isn't around to hurt anyone else.'

She paused just long enough for my heart to stop and wonder.

'I am glad that someone had the balls to kill him.'

She left that there, hanging between us like a ball waiting to be batted. Her eyes were fixed on a gnarl in the wood of the table, examining every curve of the knot so that she didn't have to lift her head and look me in the eye.

She repeated herself, slower.

'I'm glad . . . that someone . . . had the balls . . . to kill him.'

My heart was pounding. It was deafening in my ears. My skin was cold and I was acutely aware of every part of me.

'I am . . . glad . . . that someone . . . had . . . the balls . . . to kill . . . him.'

I pushed myself out of my chair, clumsily getting to my feet and rushing over to her. I dropped to one knee so I could hug her, envelop her in my arms and bury my head into her neck. Hadn't dared to expect that she would understand. Had been so terrified of her knowing, her finding out and yet she had wanted the same as me all along. Far more than I hoped for. I held her tight and smelled her, kissed her hair. My heart was bursting and I had so much to tell, so much I would spare her from but so much to share. I squeezed her, almost wanted to be inside her skin, part of her.

'Get . . . off . . . me.'

I didn't understand. I held on.

'Get off me,' she ordered.

I let go, confused. She looked at me.

'You can't make up for it by holding me now,' she said. 'It's far too late for that. I don't want an apology now.'

I didn't understand. Her red eyes blazed at me in anger.

'You should have done it. You shouldn't have left it to someone else. It's far too late to say sorry for that now.

'And now here I am, glad that a man is dead. Christ I'm glad that some . . . some psychotic freak has murdered four people. Do you know how that makes me feel? Disgusted with myself, that's how.

'You made me feel like that. You. Hope you're proud of yourself. If you had acted like a man it wouldn't have come to this.'

I fell back from her in shock. Thought she had understood, thought she had known but her anger just made me want to scream. It wasn't like that. No freak, no psycho. It was me. I had done all that.

But I saw her eyes, could see her self-loathing right at that minute. She was angry at me but she was so much angrier at herself. She had been sat there much of that day celebrating a death and by doing so she had been rejoicing at four deaths by a person she thought was a serial killer. She was right, I had done that to her.

I tried to speak, realizing for the first time that I hadn't said a word since I entered the house. Didn't know what to say to her. Didn't have a clue where to start. If she hated us both for very different reasons then she would hate us both all the more if she knew the truth. I would kill her by telling her.

'You have done nothing,' she spat at me. 'Not a thing. At least I've tried to stop bastards like him from drink-driving. I've tried to make a difference. Tried to change the law and keep the likes of Ogilvie off the street. What have *you* done? Disappeared inside yourself, hiding from the world like a coward. Did you even think about doing something? Do you even think about her?'

Blood rushed through my head like a passing train and I nearly lifted my hand to her for the first time ever. I wanted to slap her hard across the mouth. I wanted to hurt her for saying the most hurtful thing that anyone could have said to me. I thought of nothing else but her.

She saw it. Saw my rage. Saw my hurt. Saw what her words had done and she crumbled. Her own anger was gone and her hands reached out grabbing at me in apology, trying to reel me back in, sorry, sorry, sorry spilling from her lips.

I backed away at first but stopped and let her hold me. Words fell from her, telling me she didn't mean it, any of it. I knew that wasn't true. But she told me she'd have hated it if I had killed Ogilvie, not what she wanted, knew I loved Sarah, was so sorry, didn't really want him dead, couldn't believe someone had murdered four people, so sorry, what had happened to us. Why us? So sorry.

I stared over her shoulder, lips pursed, eyes straining back, fighting off all the emotions that had been strangers to me for so long. My hate for Wallace Ogilvie simply strengthened. My determination bolstered.

I squeezed her, comforted her. But my eyes remained fixed on a spot on the wall behind her. Just a random bit of paintwork, stared at it hard, burrowing into it.

'I know,' I told her at last. I didn't particularly know what I was telling her but I knew it was what she wanted to hear. Comfort words. I knew.

She sobbed into my shoulder, soaking it with guilt, grief and apologies. She was incoherent now, the pills kicking in faster than ever before, accelerated by a broken heart that offered a motorway straight into her bloodstream.

She wept and mumbled till she fell asleep. Long after she had dropped off, I continued to hold her and stare at the spot on the wall. I knew that even if I wanted to, I couldn't stop. More than ever I had to see my plan through. For Sarah and for her. I was barely more than halfway there and to stop now would ruin everything.

So much more to do.

Eventually I picked her up without waking her and carried her upstairs. I pulled back the cover and lay her, fully dressed, on the bed. I slipped off her shoes and kissed her full on the lips before tucking the duvet round her again.

I had so much more to do. The police would be here before long and I had to be ready for them. It would be Rachel Narey, of that I was pretty sure. And hoped.

CHAPTER 23

The door. It would be her.

She was prettier than she'd looked on television and in the papers. Smaller though. Her dark hair was tied back but wisps of it escaped and played with her face. I tried not to look too long or too obviously.

She introduced herself and shook my hand. Soft but firm. Textbook for a female cop probably. She made a show of looking around the room as if taking an interest in the décor. Looking for signs of something else no doubt. No signs to be seen, DS Narey. Made sure of that a long time ago.

There was a guy with her. DC Dawson. Balding, narrow eyes and wide shoulders. She did all the talking.

Small talk to start with. Weather, traffic, the house. Disappointing, I'd expected better. When I didn't bite, when I just sat and looked back at her, she soon gave up. I knew why she was there and she knew I did.

Cut to the chase, Rachel. Mention his name.

'Wallace Ogilvie.'

151

There. That wasn't too difficult, was it?

'Wallace Ogilvie. I take it you have heard that he has been murdered?'

'I'd heard. I read the papers.'

'You will know why we are here to speak to you then.'

'Is that a question?'

'If you want. We have to explore every avenue connected with his murder. You are one of these avenues.'

'Am I? I don't see how.'

'We have to wonder about people who might have a grudge against Mr Ogilvie.'

'Someone obviously did.'

'That's what we have to establish. When did you last see Mr Ogilvie?'

'Six years ago. At the trial.'

'And you haven't seen him since?'

'You asked me when I last saw him. I told you when.'

'OK. How did you feel when you heard he'd been killed?'

'Nothing.'

'Nothing?'

'I felt nothing. It's been six years. I don't care anything about him.'

'That's hard to believe. Given what he did. I know I'd be pretty angry if it was me.'

'Yes, you probably would.'

'And you aren't?'

'I'm not. Not any more.'

'After what he did?'

'I said.'

'So you did. It was a terrible thing.'

'I'm very aware of that.'

'Of course you are. Where were you on the twelfth of this month?'

'Am I being accused of something?'

'No. But we have to establish some facts. Establish the whereabouts of everyone involved at the time concerned.'

'I'm not involved.'

'I have to ask.'

'So ask.'

'Where were you on the twelfth of this month?'

'I don't know.'

'You must have some idea.'

'What time?'

'The hours around midnight.'

'Working or asleep.'

'You weren't working, we've already taken the liberty of checking with your boss.'

'Sleeping then.'

'How can you be sure?'

'I can't. But I sleep at night so that would be my best guess.'

'Can anyone verify that?'

'My wife. But then she would have been sleeping too. You can check with her.'

'We will.'

'Thought you might. She's out.'

'We will come back. If you read about Mr Ogilvie then you'll have read about the other killings.'

'Is that a question too?'

'Yes.'

'Yes.'

'And do you know where you were on the nights when they took place?'

'I have no idea. I don't even know when they were. But I am guessing you have already checked my shift rota.'

'We have. You were working on one of them and off on the other two.'

'There you go.'

'What do you think of those killings?'

'What do I think of a serial killer roaming the streets and murdering folk at random? That's a strange question.'

'I'd still like you to answer it.'

'It's sick. Scary. Depraved. I feel sorry for their families.'

'All four families?'

'Yes.'

'Including Mr Ogilvie's?'

'I said all four.'

'After what he did?'

'You asked me that already. I said I felt sorry for his family. I didn't say I felt sorry for him.'

'Do you?'

'Feel sorry for him? No.'

'You don't feel sorry for him but you don't feel angry? And yes, that's a question.'

'One I've already answered.'

'Indulge me.'

'I am doing. I don't feel sorry for him. I don't feel anger towards him.'

'He killed your daughter.'

'I don't need you to remind me of that. I remember.'

'I didn't mean to be insensitive. But you take my point.'

'Do I?'

'A man gets drunk and gets in his car and knocks down an eleven-year-old girl and kills her. I think her father is entitled to be angry.'

'Are you always so aggressive towards the families of drink-drive fatalities?'

'I am sure I would be angry.'

'You said that.'

'I'd maybe be angry enough to kill the person responsible.'

'You have a lot of anger. You should see someone about that.'

'Did you want Ogilvie dead?'

'Yes.'

'Did you kill him?'

'No.'

'Did you have someone kill him?'

'No.'

'Do you know who killed him?'

'No. Detective Sergeant Narey, I think you just accused me of being a serial killer. Of murdering four people.'

'Did you?'

'No.'

'Then I'm sorry for the insinuation. As I said, we have to explore every avenue. We have to speak to those connected to every victim whether they are connected to the others or not.'

'I do understand that.'

'Did you know any of the other victims?'

'No.'

'Had you ever heard of any of them?'

'No.'

'We are trying to establish a pattern. Trying to see if there is any link, however small, between the victims.'

'If there is I'm unaware of it. Ogilvie was the only one I had heard of or met. The papers said they were random killings.'

'They appear that way. They most probably are but we . . .'

'Need to explore every avenue.'

'Yes.'

'I don't think I am one of those avenues, DS Narey. I can't help you.'

'Would you help me if you could?'

'Of course I fucking would. I once wanted Ogilvie dead but that doesn't mean I'd do something to protect the maniac that killed him or the others.'

'I'm sorry for the insinuation.'

'So am I.'

'We would be grateful if you would agree to provide a sample of DNA. It's a matter of procedure.'

'Is it?'

'We are asking a number of people. It is so we can rule you out of the investigation. It is quite voluntary.'

'It would need to be, wouldn't it?'

There were some obligatory pleasantries then she left, saying she'd be back when my wife was in, leaving a number and an assurance she'd be in touch if she learned anything. I wasn't sure if it was a promise or a warning.

I watched her back as she and the DC walked down the path to their car which was being guarded by two kids and the black Lab cross that had been hanging around again the last few days. Dawson, the DC, got into the driver's seat and Narey went round to the other side. Before she got in, she looked back, saw me standing at the window and smiled.

CHAPTER 24

They were all talking about it now. Every single one of them. It had been two weeks since Wallace Ogilvie's death and everyone had joined up the dots. All of Glasgow knew there had been four of them. Four slain by a single hand. All of Scotland knew. Everyone in the UK too and quite a bit beyond.

There was barely a soul got into my taxi cab that didn't mention it. I always stopped short of pointing out the irony to them. They still talked about the weather and the football and argued about the quickest way to wherever they were going but now they talked about him. The killer. Me. The one they were calling the Ripper. Stupid bloody name. I didn't mind the Ripper bit so much but this 'Jock' nonsense, it really riled me. The London papers and the news had picked up on it too. The way they said the word Jock with a sneer, that pissed me off.

'A twisted psychopath nicknamed Jock the Ripper has been responsible for four brutal murders in Glasgow.'

I cringed every time I heard the word. Jock. The people

in my taxi didn't use the word. They probably hated it as much as I did. They said killer. They said Ripper.

Have you heard? What's the latest? I used to live near the third one. I don't walk anywhere now unless I really need to. What are the cops doing about this? I can't sleep for thinking about it.

Gallus Glasgow was still not supposed to show fear. I think they were afraid to be frightened. So instead they were funny, or at least tried to be. Some succeeded, some failed miserably. Jokes about serial killers were risky things.

I picked up four young guys from Esquire House on Great Western Road near Anniesland Cross to take them into town. All early to mid twenties. They spilled out of the pub, boisterous and loud, and clambered into the cab. Three of them fell into the back seat and one got onto the bucket seat behind me.

'Telling you,' the one nearest me was saying. 'Best thing that happened to Glasgow this guy.'

'Away to fuck, ya muppet,' laughed one of his mates. 'How the fuck is it?'

'Dazza, you are a sick bastard,' howled another one. 'The fucker's killed four people.'

'No the point,' came back Dazza. 'It's all publicity, isn't it?'

His pals laughed. Dazza wasn't deterred, he was loving it.

'Look, Glasgow is all over the telly, right? London and everything. America, Japan, the lot. Fucking everywhere. No such thing as bad publicity, right?'

'You're a fud, Daz.'

'Should put you in charge of tourism at the council chambers, Dazza.'

'Telling youse,' said Dazza with a cackle.

'Yer baws, man,' shouted another. 'Good crack, right enough. Tell you what I heard though . . .'

He paused for effect.

'Spit it oot, big man.'

The big man laughed.

'Well, way I heard it, it's some mad Tim that's doing the killings,' conspired the big man.

'Ah, for fuck's sake, big yin. You're making Daz sound like a genius.'

'Blacky, I've heard it all now, man. A fucking Catholic conspiracy. Yer arse.'

'Just telling youse what I heard. That lawyer was a Rangers season ticket holder, right? Cops said so. Everybody knows that Tierney worked for Alec Kirkwood an he's a big Bluenose. And that last guy, Wallace Ogilvie, come on. A Hun name if ever I heard one.'

'Bollocks. My old man knew that Billy Hutchison and he was a Thistle man. How's that fit into your theory?'

'Aye, but who did he really support?'

They all laughed. Funny guys.

'Here, Neilly. Tell them what you did with wee Janice.'

'Aw, fuck off, man,' said Neilly.

'Spill, ya bam. What did you do?'

Neilly laughed.

'She was over at mine and I was getting nowhere fast.

She was for the off so I started laying it on thick about the Ripper and all that. Didnae actually say she'd get murdered if she walked home but I think she maybe got that impression.'

'Genius, man.'

'I was giving it, "Oh the cops have no idea, could strike anywhere at any minute, wisnae safe for someone as nice as her, would hate it if anything happened to her." She caved, stayed the night at mine and I pumped her rotten.'

'Sweet. Was she safe walking home the next morning?'

'Oh aye. Sound as a pound.'

The four of them were still sniggering like halfwits when I dropped them on Bath Street. Talked about nothing except the killer. Said nothing to me except 'Kushion, driver,' and 'Cheers, mate.'

The same night two girls got in. Late twenties maybe. Obviously had a good night. Picked them up outside the Garage on Sauchiehall Street. I was third in the rank when I pulled up and saw the queue shivering in late October chill. Doesn't matter what time of year it is, Glasgow clubbers wear as little as possible. I got to the front and they tottered over in high heels, holding hands.

It took all of two minutes for the conversation to turn to the serial killer. I seemed to hear the word and read it from the blonde's lipglossed mouth at the same time. Ripper. The words before it didn't register but that one did. I heard from that point on.

'. . . Ripper, don't you think?'

'Nah, he didn't look like he could rip open a packet of

crisps. That creep in the yellow shirt though. Definite candidate.'

'God, aye. He was a freak. Weird eyes, right stare on him.'

'I think that might just have been your tits.'

'Well true, he wasn't the only one having difficulty looking at my face when he spoke to me. Disnae mean he wasn't a weirdo though.'

'Place was full of them the night.'

'No change there.'

'Ah know, but I didn't use to think there was maybe a psycho serial killer among them. Just thought they were chancers and pervy bastards.'

'Scares the shit out of me, Mel.'

'Ah know. Didnae think something like that could happen here. It's no New York.'

'Has though. Four times. Christ.'

'Mental.'

'Ah know. My old man has an Annie Rooney every time ah go out. Would be staying in till this freak's caught if he had his way.'

'Right, we'll get the driver to stop at yours first so you'll no be left on your own.'

'Naw, naw, it's cool. You get dropped off first. I'll text my dad and he can meet me at the door to the close.'

'No, I'll just be worried. Drop you off first. Then I'll no worry.'

'Yeah, but then I'll be worrying.'

'Well, why don't we both just get dropped off first and you can stay the night at mine.'

They giggled.

'Aye, your Raymond would love that.'

'Aye, he probably would actually.'

They both burst out laughing.

In the end, some sort of sense prevailed. The one whose dad could come down to meet her got off last. Didn't seem to occur to her that the danger she was so worried about was sitting right in front of her. Not that she was at any risk whatsoever, either of them. Probably safer than any other two girls in the city that night. Safe as houses.

I breathed hard after the second one got out. Their words sticking in my head. Freak. Psycho. Mental.

Sticks and stones. Girls that age, though. Made me think of my own. Some judgements hurt more than others.

It was harder now. Wallace Ogilvie was dealt with and I could feel some of my hatred going with him. But there were still things to do. Still a plan to stick to. Had to go on. Much harder now. Had to be harder to deal with that. Hard as Glasgow. Hard as those who joked to me about a killer that sat in front of them.

They wanted this Ripper to kill football managers, politicians, and celebrities. They seemed sure I'd want him to kill traffic wardens or managers from the roads department. Hard people with ready black humour. People with no understanding. They didn't know me. They didn't know why. Never would if things worked out right.

My plan. My daughter.

Didn't, couldn't, care for their opinions. Only one thing mattered. Only one person mattered.

Had to shut them out. Had to turn a deaf ear to them again. They weren't hard, they were stupid. Stupid and dull. Only thing hard was my heart. Hardened against their jokes and fears, their theories and bleatings. They weren't gallus, they were just in the way.

Fuck Glasgow. Job to do. Job to finish.

CHAPTER 25

The thing with sending out messages is that if they are not received and understood then you have to keep sending them out until they are.

Alec Kirkwood had clipped Jimmy Mac's finger and dumped him in the street with a hole in his eye. It hadn't been enough. He had broken the arms of two neds who had acted the big-man when they were asked for info. It hadn't been enough. He had had a bullet put through Mick Docherty's front window and it hadn't been enough. He had put the frighteners on everyone he could and no one had coughed with a name. It wasn't good enough.

The newspapers said it was a serial killer. Said it was a random hit. Kirkwood wasn't so sure and didn't care anyway. He had let half of Glasgow know that he wanted to know who had claimed Tierney and someone had to know. He'd made it the talk of the underbelly. The talk of the steamie and the steaming. The chattering classes like Ally McFarland spread the gospel according to Alec Kirkwood to anyone who would listen.

Yet still he didn't have what he wanted. Did they think he wasn't serious? Could they be that fucking stupid? It left him boiling that they were going to make him prove himself all over again. If he had to demonstrate to these arseholes that he was not to be disrespected then they would only have themselves to blame.

He offered them the easy way or the hard way to do things and they made the choice. They gave him no option but to behave like the bampot that fought his way out of Asher Street. He had left that slum behind years ago and knew there were other ways of doing things, but they kept dragging him back there. Well, fine.

An example had to be made and Alec Kirkwood knew just the man. There was a guy by the name of Hutton who hurt people for Mick Docherty. Billy Hutton, a violent type who liked being a bit of a name. He was flash with his cash and his mouth and had a reputation with the women. He was maybe six four with slicked-back hair and gym muscles. He thought himself a looker and by some miracle his face had escaped a doing over the years.

The little people crossed the road to stay out of Hutton's way. He was always given room and he loved it. He had three kids by three women. None of them to his wife. Hutton had been inside twice and had put his share of people in hospital. He liked his work.

He was close to Docherty and there were even those who thought Mick was afraid of him. That seemed unlikely but you could bet Hutton was happy with the idea.

Same thing with Spud Tierney. There was some talk that Hutton had stuck Spud but Kirkwood doubted it. The knife wasn't Hutton's style. A baseball bat maybe, a drop off a tall building or simply beaten to death. Not the blade though.

Still, Hutton knew folk had made the whisper about him doing Spud and he did nothing to stop it. He knew his name was floating but he didn't sink it as he should have. It was part of the game that sometimes you took credit for things you hadn't done, add a notch to your score and a boost to your rep.

The trick though was to pick and choose your moments. Playing the smart arse and letting people believe you had offed one of Alec Kirkwood's boys was stupidity. Kirky was still very unhappy. He was convinced someone had murdered Tierney to taunt him. That someone had cut off Tierney's finger as a sign.

Every time I caught the tail end of a whisper put out by Kirkwood, I shuddered. It wasn't the way it was meant to be. It had nothing to do with him.

But the word kept coming. He was saying that it wouldn't end, wouldn't be forgotten. No one would be allowed to take the piss out of Kirky. It seems he thought Hutton was doing just that.

Hutton had a council house in Christie Street in Shettleston with his wife. A typical sixties dump from the outside but inside it was kitted out with the flashiest gear that shady money could buy.

Tuesday morning and Hutton had left that council house

and began to walk down the street. He had turned just one corner when an unmarked white van pulled up and three men got out.

They grabbed Hutton and threw him into the back of the van. The big man didn't put up much of a fight.

Of course, nobody in Christie Street was able to describe the men when the police came asking. Of course, no one saw anything they could tell the cops.

It was Davie Stewart and the Grant brothers, Charlie and Frank, each as mental as the other.

The white van drove out of Christie Street at a good pace but not racing. There was a kettle full of boiling water sitting in the front seat and you don't want that spilled on your upholstery.

They drove no more than two minutes to the hill known locally as The Womb on account of the number of kids conceived there. There are few places in suburban Glasgow that are very far from bits of green that could be used by desperate teenagers.

Hutton was marched to the top of the hill at gunpoint, his hands tied behind him. Frankie Grant carried the kettle.

They kicked his legs from him until Hutton was on his knees before them. They cracked the side of his head with the gun barrel and forced his mouth open.

Frankie poured half the kettle of near-boiling water down his throat then covered him in the rest.

Hutton screamed.

He did the same again when Frankie smashed the empty

kettle off the side of his face, leaving a red welt that stained him from his cheek to his forehead.

Charlie Grant tore the trousers off him and forced Hutton to bend over, spreading his legs wide.

Davie Stewart went behind him and shoved the barrel of the gun up Hutton's arse. He forced it roughly into his hole and spiralled it as deep as he could inside him.

Hutton still played the big man. He told them to fuck off. Told them to do it. Told them to go ahead and pull the trigger. So Davie Stewart did.

There was a click and nothing else. The gun had never been loaded in the first place.

That was the point when Hutton began to cry. He sobbed a bit and laughed out of relief. Just before Davie Stewart raped him.

Charlie Grant did the same but Frankie settled for kicking Hutton hard in the balls. Each to their own.

They left Hutton on top of The Womb, bleeding, blistering and greeting his eyes out. He'd thought they were going to kill him and chances are he ended up wishing they had. The message was that were some things worse than death for a Glasgow hard man. There were worse things that Alec Kirkwood could do to you than that.

Everyone who lived and breathed in the inner city knew the value of image and dignity. Lose those and you'd be as well losing your balls. Hutton had tried to be smart with the wrong guy. Anyone else fancy trying that? Thought not.

They would be calling him a mad bastard again. That

was fine. They'd be saying he was just a psycho in a good suit and he could live with that. This time it had all been about getting that message across, not about wee Spud's killer.

As Hutton lay blubbering on the top of that hill, Davie Stewart eventually asked him who had killed Spud Tierney. Through his snot and tears, Hutton said he had no idea. Davie Stewart hadn't expected to hear much else but kicked him in the head anyway. That was for being stupid. You should have said that in the first place, arsehole.

News of what was done to Hutton was quickly fed to all corners. No point in doing it otherwise.

Had to make you wonder what he might do to the person who had actually killed Tierney. It certainly made me think. Not scared, not of what he might do. Worried that it might get in the way of my plans. A complication I could have definitely done without.

Some people asked how it was known Hutton was leaving the house at the time he did. They wanted to know how Kirky's men knew to have that kettle boiling.

Some said Hutton was a creature of habit. Others knew that wasn't true. The smart money said Mrs Hutton made a phone call. Three unanswered rings then hung up. Come on down, the price is right.

Hutton didn't go to the cops, of course, and didn't go to a hospital. He went to the flat where the mother of one of his children lived. She took one look at him and closed the door in his face.

He went to Mick Docherty's and didn't get a much better

reception. Mickey stuck a bundle of cash into Hutton's pocket and sent him on his way. It was the last anyone heard or saw of him.

Not all my fault. Hutton put himself in that world. I just put him in that situation.

CHAPTER 26

My view on other people's happiness was not what it was. There was a time when I'd have wanted everyone to be as happy as me. As us.

The day we were married. The day Sarah was born. The first day she went to school. The day she won that poetry prize. I had so much happiness that it burst out of me and there was plenty to share.

Things changed.

Other people's happiness became something I didn't consider greatly. It became something I didn't consider at all. My priorities were my own. She was my only concern. Other people didn't exist. Other people were noises that fluttered at my ears or drifted past my eyes. They were in the world but not in mine. People were obstacles and stepping stones. They thought they were talking to me and that I was listening. They thought I cared. They thought. I didn't think about them.

Oh we all live in our own self-centred little worlds but my isolation was more than that. Their selfishness was no match for my obsession. Other people live for themselves

175

but want to be loved by others. I lived only for her and had no need for love.

I wouldn't say it was callous. More indifference. Maybe that amounted to the same thing but I didn't care to hurt. I just didn't care. Other people's feelings were as irrelevant as they were, somewhere on my horizon, shadows upon shadows. That is how I could do what I had done and what I was about to do.

I picked up the *Herald*. *Glasgow Herald* as was. I didn't like it when things were changed without good reason.

Page 22 is the Gazette page. Why it is called that has never been particularly obvious to me but it didn't matter. The Gazette page is where they have the obituaries and the BDMs. Births, Deaths and Marriages.

Except in the *Herald* it is Births, Marriages then Deaths. They probably consider it a more natural order of things but I was always uneasy with the change from the conventional. The Gazette page is where people celebrate themselves in print. It is where they let their friends and neighbours know of their achievements or failures in genetics.

Weir

John and Fiona are delighted to announce the safe
arrival of their beautiful twin girls,
Victoria Susan Eilidh (5lbs 11 ozs) and Emma
Ann Marcia (5lbs 9 ozs) at 34 weeks on
22nd February 2010. Sisters for Jack. Many
thanks to Dr James Hines, Dr Ken French
and all staff at the Royal Alexandra Hospital, Paisley,
for all their care and attention.

That was not to be it.

I felt for John and Fiona though. They were pain waiting to happen. John and Fiona still thought life was fair. Beautiful twin girls. Victoria and Emma. Lovely. Victoria. Emma. Sisters to Jack. Good weight for premature twins too.

So many bad things could happen to Victoria and Emma. A world of bad possibilities. That was a fact. I almost despised John and Fiona for their ignorance. How could they be so unaware of fate, so naive, so stupid to think otherwise?

McGowan
At the Southern General Hospital on 28th February
2010, to Neil and Polly McGowan (née Rawstone)
a son Angus Michael, a little brother for Claire.

Not the one.

Angus, a good name but anachronistic. Parents really had to be more considerate when naming their offspring. We had taken two months to settle on Sarah's name. Sarah was a princess, wife of Abraham and mother of Isaac. If it was a boy it was to have been David, the beloved one.

Two columns of births. One and a half of marriages. Four and a half columns of deaths. Three of acknowledgements which was really just another three of deaths.

I looked carefully at the last seven and a half columns. Why so many more deaths than births and marriages? The population was dropping but not that quick.

If deaths were more worthy of noting in a national newspaper then that sounded more like guilt to me than honouring those that had gone. Anyway, deaths clearly didn't suit my purpose. That would have been impractical on so many levels.

It was to be the last marriage. I'd settled on that before picking up the paper. No reason. Just a random choice. Those at the end of the alphabet were at a distinct and dangerous disadvantage but that was life.

Sinclair
Gardiner
The marriage took place at Iona Abbey on
20th February 2010 of Brian, son of the
late Archibald Sinclair and of Elspeth Sinclair,
Arran, and Mary Anne, daughter of
Ian and Anne Gardiner, Inchinnan.

The newly wed Brian Sinclair and Mary Anne Gardiner. Brian and Mary. Mr and Mrs Sinclair. By the time the glorification of their union appeared in the *Herald* they had enjoyed thirteen days of wedded bliss.

It struck me that the right thing to do would be not to separate Mr and Mrs Sinclair. Wherefore they are no more twain, but one flesh. What therefore God hath joined together, let not man put asunder. Matthew 19:6.

The thought struck me but I dismissed it. God and I were no longer on speaking terms. Mr and Mrs Sinclair together would pose far more problems. The rights and wrongs of separating them paled beside the practicalities of what had to be done. Brian and Mary were both obstacle and stepping stone.

So, Brian or Mary? Husband or wife?

I was ambivalent but thought I should redress the unfairness of the alphabetical disadvantage.

And behold, there are last which shall be first, and there are first which shall be last. Luke 13:30.

God and I did not speak any more but I still remembered his words. It would be Brian. Mrs Mary Sinclair, wallowing in the blissful ignorance of the newly wed, would soon be a widow.

These days I had only misery to share. It burst out of me now.

CHAPTER 27

Brian Sinclair was a runner. Twice a day, every day, he left the house at Inchinnan overlooking the White Cart and headed onto the hill behind it where a path cut a trail through the woods. I didn't know how far he ran but he was gone a good hour each time and seemed to pick up a very decent pace. He was very fit, which was a bit of a worry. Not necessarily a major problem but definitely an issue.

Thankfully the new Mrs Sinclair was not a runner. Their inseparability did not seem to extend to staying fit together.

I'd parked half a mile away and positioned myself in the shadow of a tree that let me view their house without being seen.

I waited. And waited some more.

I was wearing jeans and walking boots, a shirt and water-proof jacket. In the back pocket of my jeans was a rolled-up newspaper. I didn't care much for papers or the people who wrote them. I'd known journalists. I hadn't liked them. Pretending they are your friend. Just there to help. Only wanting to tell your side of things. Then when they write stuff you didn't say, put it in ways that you didn't mean, then it isn't their fault. The editor wanted it that way, the sub-editor wrote the heading, nothing to do with them.

But, of course, once it is in black and white it is gospel. Once it is plastered across the columns of a newspaper everyone believes it to be fact. It is so true that the pen is mightier than the sword but it's not the only way a newspaper can be a weapon.

I felt the weight of the rolled-up paper in my back pocket and was reassured by it.

I waited.

Eventually the door opened and I saw Brian Sinclair wave before closing it behind him. He began to run. He didn't have the dog with him. That meant it was time.

I gave him fully five minutes then made my way away from the house and circled it before joining the path and walking deep into the wood.

It was a fairly steep climb but I was fit enough. I'd already worked out that I wanted to be far enough in that only one person was likely to pass me. Not so far that it would take me too long to get out again.

When I got to the point I'd picked out, I sat and waited. It wouldn't be long.

My timing was good. I'd been sitting no more than three minutes when I picked up the sound of running. He was on his return route.

It was a scratch that became a roar. Feet through leaves. Feet across packed ground. Getting closer. Louder. Scrunching towards me.

My heartbeat matched his stride as it closed in on me. I felt cold. No, hot. Heart thumping. Blood pumping. Hot through the ice that filled my veins and froze my heart. I was hot cold. Freezing hot.

Then there he was. He rounded a corner and was no more than ten yards in front of me. I hadn't seen him so close up and he was taller than I'd thought. Maybe six foot two. Cropped, fair hair. Honeymoon tanned. Happy.

He smiled when he saw me. That threw me but only slightly. For a long time now, strangers smiling at me had struck me as odd. Strangers were strange to me. I knew it was just me though. I'd lost my reason to smile. Lost my reason.

But Brian Sinclair didn't think like me. He liked people. He smiled at strangers. Or perhaps I wasn't completely unfamiliar to him. He had a look that suggested he might have seen me before. And of course he might have.

I had watched him for a month. Watched from afar. I had seen him leave the house over the river. I had seen him arrive at his dental practice. I had seen him set out on his run. I had seen him return.

I had seen them walk, hand in hand, whispering, laughing. I had seen them walk the springer spaniel. Sometimes it was Brian, sometimes Mary. Most often it was Mr and Mrs Sinclair together. They liked togetherness. They were wrapped up cosy in it.

But then I knew what they didn't.

As Brian Sinclair stood there, the look on his face was one that said 'Hey, I know you. I'm not sure where from but I do know you, don't I?'

I wasn't particularly pleased about his recognition but soon it wouldn't matter.

Sinclair saw me holding my ankle. I was sitting on a boulder, the right leg of my jeans pulled up to the calf.

Of course, I hadn't sprained it. Brian thought I had.

Are you OK? he asked. I said I was – in a voice that said I wasn't.

He looked around. What did he expect to find? A crutch, a doctor, an ambulance? He wanted to help. Brian was a nice guy.

I'd already taken the newspaper from my back pocket. It was rolled-up tight but I wrapped it tighter still. Brian might have seen it but thought nothing of it. He couldn't see that the paper was weeks old.

He kneeled by me and said he'd take a look at my ankle.

He was talking. Words about help. About being careful. About ankles. I didn't take them in. I only heard noise.

My eyes were on him. On his throat. I gripped the newspaper tighter. Then even tighter.

My breathing was heavy, I knew it. I was sure he'd just put it down to my supposed fall. I hoped he couldn't hear my heart.

He was closer, trying to lever me up. His head was by mine now. It was nearly time but I couldn't rush it. I would only get one chance. If I messed it up it was all over.

The newspaper was hot in my hand.

He took hold of my ankle, checking it for me. He was about to find out that it wasn't swollen. I saw the puzzled look on his face. He was about to ask, about to doubt.

I knew it was as much about accuracy as strength. I would get as much force behind it as I could but it was more important that I caught him in the soft of the throat. It is all about tensile strength. It makes a newspaper as good as a hammer. It makes it near lethal.

His eyes were just turning up towards mine when I stabbed at his throat with the paper. It caught him full and hard, driving against his larynx. It knocked him off his feet. If he'd looked puzzled before then he was bewildered now. His eyes streamed, he clutched at his throat, he gulped and coughed.

I got above him quickly and placed the end of the paper a couple of inches off his forehead. I used the flat of my hand as a hammer and drove the paper against his skull. He passed out with nothing more than a groan.

I was over him then. A newly gloved hand pinching his cheeks and encouraging his mouth to open.

I carefully forced the end of the paper into his mouth and turned it slowly as I fed it to him. Three, four, five inches of it disappeared easily. Easily for me.

Then it hit the back of his throat and went no further. Until I used my hand as a hammer again and hit it hard.

When it didn't budge, I hit it harder. His throat opened and the newspaper moved down it.

His eyes suddenly opened, bulging wide. They strained down, trying desperately to see what was being forced into his mouth. As if seeing the intruder would free it. It wouldn't. It didn't.

I pushed further.

Sinclair waved his arms like a drunk. No power and no direction. They barely flapped. He was choking. Slowly. Hopelessly. It was fascinating to watch.

His eyes watered. His cheeks strained red with effort. His neck was swollen, muscles stretched tight.

Then there was blood at his eyes. Amazing. He cried blood.

The strangest thing was his throat where I could see the outline of the paper. It thrust against his tight skin, trying to burst free.

I hit the top of the paper again. I forced it. I pushed down on it. I literally rammed it down his throat.

The process was incredibly simple if not particularly pretty.

He choked to death in front of me. Silent all but for a few pathetic gasps and a scream that stayed deep down inside him, strangled at birth.

I worked the newspaper back out, a far easier job than putting it in. Wet with saliva, blood and traces of vomit, it slid along his surrendered throat and out.

I sat it on the rock I'd been sitting on and took a cigarette lighter from my pocket. One spark was enough for the damp paper to light and burn and dance and disappear before my eyes. One murder weapon gone.

I swapped the lighter for the secateurs and severed his pinkie.

CHAPTER 28

The *Herald*, 18 March 2010
Newlywed found murdered in woods
Has Ripper killed again?

The *Daily Record*, 18 March 2010
NUMBER FIVE!
Ripper kills again
EXCLUSIVE by Keith Imrie

The body of a Glasgow dentist was found in woods near Inchinnan yesterday – the fifth victim of Jock the Ripper. Brian Sinclair (32) had been on his daily run through the woods when the killer struck.

It is not yet known how Mr Sinclair was murdered but police have confirmed that his right little finger was severed. Officers are bracing themselves for the finger

to be posted as has become the norm after the Ripper has killed.

Mr Sinclair had been married for only six weeks and his devastated wife Mary was last night being cared for by her family.

The brutal murder will bring even greater fear to a city already haunted by the shadow of the Ripper.

Full Story on pages 2 and 3.

The *Courier*, 18 March 2010
Dentist murdered as police fear serial killer has claimed new victim

The *Daily Express*, 18 March 2010
RIPPER STRIKES AGAIN

The *Daily Star*, 18 March 2010
RIPPED

The *Daily Record*, 19 March 2010
THE CUTTER
EXCLUSIVE by Keith Imrie

The infamous Glasgow murderer who struck for the fifth time on Wednesday has revealed himself to the Daily Record *as The Cutter. The serial killer sent a harrowing package to this reporter containing a house key belonging to murdered dentist Brian Sinclair. It was accompanied by a 'business card' adorned by the printed words 'The Cutter'.*

The package and the printing were identical to a previous envelope from the killer which contained the finger of slaughtered businessman Wallace Ogilvie.

Police have confirmed that the key was for the front door of Mr Sinclair's Inchinnan home and that he always carried it with him while out running. Strathclyde officers have also confirmed that they took delivery of a package which held the severed right little finger of the victim.

Psychologists have told the Daily Record *that by allocating himself a nickname, The Cutter was affirming his ownership of the killings. They say that it was his method of declaring that he was in control of the situation, not the police or the media.*

That and because he hated the fucking name Jock.

CHAPTER 29

Alec Kirkwood had changed tack. Ally McFarland told me so.

Number five had changed his thinking on the whole issue. Seems he now accepted that the killing of Spud Tierney was not done to taunt him. Realized that Tierney's finger wasn't a great big Get it Right Up You to him.

That was the good news.

The bad was that Kirky was still hell-bent on finding out who murdered his dealer. Maybe more so than before. He had put the word out that he wanted Spud's killer. Made sure everyone knew just how much. Kirky was used to getting what he wanted so was not a happy man when it didn't deliver. And because he had made his wishes so public, it was left all over his face when he got nothing. That just made him angry.

What bothered Kirkwood most was that people, the people that mattered, might see this as weakness. Being top dog in a world where one ate the other was always a pre-

189

carious business. If they think you are on the slide then they boot you up the arse to help you on your way.

One opening, that was all that they were looking for. Searching for a wound where they could stick a knife and twist until it was left wide and festering.

Well Kirky wasn't about to give them an opportunity. He'd fuck every one of them over before he let that happen. He needed to re-establish his authority. Smack some heads together, break some legs.

That meant finding the cunt that had killed Spud and took the piss out of him and that was what he was going to do. Maybe it wasn't all about him but that wasn't going to stop him from finding whoever shanked Spud.

This serial killer wasn't the only one that had taken the piss. Mick Docherty, still blazing about Jimmy McIntyre, the bullet through his window and the torture of Billy Hutton, hadn't missed his chance. He let it be known what a joke Kirkwood had become. How everyone was laughing at him for not being able to look after his own. How he had made all this big noise about making someone pay and then doing sweet fuck all about it.

That would have been enough to make Kirkwood furious but Mick had also been getting a bit naughty. Two pubs in Cowcaddens had been turned over. Bottles, beer and cash taken and both places trashed. Two pubs in Alec Kirkwood's pocket and under his protection. Penny stuff really but it was cheeky.

Everyone knew that it was kids who worked for Docherty who had done it. They had been selling the booze cheap and knocking back a fair share of it too. Cheeky little bastards, Kirky had said.

They were sorted without too much fuss. Three doors kicked in at the same early hour of the morning. Three disrespectful wee shits beaten about the knees with baseball bats. One of them would never walk unaided again but the other two would be back on their feet in a few months. Lesson learned.

But the boys that had robbed the boozers weren't the issue. Mick Docherty was. He might not have given them the word to plunder the pubs but he didn't stop it or turn them over to Kirky once he knew the score. That was out of order. That was ripping the pish.

Kirkwood said it was simple. His reputation. The serial killer. Mick Docherty. All three needed sorting. He figured that by doing one he could maybe do all three. It was all about coming up with a plan.

He had advantages when it came to catching a killer. Kirkwood could send his guys to talk to people that the cops couldn't. He could get answers where they would only get knock-backs or no comments. Kirky's people played by different rules.

Davie Stewart and Charlie Grant spoke to Jack Fyfe, a partner in Salter, Fyfe and Bryce. Jonathan Carr's boss. Seems Fyfe had more than a few clients on his books that were known to Kirkwood. Criminals needed lawyers like anyone else – more than most – and there were always lawyers more than happy to take their coin. Jack Fyfe was one of those.

Kirky's boys leaned on him although there really wasn't

much need. Fyfe knew which side his bread was buttered on. He provided them with a list of Carr's clients and a rundown on who might be worth talking to.

He also gave them details of Carr's extra-curricular activities. The lap-dancing clubs, the massage parlour and the redhead in Milngavie named Amanda. Jack Fyfe was the type who made sure he knew everything about his employees, particularly the potentially embarrassing ones like Carr. He survived by knowing about problems before they happened.

Davie Stewart and Charlie Grant took a trip out to Woodlands Street in Milngavie and knocked on Amanda Kernaghan's door. She wasn't best pleased to see them.

The way Ally McFarland heard it, she was much less pleased by the time they left.

I had no idea if Rachel Narey, DC Dawson or any of their uniformed friends had been out to see Amanda but if they had I was pretty sure their approach would have been different. It's doubtful they would have taken a crystal vase from a table and emptied flowers and water over an expensive carpet. Or smashed the vase against a wall. They almost certainly wouldn't have rummaged through drawers to find address books and letters. They wouldn't have stood over her and let her believe that they were about to rape her.

They wouldn't have forced her legs apart and dragged her skirt to her waist. Wouldn't have leered and stared and scowled and drooled the way Davie Stewart did. Silently pawing at her, aroused and angry, while Grant demanded to know who else knew about her and Carr. Pushing at her to tell who would have been jealous enough to kill him.

Amanda cried, tried to scream but Stewart's hand stopped her from doing that. She told them that the killer had nothing to do with her, nothing to do with Jonathan. It was a random murder, the papers said so, the police said so.

Stewart and Grant told her it wasn't, that she was a stupid cow, that she had to tell them what she knew. She cried again. Stewart stroked her thighs and licked his lips. Grant asked for a name and in the end she gave one. Some guy that had been interested before Carr was on the scene and who she had been out for dinner with a couple of times. He didn't take it too well when she said she didn't want to see him again. The guy, a computer programmer from Bearsden, demanded to know if there was anyone else and she'd said yes.

They didn't leave a mark on her. No damage to the house except a broken vase, a clumsy accident. They eased her skirt back down and encouraged her not to speak to anyone. Grant suggested that Davie Stewart might be keen to come back and pay her another visit if there was even a whisper out of her. She wouldn't say anything.

The computer geek took a doing. He told them nothing because he had nothing to say.

The cops were called but he could tell them little. Two guys in ski masks asked about the lawyer that had been murdered. Left him in a heap of badly bruised ribs when they realized all he knew was what was in the papers.

Frankie Grant and a couple of thugs were tasked with having a quiet word with some of Billy Hutchison's customers at the bookies in Maryhill. It was in the nature of things that there were punters there that owed Billy money and would have been quids in when he got a short, sharp shock and was found pan breid behind his own front door. Independent bookies like Billy strung regulars out on credit and were much more likely to let them run up a tab than the likes of Ladbrokes or Corals. Some of them could be into him for a bundle.

Debts like that could end up in the hands of loan sharks and it took no more than a single phone call for Kirky to find out what he needed. Frankie and his boys had leverage. Not that they particularly needed it because they were quite happy to break fingers or burn cars. But the threat of those gambling debts being transferred to Alec Kirkwood turned out to be a very effective laxative. It loosened tongues as well as bowels. A name that was offered to them three times was Charlie Coyle, known as Glasvegas because of his heavy gambling.

At the time Billy had popped his clogs, Coyle was into him for nine and a half grand. Glasvegas was a big up, big down punter, the kind who would sting Billy for a thousand here or there with a shrewd bet then give him fifteen hundred back with a crazy hunch. Billy would always take his dough because he was confident he'd finish up ahead. Glasvegas sold second-hand cars so made decent money without exactly rolling in it. He needed Billy's credit line and got it. But this time he'd got more of it than he could handle. Billy hadn't handed the debt over to a shark but they were circling and smelling blood. The pressure was on but Glasvegas couldn't buy a winner to get himself out of it.

There were those who reckoned Glasvegas was mad and bad enough to have done Billy in. No one made him for a serial killer though. Didn't figure him for that. Frankie Grant and his bully boys weren't thinking that far ahead though. Don't ignore the obvious was what Kirkwood had told them.

Glasvegas was walking home half-canned from a session in Munns Vaults on Maryhill Road when he was pulled into a white van and knocked unconscious. He woke in a flat somewhere, blindfolded and his bare feet in a basin of water.

Glasvegas was a gambler, a bluff merchant, a guy used to putting on a bold front. Confidence can only get you so far though. As the first tiny jolt of electricity shot through his body, Coyle would have torn up a betting slip with 'Certainty' written on it. He was a gambler not a fighter. And he fucking hated pain.

The clamps on his fingers stayed put despite his shouts to take them off and his offers to tell them anything they wanted to know.

So talk, they told him. The first words Frankie or the thugs had spoken.

Glasvegas was the kind of guy with fingers in many pies, skeletons in many cupboards and debts in many places. He didn't know where to start.

'Is it about the Skodas I got from down south? I can sort that, no probs. If it's Billy Hutchison's dosh then you're maybe family. Will pay that obviously. It's only right. Terrible shame what happened to Billy. Great guy. Salt of the earth. Wait. Is it my maw's hoose? Is it? Fuck, can't tell you how bad I feel about that. Loved that wee hoose, she did too. The Cosworth that I sold to Malky Blackstock's cousin? That it? I knew I should have got the boy to check those gears over.'

Frankie raised a hand signalling his boys to keep quiet.

'It's about your maw's hoose. Talk.'

Glasvegas spilled his guts. He'd remortgaged his mother's ex-council house and blew the thirty-five grand he got for it. Then he couldn't keep up the mortgage payments and the bank had repossessed. His mother had gone to live with her sister in Bishopbriggs. The sister with three cats and a bad back. The smell and the inconvenience wasn't the worst thing though. It was the shame. Lost that smashing wee two-bedroomed hoose. The one that she had loved showing off to her sister. The sister that was now lording it over her. Frankie Grant threw a big blast of electricity that had Glasvegas's hair standing on end. Didn't kill him, didn't even knock him out but had him grinding his teeth together as if trying to bite his own molars off. Scorch marks on his skin where the clamps had fired into his hands.

Eventually Coyle found a shaky voice.

'Bastards. Said you wouldn't do that if I told you what you wanted to know. Bastards.'

'Aye, but that wasn't what we wanted to know. That was for your maw, you fucker. And so's this.'

The charge of electricity wasn't as much as the one before but it still had Glasvegas screaming and whimpering.

'Billy Hutchison, you wee scrote. Tell us everything.'

Wasn't much to tell. Glasvegas had been into him for money for a while. Nothing too serious then a couple of big bets went wrong and suddenly he owed Billy five grand. He tried to bet his way out of the hole and one came good but then three went bad. Billy had warned him the last one was the last one until he started paying it off. Billy had told him he couldn't run a line that big and might have to pass it on. That made Glasvegas ready to shit himself. That was why he ordered the cut and shut Skodas. And why he couldn't pay for them just yet.

'And why you bumped off Billy?'

'What? No! No, no, no. Naw! What? No!'

'Did you fucking well kill Billy Hutchison?'

'No way. Not my style. Couldn't hurt a fly.'

Frankie frazzled Glasvegas for a fourth time to make sure but he was already convinced he was telling the truth.

The gambler was crying now. 'I've never killed anybody in my life. Never even won a fight since I was at school.'

Frankie Grant nodded at the other two. It wasn't him.

'Who else owed Billy money? Give us another name.'

Glasvegas eagerly coughed up two names. Two more dead ends to be chased down. In return, one last shot of electricity was pinged through his body. Just for the fun of it. Just for his mother.

It was Davie Stewart and Kirkwood himself who went after contacts of Wallace Ogilvie at Glasgow Council. One of them was in the planning department and the other a Labour councillor. Men bought with fine wine, expensive meals and timeshare apartments. Brown envelopes stuffed with used notes were so 1980s.

The planning officer, a senior guy there named McMartin, wasn't for playing ball at all until Davie Stewart threw his cat out the window of his penthouse flat in Finnieston. Until the point that Stewart grabbed the thing by the scruff of its neck and opened the window, this McMartin still seemed to think he was used to playing with the big boys and had no need to worry. He knew people, he thought. Problem was he didn't know people like Davie. The window was shut with the cat still learning how to fly. That was when McMartin got the message.

He gave them the names of people who Wallace Ogilvie had business dealings with, including those that were off the books. He told them of people that had grudges against Ogilvie. A worrying development.

The planning officer was patted on the head and told to give it ten minutes before he went looking to see if his cat had eight lives left.

The councillor wasn't named but he was old school, ex-union official, and a friend of a friend of Kirkwood. This guy was not averse to talking to friends of gangsters. It was part of how he got where he was. That's why Kirky was doing it himself. The councillor wasn't going to respect common or garden crooks or be frightened by them. Top man or nothing for this job.

He told them how contracts might be won and who might have lost them. He wasn't naive enough to give them chapter and verse on the subject but they got what they wanted. He gave them names, individuals and companies, and pointed them in the direction of deals that didn't turn out to be what they promised.

The councillor also gave two names from Kirkwood's inner city. Two men that Wallace Ogilvie didn't deal with directly but who were associates of his associates. Nothing unusual in that. Do business in a city like Glasgow and you are no more than a couple of degrees of separation from a criminal, of either the organized or disorganized variety.

It was the names that interested Kirkwood. One was Alan Devlin who ran one of the biggest security firms in the city and had recently guarded the building of new homes for three housing associations in the city in return for taxpayer's cash. Kirkwood knew Devlin well and he wouldn't have hesitated to kill Ogilvie if he had screwed him over in a deal or even if he had just looked at him the wrong way. But freezing the cunt to death was hardly his style. He'd have had him decapitated or buried under a block of flats. Or both.

The other name was Mick Docherty. As well as dealing drugs and shooting off his flash mouth, Docherty had a line in providing cheap labour, all foreign and all off the books. The suggestion was that Ogilvie had his fingers in the building of a new school and a contact of his had been in charge of labour for tarmacking the driveways. The councillor said that the middle man was dodgy enough to have gone to Docherty to provide the workers. It wasn't much to link mouthy Mick to Wallace Ogilvie but close enough for Kirkwood's purposes. Just perfect, in fact.

Kirky had already let it be known he would catch the

man they were now calling 'The Cutter'. Said he would do what the cops couldn't. Said he would do their job for them. That was why he had made sure everyone knew he was chasing leads, letting slip bits about Glasvegas, council contracts and baseball-bat beatings.

Everyone in Glasgow wanted this guy caught. They were prepared to buy into anyone that could do it. Anyone. City was crying out for a hero.

The councillor had given him the name of the middle man in the school building project, a guy called Archie Kepple. It wasn't clear if Kepple knew Docherty's labourers were wetbacks or if it suited him not to know. Either way, it was time for Kirky to pay Mr Kepple a visit.

He had an office on the first floor of a building on Renfield Street, not far from the lawyer Carr's. When Kepple's secretary was told that Alec Kirkwood was there to see him regarding Wallace Ogilvie, she asked if he had an appointment. Kirkwood said he was confident that Mr Kepple would see him and he was right. He was to be shown right in.

Archie Kepple was a nervous little man who kept playing with a glass paperweight on his desk. Kirky was used to people being nervous around him and didn't take offence.

To begin with Kepple was very evasive about Wallace Ogilvie. Made out he had to think about the name, which was pretty stupid given that he had been all over the papers as a victim of the serial killer. It's the kind of thing you would remember.

Then he tried to play down his business involvement with Ogilvie, said they had only had a couple of dealings.

That's when Kirky smiled and told him to cut the crap. They were both businessmen, men of the world, they could talk straight. The paperweight was going like a yo-yo.

Kepple nodded at Kirkwood's suggestion. Yes, businessmen.

Sometimes need to cut corners to get deals done, said Kirky. Yes, sometimes, agreed Kepple. Need to deal with people that we normally wouldn't, declared Kirky. Kepple blinked a lot but nodded.

Kepple's fiddling with the paperweight was starting to get on Kirkwood's tits. He glared at it and Kepple promptly put it down and shoved it away from himself.

'People like Mick Docherty.'

Kepple opened his mouth and closed it again. Opened it again to say no more than 'Em . . .'

'It's OK, we all do it. Docherty is a piece of scum and I'm sure you wouldn't work with him if you didn't have to. Hard times in the building trade. Needs must, eh?'

'Mr Docherty is, um, an associate but I've no reason to think . . .' Kepple's voiced trailed off unconvincingly.

'Of course you haven't,' smiled Kirkwood. 'Best not to, don't you think?'

Kepple's head dropped as he nodded again.

'Did Mr Docherty ever meet Mr Ogilvie?'

'No.'

Kirkwood stared at him.

'No, yes, once. I was having a drink with Wallace when Mr Docherty came in. I introduced them. That was all though.'

'It's possible that they met after that though, isn't it? Once they knew they had a mutual business acquaintance? It is possible.'

'Well, yes. I suppose so.'

'It is, isn't it? And you do know that Mr Docherty has a rather . . . unsavoury reputation?'

'Yes.'

'Has it never crossed your mind that he might have killed Mr Ogilvie? A man like that, capable of anything.'

Kepple looked close to shitting himself. He swallowed and shrugged a nod.

'Leaves you in a tricky position, Mr Kepple. You knowing what you know. Mr Docherty knowing what you know . . .'

So it was that Archie Kepple phoned Mick Docherty. Asked him to meet in the office in Renfield Street after hours. He mentioned a housing association contract on the south side. Big money and a lot of manpower needed. All under the radar for now though. Mick needed to keep it quiet and come on his own. Greedy Mick was happy to agree.

The details on what happened in that office once Mick Docherty had turned up were few and far between. Suffice to say that Mick was never seen again. Some said he was strangled, others that he was stabbed. There was even talk that he had been given a huge overdose of the stuff that he helped put on the streets.

Archie Kepple's nerves and conscience ensured he couldn't keep his trap shut completely and he let it be known that he thought Docherty had something to do with the murder of poor Wallace Ogilvie. Never any mention of any other prominent Glasgow businessman though.

Kepple's trade contacts took a bit of a dunt with the disappearance of Docherty but he found himself a new partner who was happy to pick up the slack and provide bodies to lay the black stuff and the bricks, all foreign and all off the books.

Together they helped build sparkling new southside housing with a nice little wedge from the taxpayer. Alan Devlin's boys made sure the building site was safely secured night and day in case anyone came around stealing or snooping. Lovely houses they were too, solid as a rock and built on a very sound foundation.

Docherty sorted, reputation sorted. Kirkwood wasn't so daft as to think he had sorted the serial killer too. That box still needed ticking. According to Ally McFarland, Kirky felt he was on a roll and had all sorts of useful information to work with.

CHAPTER 30

She's sleeping.

I'm downstairs. Television on. I'm staring at the screen. No idea what programme is on. No interest.

I've eaten. Hours ago though, I think.

I'm thinking. Remembering. Planning.

I won't close my eyes. I know I'll see her. See him. See them.

Have I put the hall light off? I'm sure I did. I know I did. Better check.

I check. I had put it off. I knew I had.

Ideas run round my head. So many thoughts. Can't stop them, can't slow them or reduce them.

I want a drink but won't do it. I want control. Need it.

Not being alone but being lonely is a hard way to be. That's why I sometimes turned to my pal Jack for help. Sometimes my mates Jim or Arthur too. Mr Daniel's, Mr Beam and Mr Guinness. Best friends a lonely man could have. I liked drinking. It helped.

But sometimes it didn't help. Like now.

Remember when Sarah fell off her new bike and tore the skin off her knee? She refused to cry, just wouldn't do it even though there was blood running down her leg.

So many plans to make. Got to make sure things are done right.

There's a feeling rooted deep in my gut. An irritation that won't go away. It nags at me, gnaws at me. It eats me. I try to stop thinking about it but it churns my stomach, beats my head. It's there, always there. I fret because of it, continually aware of it. I worry because it is always there and it is always there because I worry about it. Can't break that loop. Not a loop, a spiral. Downward. There is a constant urge to scream.

Did I put that light off? The hall light? I know I did but maybe I better check. I know I did. Check anyway.

I check it. It was off.

Glass of Jack Daniel's. Just the one. Driving later. Largish one though. Beyond caring.

The newspapers have been full of things I've done. This street too with all its talk of killings. Kids write stuff on walls. That dog has been hanging around again as if it is stalking me. Not a happy place.

What's happy?

So much planning to do. So much to remember. So much to forget.

I want to wake up in the rain with her sheltering beneath my arm, raindrops falling off her smile and her feet shaking with the fun of it. I want her to rain-dance and twirl. I want her to pretend she is showing off. I want to open my eyes and see her looking up at me then looking down at rain dripping off her nose, her licking it the way she does. Did.

It is hours since I've eaten. Hungry now.

No time though. I've got to go out soon. How long is it since I had that glass of Jack?

Punters in the taxi been talking of nothing except him. The Cutter. Him not me. Kept going on about the dentist. Sinclair. Saying what a shame it was. Sin for his wife, they said.

What did they know about sin? Sin everywhere.

Woman actually cried in the back of the car. Husband had to hold her. Crying for a woman she didn't know. I caused that. Wallace Ogilvie caused that.

No more Jack. Haven't eaten. No more Jack on an empty stomach.

Shit. Have to shake that gnawing. Stomach all over the place. Maybe a glass of Jack would sort it.

They were saying that Sinclair was the worst one yet. Just married. Said surely if killer had known that he wouldn't have done it. How could anyone do that? they asked.

Pour another glass.

Might not make work. Don't want to hear them talking. Could phone in sick. True enough anyway. Sick in the stomach. Sick in the head.

Sarah was off school for nearly two weeks with chicken pox once. Poor wee thing was covered in spots and had the cough and a really bad headache. Plenty of fluids and calamine lotion. Don't scratch.

Taxi passengers been boring into my head. Harder and

harder to shut them out. Why couldn't they just shut the fuck up?

Not going in. Decided. Need to phone before having another glass. Keep voice together. Cammy doesn't sound best pleased. Feels sorry for me though. Know that. Still not happy.

No work though. No passengers. Why do they keep asking if I have heard anything? Just because you drive a cab doesn't mean you get loads of gossip. No, heard nothing. Shut the fuck up.

Seemed to be more people taking taxis. No one wanted to walk anywhere any more. People were scared. Even in Glasgow.

Did I put the light off in the hall? Sure I'd checked that already.

Sat back down. Last Jack.

Still got to plan. Still lots to do. Dice move next.

Maybe not best time to plan. Mind full of Jack. Mind full of Sarah. Mind full of Sinclair.

I keep hearing Sarah's voice. Always been the way. Would hear her in shopping centres or calling to a pal in the street. Would be sure it was her. And every time I remembered it wasn't, couldn't be, it was like her dying all over again. But now I hear it without anyone talking.

She was talking through Jack. I was thinking through Jack.

Man gave me a ten-pence tip last week. Fare came to £6.95 and he handed over seven pounds and a five-pence piece. Why do they bother doing that? I threw the coin out the window behind him. Shouldn't have done that.

Jesus, my guts were churning. Not nerves, just everything. All the shit rolled together. Should have been at work by now. Should have been on the street. Couldn't now even if I wanted to.

Not going to check that light again. Know I've checked it.

I miss you. I say it out loud. I really miss you. Am I saying it out loud to prove it in case she's listening? Don't know. Shouldn't have to prove it. She knows I love her.

Don't feel guilty. Doesn't matter how many people say how bad it all is. Just because he was recently married. So what? Random. Way it has to be.

The woman who was crying was doing so for herself. Not for the widow. Her own fear of being alone. Selfish bitch.

Glasgow was full of fear. Could smell it from them. All their talk, all their gallusness meant nothing. All worried about their miserable little lives. Five fucking deaths and their front disappears like snow off a dyke. Could see the strain in their eyes, hear it in their voices. Smell it, see it, hear it, taste it, touch it.

Can't make plans with all this Tennessee firewater in me. Drunk plans are bad plans. Need to do things right. Owe it to her to do it properly. Getting caught would blow everything. Shame her. Shame both of them. Can't do that. Can't have that.

Need control.

Put half glass of Jack aside. Not finishing that.

Rachel Narey is suspicious. Maybe she is just suspicious of everyone. Maybe half of Glasgow thinks she suspects them. They had nothing to hide though. Nothing to protect. She is getting a hard time on telly and in the papers. Scared people demanding answers. Police getting called for everything in taxis and on the street. Feel sorry for her. Not her fault. Their Cutter is too clever for them.

A wee bit more of the Jack. Just what's in that glass though. No more after that.

Wonder what the cops really think. Must be saying lots they aren't letting on to the press. Must have theories. Must have leads. Must be fucking furious that the piss is being taken out of them. Must be doing so much that I haven't got a clue about.

Getting tired.

Sarah once said she wanted to be a policewoman. And a lawyer. And a pop star. And a nurse. And look after old people. She was really bright. And so kind. A warm heart.

She and her pals found some kittens in the river when she was about seven. Some farmer had tried to drown them in a sack. She took the two surviving ones from house to house for hours until she found a home for them. It didn't matter how many times people said no, she just moved on to another house with big eyes and a soft sell until the cats had good homes.

Last drops of Jack clinging to the side of the glass. The rest deep inside me. No more.

Tired.

Just going to close my eyes for a second. Rest them. Need rest.

Sarah. Narey. Sinclair.

Traffic lights. Traffic jams.
Wallace Ogilvie. Ogilvie. Ogilvie.
Fighting back.
Car door slamming shut somewhere. Black dog barking.
So tired.
Is the light switched off in the hall?
So very tired.

CHAPTER 31

The *Daily Record*. Wednesday, 25 March 2010. Page 1.
CLUELESS
'CSI' psychologist admits Cutter cops are baffled
EXCLUSIVE by Keith Imrie, Chief Reporter.

The forensic psychologist assisting Strathclyde Police with The Cutter murders has admitted that the force have 'no worthwhile leads' in their hunt for the killer. Dr Paul Crabtree, a consultant on US drama CSI, said that officers were out of ideas and resorting to 'hoping that something would turn up'.

A week on from the vicious murder of Cutter victim number five, Inchinnan dentist Brian Sinclair, the revelation will be seen as a devastating blow to the police investigation. Criticism has continued to mount against the police as the hunt goes into its thirteenth month without any tangible success. There are believed to be deep rifts within the investigation team and there are widespread rumours of officers from an outside force being parachuted in to 'assist' with the case.

Speaking exclusively to the Daily Record, Dr Crabtree gave a remarkable insight into the profile he has drawn up for officers as well as a depressing assessment of their progress. 'I am firmly of

213

the opinion that this killer is striking randomly and that there is no discernible pattern to either when or who he strikes,' he said. 'That makes him extremely dangerous and, by extension, extremely difficult to apprehend. However there are certain characteristics that we can confidently assign to him and these can form a basis of elimination as well as inclusion.

'I believe that the killer is a man, aged between 18 to 50 and with his own car. He seems to have issues with men rather than women and may well have close ties to a female figure in his life, probably his mother. This has manifested itself in deep-rooted hatred of men and it may be that his significant female figure may have been significantly abused or hurt by a male figure.

'It may be too that he has a grievance against the city of Glasgow and that is an avenue worth exploring.

'He is also likely to have issues with authority as he seems to be taunting the police over their inability to catch him. He sees himself, quite wrongly of course,

as omnipotent and far smarter than the police. Indeed I fear he is possessed of what we term Roman Emperor Syndrome, the quest in the killer for something even beyond omnipotent control, for the complete subjugation and slow destruction of others.

'The sending of the victim's finger to police is a clear indicator of his belief in his own invulnerability and his desire for publicity. He believes he is untouchable but moreover he wants everyone to know about his power.

'These particular murders are unusual because they are crimes with no obvious indication or links as to why they would happen. In most cases there are clear connections but not in these.

'I have to say that police are at the stage where they have exhausted all logical lines of possibility and are simply hoping that something will turn up or that the killer will make some fundamental mistake. There are no worthwhile leads and they are praying that one surfaces before he strikes again.'

Dr Crabtree, who was brought into the investigation after the third murder, that of Thomas Tierney, has been critical in the past of the force's reluctance to use forensic profiling techniques. There have been persistent rumours of friction between Dr Crabtree and DS Rachel Narey, the officer in charge of the investigation. Sources suggest that the two have argued in front of other officers on many occasions with DS Narey openly critical of the psychologist's assessments. It is thought that she disagrees with his opinion that there is no connection between the victims.

While not confirming those suggestions, Dr Crabtree said that there had been some disagreements over strategy.

'Differing members of an investigation team often take differing approaches,' he said. 'This is not unusual and may even be seen as constructive. It is important that everyone keeps an open mind on all avenues that may be conducive to bringing this case to an end.'

CHAPTER 32

A time will come when a person will be declared insane when they believe that 'I am he who is X, Y and Z, and X, Y and Z only.'

It's a line from a book called *The Dice Man* by a guy calling himself Luke Rhinehart. It was a cult novel written at the height of the hippy revolution and featured free sex, rape and murder. The dust cover said it was subversive, controversial, and dangerous. Banned in several countries, it promised to change the reader's life whether he liked it or not. It was about a bored psychiatrist who spiced things up by letting his entire life be ruled by the roll of the dice. No going back, no changing the rules, just follow the dice and let chance sweep away what he said were the illnesses of reason and seriousness created by modern society. It championed freedom over free will, chance over choice. It took away the moral or ethical responsibility that came with choice and replaced it with risk, variety and impermanence. You couldn't be held accountable for something that happened at random and there was no point in worrying about

217

the consequences of any action when the next throw of the dice took you in an unrelated direction.

It was of course a massive piss-take.

All that mattered though was the premise and the premise was simple. The dice decide. Or the die decides. Die is the singular of dice. Die, die, die. For my purposes, it was all rather neat. The die decides who dies. Homicidal tongue-twisters r us.

The line about he who is X, Y and Z means that it's crazy to believe a person is just what he is and nothing more or less. We are all more than we seem, even to ourselves. We are all capable of much more than we or others might think.

None of us can be sure of who we are or what we are, far less of what we might do. One event, one roll of the dice, one chance happening, one flutter of a butterfly's wing and all that we think is set and sure is suddenly very different. Your world is arse over tit just like that. Chaos rules. Your X, Y and Z is gone and you find that you are X, B and W. You are more and you are less.

My instruments of chance were a pair of dice liberated from an old Monopoly set. Rhinehart's nonsense is no way to live a life but it seemed a perfect way to orchestrate a random death.

The dice man cometh.

I split Glasgow into two areas, north and south of the river. An odd number meant north, even was south. A four and a six. South.

Wikipedia lists sixty-two districts south of the Clyde in alphabetical order from Arden to Tradeston. I split them into five groups of twelve with two left over. I threw a single die and threw a one.

That left me with Arden, Auldhouse, Battlefield, Bellahouston, Cardonald, Carmunnock, Carnwadric, Castlemilk, Cathcart, Corkerhill, Cowglen and Craigton.

Leafy suburbs, skyscraper hellholes, Victorian villas, tenement graveyards and conservation villages. Rat runs, estates, schemes and bombsites. Someone in one of them would fall into in the crosshairs of the dice.

I'd need to throw a pair of dice so that left only Arden as being safe. Perhaps a first for anyone living there.

I threw some practice dice in my head. Think of a number.

Eight. Castlemilk. Château Au Lait or Castlemanky depending on your point of view. It had one pub and seven hundred hungry weans testifying that you couldnae fling pieces oot a twenty-storey flat. If it was butter, cheese or jeely, if the bread was plain or pan, the odds of it reaching earth were ninety-nine to wan. Numbers everywhere.

Ten. Corkerhill. Home of the Paka, a canal or train stop for Paisley, refurbished commuter land and not half as bad as it was painted or as it used to be.

Seven. Carnwadric. Another tweeny war housing scheme on the fringes of civilization, east of safe Arden and north of Thornliebank. I'd say it was a shithole but that would hardly distinguish it from so many of the badly thought out schemes thrown up to take the spillover from the old slums.

I threw the dice for real.

A two. A three.

Five. Cardonald.

I knew there was the college, a cat and dog home, the Bute and Cumbrae multis and not much else of note except the bus into town. Cardonald it was.

Random step number two.

I opened an email account in the name of Wayne Wayne. Wayne.wayne@live.co.uk. I then opened a Facebook account in the name of Wayne Wayne. As good a name as any, better than most.

Wayne is the most common middle name of America's most prolific murderers. It's all big John's fault. Over 150 of the USA's most vicious serial killers had the middle name Wayne. John Wayne Gacy, 36 victims. Elmer Wayne Henley, 27 victims. Conan Wayne Hale, Jimmy Wayne Jeffers, Robert Wayne Sawyer.

Blame the parents. Give a kid a name like that and don't be surprised if he grows up just a little more aggressive and macho than you expected. Wayne Wayne it was.

Facebook search engine. Type in the word Cardonald and hit enter.

Top of the list of over 500 names was Lara Samoltowski, the unwitting victim of the social networking revolution. It was all Google's fault for opening Facebook up to their search engine and so opening her up to me. She really ought to have listened to those warnings on privacy settings.

A look at her profile told me a lot. Where she studied. What bands she liked and so what concerts she might go to. Where she liked to eat. Where she liked to drink. Where she liked to shop. The lack of a boyfriend. Her vulnerability.

So much networking. So much information.

I was the most patient of impatient killers. It took three meals at Gambrino on Great Western Road. It took three times of wandering carefully through Zara, H&M and Oasis. It took four fairly uncomfortable visits to Oran Mor and the pubs of Ashton Lane before I saw the face from Facebook.

It was in Jinty McGinty's on Friday 3 April that I eventually saw her. She was sitting at a table in the corner with three other girls. I knew them immediately. Maz, Christine and Ash. Her Facebook friends, her best pals. Fellow students who didn't know how lucky they were. But they would.

Maz was a hotshot netball player, had a thing for guys with glasses and the only thing she loved more than vodka and cranberry was *Ugly Betty*. They all thought Christine was the best-looking girl in college. Chrissie had loved Take That since she was seven but now she was big time into the Chemical Brothers and missed her dog Robbie who was at home in Elgin. Ash was a party girl, hated studying but loved Greggs steak bakes, Pinot Grigio and tablet.

Then there was Lara. She wasn't one of the new Poles who had flooded into Scotland since EU expansion. She was fourth generation. Her dad couldn't even speak Polish. Lara wanted to save the planet, the environment, the whale, the proboscis monkey, the Penan forest people of Malaysia and the old Atheneum theatre. She'd have been better off trying to save herself.

She loved hillwalking and clubbing, lusted for Ashton Kutcher and admitted a guilty fancy for Al Gore. She barely looked her twenty years. Slim and pale. Long, dark curly hair. A near constant, guileless smile on a pretty face.

One of the other girls, one of the lucky ones, sat with her back to me. Whatever she was saying, Lara smiled, laughed and nodded. Quick impressions were that she was smart and lively, an intelligent face, not too loud, interested. Nice. Beautiful. All to live for.

I saw a couple of other guys in the pub looking at her too, checking her out and nudging their mates. That helped. It wouldn't seem so odd if someone caught me staring at her. And I did.

In fact, I couldn't take my eyes off her. Lovely, laughing, lively Lara.

But I wasn't looking for the same reason the other guys in the bar were. It wasn't the slim waist, the long hair or the beautiful smile. I was staring because I was going to kill her.

I wasn't like them. I wasn't gawping at her slim neck because I wanted to kiss it. I wasn't like them at all.

I wasn't like anyone. Not in that pub or anywhere else. I hadn't been like anyone else for a very long time.

Not since my wee girl died under the wheels of Wallace Ogilvie's car. Not since I had taken the lives of Carr, Hutchison, Tierney, Ogilvie and Sinclair. And I would be a lot less like anyone else after I disposed of the young girl sitting a few yards away from me.

I had no choice. There was no choice. The dice said so. Facebook said so. The others, Ogilvie apart, were the unlucky losers in my Cutter's lottery. She was part of the afterthought, the camouflage, the extra padding, the rest of the plan. Not the way a young life should be described. Not the way things should turn out.

There was something about her neck though. My eyes kept being drawn to it. A pretty neck but slender. Fragile.

I'd watch what she was doing – taking in her friends, her movements, trying to pick up more clues about her – but again and again my eyes went back to that delicate neck. Brass neck. Won by a neck. Red neck. Up to your neck in it. Dead from the neck up. Pain in the neck. Stick your neck out. Millstone around your neck. Hung from the neck until dead. Broken neck.

She would be just a couple of years older than Sarah would be now. Maybe Sarah would have been at college or university now too. A young woman. Out on the town with her friends. Her life ahead of her.

I shook my head. Shook the interfering thoughts out. No time for that. A distraction I didn't need. I mentally apologized to her for doing so but it had to be done. Out damn thoughts.

They kept coming back though. Maybe Sarah and Lara would be friends. Maybe Sarah would have been on her Facebook list, swapping messages with Maz, Ash and Christine. Maybe she'd have been in that happy group in Jinty's with white wine, vodka and cranberry and bottles of beer.

I'd been mugged by my memories again. Sarah came flooding back, pushing at me, arguing with me. She was saying no, I was saying it had to be. The plan, the dice, Facebook. They all demanded it.

I shook the thoughts out of my head again and screwed my convictions to the sticking place. It had to be done. That neck. I was still looking at it when I became aware of someone standing at my shoulder. I hadn't paid any attention to the door opening or the two sets of feet that had walked near me.

I looked up and saw the inquisitive face of Detective Sergeant Rachel Narey looking back down at me.

CHAPTER 33

We were back outside the pub, standing on Ashton Lane, groups of people passing by on their way to the Loft, Vodka Wodka or Brel.

Me, DS Narey and wide, balding DC Dawson.

'How nice to see you again.' DS Narey.

'Is it?'

'I'm just being polite.'

'Oh well, they say it's nice to be nice. You not making house calls these days? I missed you the last time when you came round to chat to my wife.'

'She confirmed that you were with her and asleep when two of the killings took place.'

'I know. Strangely enough it did come up in conversation.'

'You must be pleased that she put you in the clear. And yes, I suppose that is a question.'

'Hardly. I had no need to be put in the clear. Instead I had to comfort an already troubled woman after her husband was accused of being a serial killer.'

'I'm sorry about that.'

'No, you're not.'

'OK, maybe I'm not. I didn't accuse you of being a serial killer but I understand why you might resent the suggestion. I had to look into all aspects of the case but then I explained that to you before.'

'You did.'

'You see we are trained to always look close to home before examining the possibilities that a murder might have been committed by a complete stranger.'

'Are you now?'

'The percentage of what we call stranger murders is pretty low. Most victims know their killer. There is usually a reason for it in my experience. Random killings just don't happen very often.'

'But they do happen?'

'Oh they do, yes. But I'm an awkward sort. Someone tells me something I tend to doubt it. I blame my parents.'

'I'm sure they are very proud of you. The newspapers seem certain that these murders are being done at random.'

'Don't you know you shouldn't believe everything you read? I wouldn't believe the date on half those rags. Maybe they're right but I'm keeping an open mind on things.'

'Well done. So is that why you are speaking to me again?'

'Yes.'

'Oh good. And are you having me followed or did you just pop in here for a quiet drink with DC Whatsisname here. I thought they frowned on officers drinking on duty.'

'They do if we get caught.'

'Does that go for serial killers too?'

'Oh most definitely. But no, my visit wasn't entirely accidental. I fancied a quick word with you and a wee birdie told me you were in here.'

'The wee birdies are awful well informed. So why do you want to talk to me then?'

'Oh it's not just you. All aspects of the case remember? All of the victims of this killer had given someone a reason to want them dead. Just that in some of the cases we maybe don't know what the reason is yet. In your case, maybe we do.'

'I told you. I didn't kill him.'

'I know you did. And I told you I'd understand it if you had wanted to. I don't have children of my own but I think I know how you must have felt.'

'Believe me, you don't. Not even close.'

'A drunk that knocked and killed a daughter of mine? I'd want him hurt. I'd want revenge. I'd maybe do anything to make him pay.'

'Maybe you would.'

'I understand that need to make things right. That's my job. To sort things.'

'You don't seem to have made too good a job of it, DS Narey. No offence.'

'None taken. You can surely see why you would make a good suspect for the killing of Wallace Ogilvie though.'

'Maybe. But I didn't kill him. And I certainly didn't kill the rest of them. You tell me what makes me a good suspect for the others.'

'Nothing does. Not a thing. That would be a puzzle right enough.'

'I'll leave you to your puzzle then, DS Narey, if there's nothing else. Was there anything specific you wanted to ask me?'

'Oh no. Just a wee chat. Helps me get things straight in my mind. I might need to chat to you again sometime.'

'You do that. If you get a spare minute from catching the serial killer that is terrifying Glasgow then you come and have a chat.'

'Thanks. I'll do that.'

I had just turned away from her and could hear the two lots of detective feet ringing on the cobbles when the door to Jinty's opened. Out came Christine, Maz, Lara and Ash. They were on their way to the Loft, I heard Christine say so. They were on their way for some food and some more drinks. They were on their way to sanctuary and salvation for Lara.

If I ever saw her again it would be pure chance.

I wanted to turn and watch them walk across the lane but I was aware that the two cops might also have turned and might have been looking at me. I caught the door to Jinty's that they had left swinging behind them and went back in to finish off a pint of Guinness that was about to taste sweeter than it did before. A voice in my head said 'Good' and I didn't disagree.

I silently wished Lara Samoltowski a long and happy life.

CHAPTER 34

I was doing everything I could to avoid conversation with her. Wasn't too difficult. I badgered Cammy for as many back or night shifts as were going. He was happy to oblige.

It meant she was out all day on her pointless crusade against drunk drivers while I slept or planned. I was on the streets while she was in bed. At most it left a short awkward time when she got in from her day and before the pills kicked in and sent her to dreams, nightmares or nothingness.

I was quiet, reluctant. She was used to that by now. Didn't put her off talking. Got little back in return but ploughed on regardless. I could see the topic coming a mile away and would do my best to head it off. Sometimes wondered if she noticed that I spoke most when I was trying to avoid saying anything. She could never resist it for long. Probably like every other household in Glasgow. But ours was different. We were touched by it.

Maybe they all thought they were. No more than six degrees of separation between them and a victim of the man they called The Cutter. Heard that all the time when I was driving.

'My sister works beside this guy who's dad knew that Billy Hutchison. You know. The bookmaker. Says the guy was in the bookies the very day that the man was murdered. Terrible, ain't it?'

'My cousin Johnny is going out with a girl who was a patient of that dentist Sinclair. Brian, isn't it? Was. She hadn't seen him for a while right enough. Good teeth this girl, our Johnny says. Anyway she says he was a really nice guy. Very professional. Sin what happened to him, wasn't it?'

When you live in a village like Glasgow then you can be sure everyone would have known someone. All over the papers. All over the TV. Only thing anybody talked about. That and the football.

Different for us though. We were glad Wallace Ogilvie was dead.

We were just one separation away from it. A single step. And we were glad.

We didn't say it. Not to each other or anyone else but there was no doubt about it. She denied it after that first time when she read about his death and broke down and swore. She maybe even denied it to herself but she was glad. And I was very glad. It meant she wanted to talk about the killings every chance she got. She never missed a news bulletin. Just in case.

There had been a special report on the BBC the night before. A *Crimewatch* special. The whole programme devoted to it. Reconstructions. Witnesses of sorts. Relatives. Police. So-called experts. She stayed up to watch it, of course. Left her pills till later. Didn't want to take the risk of snoozing through it.

Rachel Narey was live in the studio. Whisked down to London to film it then doubtless back up to continue the chase. She looked good. Camera still liked her. Dressed well, composed, in charge. Strain behind the eyes though. Could see that. Couldn't miss it. Taking its toll.

The presenter was asking her to reassure. Asking her what the public could do to help. Not a whole fucking lot it seemed.

Rachel said that someone must know who the killer was. Said that there must be someone in Glasgow whose behaviour had changed, who had unexplained absences, whose actions were causing suspicion. Urged anyone who had doubts, even about a partner, a member of their family, to contact the police.

I looked at her out of the corner of my eye. Watched for a reaction but there was none. Nothing at all.

Rachel had practised this, I was sure of that. So smooth. Full of nothing but well delivered. There was a plea from the heart from Sinclair's widow. The recently married, recently widowed Mrs Sinclair. She looked like shit.

Could barely look at the camera. Hadn't slept since it happened. Hadn't stopped crying since it happened. I didn't need to see this. Looked at my wife and saw in her some of what Mary Sinclair was going through. Tired. Haunted. Gaunt. Shocked, still.

Programme ended with yet more showings of the numbers to call. All treated in the strictest confidence and you may be eligible for a reward. Businessman from Glasgow had put up £125,000. Others had put up smaller amounts.

She sank deeper into her chair and breathed out. Like she'd been through a boxing match and had taken a beating. She didn't say anything for a few minutes and I certainly wasn't going to. Then she started.

'Still can't believe this. What's happening to this place?'

She was glad.

'Did you see the state of that poor woman? Shocking. How could anyone put her through all that? Would have been better killing her too.'

She was glad.

'Someone must know something. That polis woman is right. There's no way you wouldn't know if it was one of yours. Your husband or your son or your brother. How could you not know? Someone must be hiding him, covering for him.'

I knew she was glad he was dead.

'Maybe someone's too feart to speak out. Murderer like that it stands to reason. Things he's done. Unbelievable.'

She was glad.

'Because there's no way you wouldn't notice. Guy must be a lunatic. Might pretend to be normal but he couldn't keep that up for long. Capable of doing all that then how can he act like nothing's happened? What do you think?'

I think you're glad Wallace Ogilvie is dead. That means you are glad they are all dead. Think the killer can act normal because he is normal. He has a job to do. He has a promise to keep. He is doing what is right and you are glad.

'I don't know,' I said. 'People are strange. Never know what's going on in someone else's life.'

'Well, no. That's true. But, oh my God, how can he do that? How can he get away with it?'

He does it because he has to. Because a wrong needs to be put right. Because a drunken bastard killed the most precious thing in his life. Because you cannot let a person get away with something like that.

He gets away with it because he is smart, because he plans well and because he has thought it all the way through. He gets away with it because what he is doing is right.

'I don't know. Who knows what people are capable of doing? I'm sure the police will catch him eventually.'

'Eventually? Eventually? How many more are going to die before that happens?'

Two more. And you are glad it has happened. You are glad they are dead. We both know that.

'I'm sure they will get him soon. Don't worry about it. You have to stop thinking about it. Isn't your soap opera on the other side?'

'Can't watch that. Not now.'

Her eyes were wide. As if I'd suggested she go swimming at midnight or walk to London. She was glad.

'Well, I'll get you a cup of tea then.'

'No, no tea. I don't want tea. Do you, do you think he . . .'

She rarely mentioned him by name.

'Do you think he was picked somehow because of what he had done?' Her words trailed off quietly.

'Don't know,' I mumbled.

'But you've thought about it. Don't tell me you haven't. You have. Do you think that was why he was picked?'

Yes, of course it was. It was why he was killed. It was because of what he did that they were all picked. Why they were all killed.

'No, it was just coincidence. Police have said so.'

'Too much of a coincidence. That Thomas Tierney was a drug dealer. Maybe that's why he was picked out.'

She was glad.

'Not what the police say. Anyway, the others hadn't done anything wrong.'

'Well, not as far as we know. Might all have sinned.'

Everyone sins. Stop talking like that. You are glad. Admit it. Thank me. You are fucking glad.

'There has been nothing in the papers about any of the others doing anything wrong,' I said. 'What about that dentist? What did he do?'

She looked at me in despair. Reaching for an answer.

'I'm going to take my other pill. Should have had it by now. Getting late. I'm tired.'

She was glad. She was glad he was dead. She was glad they were all dead.

Within fifteen minutes the questions had stopped. Another quarter of an hour and she was going to bed.

I was left alone again, safe from her conversation and her worries. No more theories or guilt trips, no more pretending. No more talk of sin or reason or knowledge. No more fucking words. Just give me the silence of the room and the night and the road and the city. Give me peace.

Give me fucking peace.

CHAPTER 35

My boss, Cammy Strang, ran a legit taxi operation. As legit as a private hire firm gets in Glasgow anyway. Cammy was ex-army. He would look after himself and his drivers and sometimes that meant hurting people. But an occasional swing of a baseball bat didn't make Cammy a bad guy. Not compared to some.

Bribes and bungs, threats and lies, punters hijacked and flyers taken down. That kind of stuff was just business. It was what you had to do to survive, what was needed to turn a profit but it didn't make you a crook. Not compared to some.

He'd started out with just one cab, driving it himself. Established private hires tried to put him out of business but Cammy wasn't having it. He paid a couple of late-night visits and made his point.

He bought more cars and took on more drivers. Ended up with a fleet of eight, made himself a bundle.

Working for Cammy was a good deal. You could work hours that suited you both and he'd be straight with you.

No need to worry about all your money being there or that he'd take someone else's side over yours. Play fair by Cammy and Cammy would play fair by you. Above all, if you got a call for a job from Cammy then you knew there would always be someone in the taxi. Sounds obvious enough but elsewhere, other firms, that wasn't always the case. Plenty of them ran 'drops'.

The driver would get a call, pick up a package rather than a passenger and deliver it. No chat from the back of the cab, no tip. Door-to-door drugs. Class A all the way. There had never been drops in any of Cammy's cabs. He held a hard line on drugs, would have nothing to do with them.

But the wolves were out there, getting closer. Three other private hire firms had been bought out in the past few months alone. Word was that all three of them now did drops. Word was one guy was playing monopoly.

The more cab firms that were taken over, the less chance of getting a job with another company. Less chance of another job, less scope for saying no when asked to do a drop. Just business.

Cammy knew that the guy was coming and knew he could do nothing to stop him. Cammy had one baseball bat, the guy had a whole team.

Time to retire, Cammy told us. Tenerife for him and the missus. An offer he couldn't refuse. We knew.

Who's taking over the firm? asked one of the boys. I held my breath.

'Guy named Arthur Penman,' Cammy said. I breathed again. Sometimes it's better the devil you don't know.

Cammy didn't say goodbye. The handover was to be on the Wednesday and he went home Tuesday night as per usual. Wednesday came and there was a new face behind the desk and a couple of new faces in the cabs. Handover done, Cammy and Jean halfway to Santa Cruz.

Penman was a lanky guy with glasses and a nervous cough. Studious looking. I recognized an accountant when I saw one. Penpusher not drugs pusher.

Penman wasn't the man.

Our jobs were safe, he said. Business as usual, he said. Even giving us a couple of new drivers. He owned other cab firms, he told us, so he wouldn't be there all the time. He'd pop in regularly though, just to keep us on our toes. The radio controller would do the rest. And the new drivers, Tobin and McTeer. He knew them already and they'd help things tick over when he wasn't around.

Nobody said much. Wasn't much to say.

The radio controller was new too. A grumpy big guy with close-cropped hair and an angry, pock-marked face. Old Annie had gone into early retirement. Tollcross for her, not Tenerife. Spending the rest of her days smelling the McVities biscuit factory. Which was a bit ironic really.

Penman's new drivers were sullen and sure of themselves. They only spoke to each other, seemed to drive when they felt like it and spent a lot of time holed up in the cab office with crabbit Robert the new controller.

A week went by and nothing much changed. I still drove a cab with passengers in it and Penman's was the only name above the door. There were moans and mutterings amongst the drivers. I dodged most of the gossip because there were things I didn't want to know. A name I didn't want to hear.

Then on the third Wednesday, two weeks after Penman first showed up in the office, he was back.

I heard the sound of laughter as I went in. Penman was sitting on the edge of the desk, long legs crossed in front of him and arms across his chest. He was listening like everyone else, a smile on his face.

A few feet from him, a man with his back to me was holding court. All I could see was a smart suit stretched across broad shoulders, neatly cut hair and arms going. He was tugging at his cuffs as he spoke, then arms open wide. Inviting. Including.

The guys were laughing, lapping up the routine. They liked this guy. Funny man. Stand-up comic, stand-up guy. Written all over their faces.

I didn't want him to turn round. Didn't want to see him. Didn't want him to see me.

I sidled round the side and joined the edge of the group. Stood next to Tobin, one of the new guys, who turned and took me in with a slow look, saying nothing.

The suit was still talking, winding up his spiel now. Saying how pleased he was to be an associate of Mr Penman, saying how things could go on as they were under Cammy, maybe be even better. Maybe more money to be made.

He threw in another couple of jokes and started glad-handing the troops. He shook hands with them, beginning at the other end of the line and working his way along. Chatting with some, listening to others as if they were saying the most interesting thing he had heard in his life, laughing at the funniest jokes he'd ever heard.

Eventually he got to me. Alec Kirkwood reached out for my hand and looked into my eyes, a smile playing on his lips. He didn't say anything, just nodded. Placed his other hand over the one that was holding mine. Felt like I was being blessed by the Pope or measured for size by the Devil.

Held my hand. Held my eye.

All sorts of thoughts. Most of them bad.

I had been on the edge of Kirky's world and that had suited me fine. Knowing people who knew people who knew him had been close enough. Now he was in my world and me in his. Glasgow's two scariest men, some would say. Face to face, hand in hand.

Except I wasn't scary. Not in my head. Not in my scary head. I was just me, doing what I had to do. He was a professional psychopath. He was in front of me and in my way. I was in front of him and in his sights.

Kirkwood had taken my hand with a knowing smile and released it the same way. All the time I wore my best dead look. Cold eyes, corpse expression. Nothing inside, nothing to read.

Still, he smiled and nodded as if I was an open book.

He moved on into the cab office and Tobin followed him. He too looked at me as if he knew something.

But they couldn't. OK, they could but if they did then why slow-play their hand? Why not string me up and electrocute my bollocks or whatever they did? Maybe Kirkwood was being cute, wanted to be sure, wanted to flush me out.

He knew where I was – right where he wanted me. I wouldn't, couldn't go anywhere. He was trying to unnerve me, break me.

Shit, if that was his game then I was playing right into his hands. Get a grip.

Kirkwood had been buying up private hire firms all over Glasgow, it was obvious he was the monopoly wolf. No surprise then that he bought out Cammy. Coincidence. And all he had done was smile at me. No more than shake my hand and look at me. Get a grip.

If Kirkwood knew then I would be dead. He was my boss now and I was on his radar as well as his payroll but that was it. Grip. Stay calm, give nothing away and it will all be OK. Being crazy wasn't helping.

Yet all the time, a voice called to me, telling an old joke that wasn't funny. *Being paranoid doesn't mean they're not out to get you.*

CHAPTER 36

The *Daily Record*. Saturday, 4 April 2010. Page 4.

Calls for Cutter cop to stand down
By Keith Imrie, Chief Reporter

There have been calls for the officer leading the hunt for The Cutter to stand down from the investigation. DS Rachel Narey is coming under severe pressure to excuse herself from the hunt for the five-time killer who is terrorising Glasgow. It is believed that DS Narey's bosses have already asked her to consider stepping aside for the good of the investigation and the force. A source close to the case said that officers are openly questioning her ability to lead The Cutter hunt and are asking why a detective sergeant continues to run an inquiry which is now the biggest in the history of Strathclyde Police.

'No one is saying that DS Narey is incompetent but they are wondering if she is in over her head. We are getting nowhere with this case and maybe it is time for more experience or someone with fresh ideas to be taking the lead.'

Demands for DS Narey to stand aside have also come from families of The Cutter's victims. Agnes Hutchison, widow of bookmaker Billy Hutchison, said yesterday that she would welcome a change at the top of the investigation.

'It is nearly a year since my husband was killed but the police are getting nowhere. It is over a month since anyone from Strathclyde Police even talked to me or my family. I don't think that's good enough.

'I have grandchildren asking me when the man who killed their papa will be put in jail. What am I supposed to tell them?

'I am sure that Ms Narey is doing her best but there must be plenty of officers in Strathclyde with a lot more experience that could take this on. It wouldn't be about her if someone else took over. Catching this killer is the only thing that matters.'

A spokeswoman for Strathclyde Chief Constable Andrew Chisholm would not comment on whether DS Narey's position was under threat but did say that the entire case was constantly under review.

'We do not comment on operational matters of this kind nor on the role of individual officers within an investigation. However, every case, particularly one of this importance, is continuously reviewed and monitored. We always have an open mind on the direction it will take and are completely aware of the level of expectation of the general public in catching this killer.'

DS Narey would not comment on the issue of her being replaced when contacted by the Record yesterday.

CHAPTER 37

Funny thing. The newspapers were going on and on about the whole of Glasgow being terrified of the man they were calling The Cutter. All except me.

Me? I was getting scared of a man called Alec Kirkwood.

I hadn't expected fear. Had thought that was an emotion that had gone along with others. I'd told myself that I was already dead inside, that he couldn't kill me. He'd hurt Jimmy Mac badly but that hadn't worried me too much. He'd done worse to Hutton than kill him and Hutton hadn't done anything. What would he do to me?

I was getting some hints. There's a pub in Royston called the Star Bar. I'd passed by it often enough but had never ventured inside. Probably just as well. It's the kind of pub, once you get out of the city centre, that Glasgow specializes in. The sort that if you didn't know any better, you'd probably take one look and think it had been closed down. The windows were boarded up even though they also had bars on them. Belt and braces Royston-style.

No bouncer on the door. None needed.

I'm told that inside the bar looks like any other dodgy dive in the city. Torn fake leather upholstery, sticky floors, mismatched chairs, a fruit machine and galleries stocked with 'house' spirits. It smelled rancid but if you drank there often enough then you didn't notice. Or if you drank enough.

Any face that didn't fit or wasn't recognized was guaranteed hard stares and would be well advised not to go to the toilets alone. The staff stood for no shite from anyone except friends of the management. They could do what they liked.

The Star had the worst karaoke in Glasgow. Women in their sixties singing Tammy Wynette and Madonna like drunken cats. Nobody having the heart or the balls to tell them how bad they were. Suggestion like that in the Star is reason enough for husbands or sons to want to stab you.

Want anything? Get it in the Star. Drugs, a dodgy telly, guns, a house burned down, a new fridge, someone's legs broken. But don't ask if you're not known. That will only get you a doing.

My info on the Star Bar came from Ally McFarland. He had managed to become a bit of a regular there through his shady mates and was happy to bump his gums about the place. Ally loved the idea that he was in with that crowd. He was someone who knew someone. He did favours for important people. He could get nods back from guys at the bar. He'd get chat.

Suited me of course that he did. Ally talked, I listened. I asked questions too, almost without him realizing it. With

a man like Kirkwood on your tail, it pays to know some of
what he knows. Forewarned, forearmed.

Ally had also told me before about the basement at the
Star Bar. Told me what happened sometimes when last
orders were called, when the place was cleared of drinkers
and the lights in the bar turned off. Ally had been there.

Sitting on Royston Road, it's a typical, big Victorian pub.
Purpose-built for the job with a basement that had been
big enough to take every barrel of ale that a drayman wanted
to drop off from his wagon.

These days it was kitted out for a different purpose alto-
gether. Once a month, groups of men gathered in the bowels
of the Star. Under the street, deep down where a century
of brick kept in the noise. And there was plenty of noise.
The Star Bar was owned by Alec Kirkwood and he used the
basement as home turf for dogfights.

Ally loved it. Not just that it was seriously dodgy and
that he had an invite. That would have been enough in
itself for Ally to get his rocks off but he actually loved the
fights. He had bloodlust. He'd tell me about what went on
in detail that made me squirm.

I know. Irony.

*It's amazing, man. You have to see it to believe it. These dugs
tear at each other like wild animals. Fierce as fuck. There's rules
though. Got to have rules. The rules go back to like the 1800s.
Amazing that, is it no?*

*It's like a code of honour. Marquess of Queensberry for dugs.
Kirky is a big man for the rules. It's like ceremonial, you know
whit I mean? And they take it pure serious. They train these dugs*

247

like naebody's business. Have them running on treadmills and everything.

Kirky's like aye, let the cops ask me about the treadmills. Nae problemo, he says, just tell them it's to keep the dugs fit. Says he'll tell them he got the idea aff Blue Peter. Quality. Train up the dugs' jaws and all. They have them chewing on tyres and wooden sticks to make them stronger. Crazy, man.

They look after the dugs proper. They sometimes get some wido vet who they'll bung to come in and treat them after the fights but most of the time they do it themselves. Have proper kits with staples and drips and all kinds of stuff though. They look after them dugs. People say it's cruel but the Grand National is much crueller on horses if you ask me. The pit's about twelve feet by twelve and it's fenced aff with wooden boards about two and a half feet high. There's carpet on the floor, General George's finest offcut, so that the dugs can get a good grip. It's like the fuckin' Coliseum, man.

They weigh them before the kick-aff. Dugs have got to be more or less the same weight. Stands to reason. They agree on a top weight beforehand and if either dug is over that then he's bombed oot.

They wash them down before the fight too. Stick a hose on them and give them a right soaking. That's because some smart bastards have been known to put poison onto their ain dug's coat so that when the other dug sinks its teeth in it would get a right dose of it. Soon be half asleep and there for the taking. Try anything some of them.

The only folk in the ring are the owners and the ref. Everyone else is better off well oot of it anyhow. Time the dugs get into it then no one can go near them. These dugs are mental. Simple as that. They will tear into anything once they get a head of steam up. Herd of elephants? Nae bother. Bring it on.

It's a proper sport, man. A good fight is a thing of beauty. Up at Kirky's place the other night, should have seen it. A classic, a proper classic. There were these two cracking dugs. Both American pit bulls. Fucking monsters, the pair of them. Reaper is Big Kirky's dug and he was up against this beast called Bandido belonging to Charlie Dunn fae Edinburgh.

Plenty of money on the pair of them. There wis a shade more on Bandido though seeing as he was a bona fide champion. That means he has won three fights like. If he beat Reaper then he needed just wan mair win to be a grand champion and there's no many of those aboot.

Reaper had won two fights himself though and he's as game as fuck. Kirky fancied his chances and backed it up with big bucks.

Fair crowd down in the basement of the Star. Maybe a couple of dozen folk. No just anybody gets in. Have to be in to get in, know what I mean? Guys have been known to get a right doing if they turn up without a dug or a story that doesnae hold up.

It was Reaper against Bandido but everyone knew fine it was Kirky against Charlie Dunn. You know? Serious stuff.

These dugs were up for it. Couldnae wait to get going. Ref gives the signal and they let them go. Man but they just explode oot of the corner. Like two bullets coming oot of guns. Spit, hair, blood and teeth everywhere. The room's like a nuthoose. Every man on his feet, roaring his heid aff, shouting on his dug.

The Bandido thing gets a hud of the Reaper's leg early doors and looks like it is gonna tear it aff. Right sair yin Reaper's got but it keeps going back for more because it loves big Kirky. And Kirky loves that dug.

Then Reaper gets a grip under Bandido's throat, rips a chunk oot and there is blood dripping everywhere. Rolls on him and breaks one of his front legs then another. There is plenty of blood coming from Reaper an all but he has the upper hand. You can see Charlie Dunn thinking about pulling his dug out. He doesn't though. Must know it has no chance now but he lets it fight on. It's big Kirky he's up against and you just know he'd rather let the dug die than be seen to give in.

End up, Reaper locks his jaws on this big bleeding hole in Bandido's chest and rips it open. Had to see it.

Dunn's dug is dragged back to his corner. Useless by this time, but this Bandido right, he had to have one last look across the pit at Reaper. Man, its eyes were all glazed over but it still needed to stare down Kirky's dug. It was still looking at Reaper when Charlie Dunn put a bullet through its brain. Poor dug. Shows the bastards love those beasts though. Enough to put them out of their misery.

Some night though, man. Some fight. Classic.

It was about six weeks after the fight between Bandido and Reaper when Ally got word to go to the Star Bar after hours. The call came with just half an hour's warning but that was hardly unusual. Fights can be organized months in advance but everything's got to be kept hush until the last minute. Davie Stewart had left a message on Ally's mobile saying that Reaper was going for win number four. Ally was beside himself at the thought. Reaper would be just one win away from being a grand champion. Magic.

He was let in to the Star by some shady on the door. He got a nod and headed for the basement.

Down the stairs and there was Kirky. No one else. Just

Kirky. Kirky standing with a foot resting on Reaper's cage. Just Kirky and Reaper.

Ally had been asking Kirky questions. Lots of them. He asked them because I had pushed him to do it. Persuaded him. Conned him into doing it.

He had asked Kirkwood and his boys about The Cutter and if they had any idea who he was. He probed them for anything they might have known.

Ally wasn't the sharpest tool. I'd known that. It was part of how I was able to get him to think I was so into all the newspaper stuff about The Cutter. Oh and I was buttering him up big style when he came back with answers. I was well impressed with his inside knowledge. I lapped up his stories. Puffed him up and made him keen to come back with more.

And every time I got him to press Kirky and his boys for more info on what they knew about The Cutter and how close they were getting to catching him, I pushed him a step closer to his death. Ally asked too much and didn't do it with the guile it needed. Kirky saw it for what it was and he wasn't a happy man. He had brought Ally to his lair and was about to show him the finer arts of Reaper's fighting skills. First hand.

I imagined Ally joking at first. Thinking he was early for a change. Thinking maybe he'd got a special invite. He'd soon have realized he hadn't. The look on Kirky's face would have told him that. Kirky would most probably have let Ally babble on. Let him blurt out his guilt. Except of course, Ally had no guilt to spew. He had nothing to tell that would save him.

Kirky would have stamped on the roof of Reaper's cage, both to attract Ally's attention and to rouse and irritate the dog. Ally wasn't so daft that he wouldn't have got that message. He'd have been sure what Kirky was threatening. But he'd still have been incapable of telling Kirky that he was the one that killed Spud Tierney and the others. And that was the only thing Kirkwood wanted to hear.

Kirky might have opened that cage but kept a grip on Reaper's collar. Last chance Ally.

No chance at all.

End up, Kirky would have seen that he had no choice. He'd have let go the dog and it would have been on Ally in a split second. Four stones of fighting machine. Amazingly strong and agile. Reaper would have flown at Ally, knocking him off his feet and going for the throat. Jaws like a vice. Gripping Ally and mauling at his neck. It would have been hungry to please its master.

That dug kept going back for more because it loves big Kirky. And Kirky loves that dug.

Maybe Kirky had only meant to send out another warning, maybe he had hoped Ally would eventually have talked about why he had asked so many questions, maybe he just didn't give a fuck.

Maybe Reaper was just more than either of them could cope with once he got a hold. You can't break a pit bull's grip. Hit it over the head with a baseball bat and still you can't shake it.

Either way, Ally was never seen again. Word got out of course, no point in doing it otherwise. Win number four for Reaper. A grand champion. Not one bit of Ally McFarland was found. Probably never would be.

I had killed him. Every bit as much as I'd killed Carr, old Billy Hutchison, Tierney and Sinclair. And Wallace Ogilvie.

I had never regretted any of them before. Even in the darkest moments when I looked at myself in the mirror. Even when the demons came calling. I'd done what I had to do for her. This was different though. Ally McFarland was guilty of nothing more than being a daft boy. If it wasn't for me he'd still be alive.

I sat quiet in front of the television, taking nothing in. All I could hear from the screen was Ally McFarland's voice. I saw that big black Labrador cross outside our house and all I could think of was Reaper with its jaws locked round Ally's throat.

Made me think and that wasn't something I was comfortable with. Made me think about the others, made me look at things. For the first time in nearly seven years I had feelings other than hurt.

Carr. Hutchison. Tierney. Sinclair.

Guilt. Remorse. Penitence. Regret. Shame. Only shades of each but it was there.

All except Wallace Ogilvie, of course.

But there was something else. Fear.

It occurred to me that there was just one thing that Ally could have told Kirky. He could have told him who had got him to ask all the questions. He could have given up my name. But I was fairly sure he hadn't done that.

After all, I was still breathing.

Still, maybe it suited Kirkwood to wait. To let me wonder. To let me pish my pants. To give him time to conjure up something worse than death for me.

Maybe.

CHAPTER 38

The *Herald*. Tuesday, 28 April 2010. Page 3.
By Gregg Morrison

Detective Sergeant Rachel Narey, the officer who has been leading the hunt for the Glasgow serial killer, has been replaced as the principal officer on the investigation. Strathclyde Police have denied that DS Narey has been removed from the case and have maintained that the officer with overall responsibility for the case was, and remains, Detective Inspector Lewis Robertson.

However, they have confirmed that DI Frank Lewington of Nottinghamshire Police has been seconded to the investigation and will assume much of the day-to-day responsibility for the inquiry.

He will be joined by five other officers from Nottingham but all will be answerable to DCI Robertson and beyond that to Strathclyde Chief Constable Andrew Chisholm.

A force spokeswoman said that DS Narey will still be a senior member of the investigation team but that the emphasis of her role has shifted and that she will no longer be tied down by the everyday routines of the inquiry. DS Narey was initially the second officer in charge of the so-called Cutter murders but was given lead responsibility after being contacted directly by the killer. It was felt she had established dialogue with him and that it would prove beneficial if she was in charge of the case.

A senior source at Strathclyde Police says that it is felt that dialogue has now run its course and is no longer an asset in trying to track the murderer. DI Lewington, in a statement released through Strathclyde Police, said that he was determined to bring a fresh approach to the case and was convinced that the murderer would be caught.

'I am grateful for the chance to be involved in this investigation and to build upon the excellent work already carried out by my colleagues in Strathclyde. I and the other officers from Nottinghamshire will hopefully bring a fresh set of eyes to the investigation of these horrendous killings. DCI Robertson and DS Narey and their team have worked long and hard to catch the killer and we will do everything we can to take the inquiry on from here.

'We will be relying heavily on local knowledge but we will also bring a fresh approach and fresh ideas to bear. The people of Glasgow can rest assured that no stone will be left unturned to catch the person responsible.'

CHAPTER 39

So sweet Rachel was off the case. Gone. The men in suits had bowed to their own bad press and had booted her. She would no longer be tied down by the everyday routines of the inquiry. The emphasis of her role had shifted.

A bit of me was relieved. Couldn't deny that. Narey wasn't the same as the rest of them. Just as I wasn't the same as the psycho that they thought I was. The rest of them saw bodies piling up and newspaper headlines and swallowed every word that I had fed them. They were robots. Almost too easy to toy with. She seemed to be the only one that doubted what everyone else saw to be true.

They all looked for the one they dubbed The Cutter. She left room for other possibilities. Of course she hadn't established a dialogue with me. I had established it with her. I wrote to her. I posted to her. I brought her to the fore of their investigation. I made her. I put her in charge.

They had no right to remove her. My choice. I was in charge here. It was me who was in control. And she was smarter than them. Maybe too smart. Maybe it was better without her. But it was my choice that she was in charge of the investigation, not theirs. They had dismissed her because they were under pressure. MPs, media, the public. Journalists and television stations from all over the world were coming to Glasgow to write and talk about their so-called serial killer. And every word that was written made them sweat. Every word that was spoken made them look bad. Couldn't be their fault. Oh no. Had to be someone else. Call for a scapegoat. Call for Rachel.

They didn't know they were doing me a favour. They were taking away the one threat, other than Alec Kirkwood, that didn't buy into everything that I put before them. It made me laugh. Made me angry.

I had thrown the paper across the room when I read about her being ditched. About her being replaced as the principal officer on the investigation. She was a threat to me but that was my choice to run that risk. I think I had known from the first time I saw her on the TV news that she was a bit different. I certainly knew the day she first came to the house to interview me. Someone had to come, I'd known that. Matter of procedure. Had to question me, had to consider even in the face of all the other evidence that the killings weren't linked, that they weren't personal. That had to be done.

But it would be cursory, I'd been confident of that. No sane person could think that one grudge connected to only one victim of a four-time serial killer was the motive for them all. Yet Rachel had been persistent. She had needled me. I'd risen to it. Just a bit but I had risen to it. Maybe that was what got her interested, maybe she was just thorough, maybe she was just a genius or a complete fucking bitch. Maybe she really did stick to those principles of policing that said random killings don't happen very often and that they should always look close to home before thinking a murder might have been committed by a stranger.

Whatever, I knew she had not ruled out the chance that it was me or that I had something to do with it, unlikely as it seemed. She was a risk that I was happy to run with.

It was felt she had established dialogue with the killer and that it would prove beneficial if she was in charge of the case. Almost right. I was in charge. Not her. The dialogue, my dialogue, was beneficial to me. She would have known nothing unless I chose to reveal it.

Strathclyde Police said they now felt that dialogue had now run its course and was no longer an asset in trying to track the murderer. No shit, Sherlocks. I would decide when the dialogue had run its course. I would decide when it would stop. The murderer would not be tracked down.

I could restart dialogue with Rachel any time I wanted. As long as it was still an asset. They couldn't tell me who to talk to at Strathclyde. Not their decision.

I had no idea who this jumped-up English bastard Lewington was. Lewington of Nottingham and his five other Nottingham cops could get to fuck. I would deal with who I wanted. The Englishman would bring a fresh approach he said. Convinced the murderer would be caught. Bollocks. They had taken over because the men in suits had said so. Brought in to show the Jocks how it was done.

He said he would build upon the excellent work already carried out by his colleagues in Strathclyde. Probably laughing at them. Laughing at Rachel. Well, he could get to fuck. Robertson and Narey have worked long and hard to catch the killer, he said. Patronizing cunt. He means they tried but weren't up to the job. You think you are up to it, Lewington? You won't catch me. Guaranteed. Will take a header off the Science Tower before that happens.

Says he will rely heavily on local knowledge. Thinks the Glesga plods will do the dogsbody work for him and he will take the credit. Wise up. I'll decide what happens from here on in. Just like I have up to now.

I'd thrown that paper across the room and had sworn out loud. Raged at their nerve. I wasn't dealing with this Lewington, he was getting nothing from me. It was Rachel or no one. I'd kill who I fucking wanted, post to who I wanted to fucking post to. This was my plan, my rules.

But maybe this was what they wanted. Was that their game? Were they messing with me, trying to throw me off balance? Were the cheeky bastards trying to fuck with my head?

Think, think. I was posting to Narey. They said she had established a dialogue with me. Knew it was me that had started that dialogue. They knew that. They were trying to take that away from me. Break that connection so that I couldn't get what I wanted. They were cutting me off from her so that I would make a mistake. The bastards.

They thought they were smarter than me. Thought they could control my mind.

I'd seen through them. Saw their little game. They'd need to be a lot cleverer than that. I wasn't rising to it, not angry any more, I was in control. I picked the paper up and sorted the pages. Placed it back on the table, smoothed it down. In control. Patted the paper so it looked untouched.

But what if they weren't clever at all? What if they weren't trying mind games and had simply kicked Narey into touch?

Head bursting with this. Needed to think straight. Concentrate. Sort it.

Bastards. Messing with me. My plan. My rules.

Stick to the plan. Whatever their game was I would stick to the plan. They wanted me to switch course and make a mistake but I'd do what I intended to do. When I wanted. Wouldn't be rushed. Wouldn't be panicked.

I knew my next move and I'd make it when I was ready. I'd decide. They'd made me think but they couldn't make me change course. Too long in the planning, not for changing for anything. I resented them getting rid of Rachel Narey, for whatever reason they'd done it. But I wasn't getting angry, not for long anyway, I was getting even.

CHAPTER 40

I got on a bus. The number 40 from Maryhill into town.

Three of us at the bus stop. Me, a drunk and a woman doing a fair impression of Maw Broon. They were safe. Whoever it was, it wouldn't be them.

The drunk was making a fair bid to be elected, right enough. He was doing the lurching tap dance and mumbling to himself. A look in his direction brought a glare, that special Glasgow glare that happens when a guy has drunk enough to think he is six inches taller, two stone heavier and a whole lot harder than he actually is.

I let it go. Other fish to fry.

When I wouldn't play the game, he tried Maw Broon instead but she had seen plenty of his kind and didn't bat an eye.

'Who do you think you are looking at?' she demanded.

'Eh?'

'I said who do you think you are looking at? Don't fucking look at me like that. Away and fuck off.'

'Aw, c'mon missus. Nae need for that.'

263

'Don't missus me, ya wee arsehole. Any ay your shite and ah'll shout ma man doon here to sort you oot.'

It wouldn't need her man to come down and sort him out. In a square go, my money was on Maw. Straight knockout in the first round, no problem.

The drunk was drunk enough not to have worked that out though.

'For fuck's sake. Get him doon here then,' he came back. 'Ah'll tell him how sorry ah ah'm for him, being married tae you and that.'

Mrs Broon breathed in an indignant harrumph and I was sure she was just about to deck him when the number 40 swung round the corner and pulled up in front of us.

The drunk threw her a lopsided smile and stood aside, letting her on first with an exaggerated bow and a low sweep of his arm.

She stormed past without looking at him and took up residence halfway up the bus, her handbag pulled tight to her formidable bosom.

The drunk pulled himself into the first empty seat and let his head smack off the window as it lurched off, feeling no pain.

I sat four rows behind Mrs Broon and had a quiet look around. There were maybe twenty people on board the 40. Glasgow in miniature that bus. All human life was there. White and Asian. Young and old. Shoppers and office workers. Crooks and cops. Prods, Papes, Poles and Pakis. Enough racist opportunity for everyone.

Wee boys in bad suits heading for call centres. Neds in

tracksuits heading for street corners. Guys heading for the bookies and the offie.

A couple of kids were pushing and shoving at each other. The first one slapping the second round the head, the second calling him a fud and the pair of them giggling. The wee bastards should have been at school.

A mother with two kids and two big bags of shopping. The five of them squeezed into two seats, her on the outside and them and the messages trapped between her and the window. Weans wriggling like eels, shopping bags bouncing. Trapped but trying to escape.

Another mother. This one no more than mid-twenties and with three kids. Every person on that bus soon knew their names. Chloe. Chantelle. Candice. Chantelle in particular was a real charmer, swinging on the post at the front of the bus, drawing daggers from the driver and shouts from her mother.

Fuck. This was getting harder. So much harder. Had been from the moment that Wallace Ogilvie died.

There was a hard case in a torn leather jacket. His face torn too, an old knife wound scarring him from ear to lip. He was staring at the back page of the *Daily Record* and shaking his head. The front page had the latest on The Cutter but all he was interested in was who Celtic were supposed to be signing.

Two rows behind him was a junkie, no more than seventeen and off her face. Her scrawny arms tugging at her hair, head twitching. She was bouncing in her seat, bouncing more than the two kids. Energy was bursting out of her. Life leaking out. She must have been good-looking once.

Two guys in white overalls, painters maybe. One of them sleeping on the other's shoulder. His mate looking out the window at every bit of passing skirt. Knocking on the glass at a couple of them. Winking. Waving with the free arm, the one that wasn't squashed in by his pal.

Glasgow in miniature. Didn't look much like a city living in fear, a city living in the shadow of The Cutter. Though it should have done. This bus more than anywhere else. I had already decided it would be the first person who got off at the Viking on Maryhill Road. No particular reason.

The mother had already got off two stops earlier, pulled and pushed down the stairs off the bus by the weans and the shopping. I was glad to see them go. The kids who were plugging the school were still on but I was sure they were headed all the way into the town. Hoped they were. Had to be.

Approaching the Viking. Any time now. I could feel the tension in me. Could feel my heart rate pick up. Any one of them. Anyone.

The hard case in the leather jacket moved in his seat and my eyes turned to him. He'd do. But he was just turning the inside sports pages, settling himself again. Wasn't him.

One of the two boys stood up and my heart dropped a foot. My breathing stopped. He skelped his pal on the back of the head, got his own back and sat down. Wasn't him.

My breathing had just started again when a woman

brushed past me. She was getting off at the next stop. All I could see was her back. She was as wide as she was tall, just squeezing between the seats. Short and round, thick legs perched on sensible black shoes. A dark raincoat and a scarf. All topped off with a bowl of reddish hair.

She was getting off at the next stop. She was the one.

The woman stood at the front waiting for the bus to come to a halt and copped some chat from the drunk that had already chanced his luck with Maw Broon. I couldn't hear what he said or what she replied but there was no doubt who had won. The roly-poly snapped something at him and he turned to the window, wrapping his arms round his ears and his head in exaggerated protection. Just wasn't his day. Slayed by two of Glasgow's finest within twenty minutes.

I waited until the bus had stopped before getting up from my seat and making for the exit. By that time a couple of people were trying to get on and I earned a bit of a glare from the driver. It was worth it though, the roly-poly was off and waddling down the street without ever catching sight of me.

As soon as she got off the bus, she'd reached into her handbag and took something out. Whatever it was, she moved it from hand to hand and then seemed to put it back in the bag. She went just a few yards then repeated the exercise.

Maybe ten yards further, just as she'd passed the Viking itself and crossed the road, she was back into the bag again. She took out whatever it was and this time huddled over

it for a few moments before walking on. She'd lit a cigarette.

I was still on the other side of the road, watching her
turn right and head back in the direction we'd come.
Watched her charge purposefully ahead, fat but fast, rolling
like a battlecruiser in stormy seas.

Then suddenly she took a sharp pavement left and turned
into the Tesco on Maryhill Road. I followed, grabbing a
basket for cover. Cameras saw me enter the store but it
wouldn't matter. I was one among hundreds. Hundreds
today and thousands this week.

I walked up and down the aisles but couldn't see her
anywhere. Fruit and veg, toiletries, dog food, tinned foods,
all the way to the butchers and bakers without sight of the
roly-poly. I started to walk quicker, doubling back, scanning the heads of all the shoppers.

Nothing.

Fully five minutes, up and down, back and forth, getting desperate, had to find her. Surely she couldn't have
gone in and out so quickly. Had to still be there. Panicking
a bit.

Then I saw her. Not in any of the aisles but sitting behind
a till. Ten items or less. The roly-poly had been on her way
to work at Tesco.

I picked up enough things to make it look like I had
actually been shopping then joined a queue already three
deep at her till. There were shorter queues but not so many
that it would have looked odd that I chose this one. Just
like a once a month shopper who didn't know any better.

Women were probably shaking their heads at me and smiling patronizingly.

She looked up and saw me standing there, another imped-iment to an easy day. She exhaled noisily and shook her head at my stupidity. Keep shaking it, I thought. She was maybe fifty-five although I had the feeling she wasn't as old as she looked. She'd made herself old. She'd smoked her face old and scrunched it up into a meaner, harsher version than her God had intended. If she looked fifty-five then she was forty-five tops. Her podgy face was framed by that bowl of red hair and set off by a pair of practical specs and a permanent scowl.

You wouldn't want to take a burst pay packet home to this one.

Her name badge said she was called Fiona. Then the young girl on the next till called her Mrs Raedale. Fiona Raedale. Welcome to my world.

She was unpleasantly plump and dressed older than she looked. Which meant she dressed at least ten years older than she was. Fiona Raedale was someone in an eternal bad mood. She didn't like people. Maybe she thought people didn't like her.

The woman being served had a wee girl with her, maybe three or four years old. She was hanging near the till and obviously wanted to help. She was reaching for the food as it came off the conveyor belt and a couple of times she made a grab for it before Mrs Frosty Drawers had the chance to pass it across the machine that reads the bar code.

If looks could kill. Raedale snatched a packet of HobNobs

out of the wee girl's hand and treated her mother to a glare that could fry eggs. The woman looked back at the queue with raised eyebrows and I shrugged in some sort of sympathy.

They moved on and it was soon my turn. Raedale didn't look up but surveyed the contents of my basket with a cold glower. She didn't take anything out but just looked at it, her small eyes flitting across the milk, bread, and processed foods that I had picked up. She was counting them. She was actually fucking counting them, the bitch.

Raedale must have recounted the stuff in my basket because I saw her eyes go over them again. By this time I had counted them myself and knew there were ten items. She seemed disappointed to find I wasn't attempting an illegal till transaction.

She raised her eyes slowly and they settled on mine. Lucky, she was saying, lucky for you. Her fat, painted lip turned down at one corner in a barely-hidden sneer.

She didn't look at me again. Picked up the ten items, one at a time, scanned them and dropped them onto the belt.

Roly-poly Fiona Raedale. Fat fucking bitch.

A voice raged inside my head. I am the scariest man in all of fucking Glasgow. Everyone in this city is living in fear of me and you sit there and fucking sneer at me. You fat fucking bitch. Bitch. Count my fucking shopping? You fat fucking bitch.

I could tear your fucking head off right now. I could strangle you with my bare hands. I could take those scissors that are at the side of your till and rip a hole in your throat.

I didn't do that of course. I smiled quietly, put the items in a carrier bag, paid in cash and left.

CHAPTER 41

Raedale was a forty-a-day woman trying not to be.

I watched her. To Tesco, from Tesco, in Tesco. To the multi where she lived in Gilshochill in Summerston. To her mother's house in Shiskine Drive. To regular Friday nights out with girls from work. To the one night a week with her mother to County Bingo across the road from her work.

Time and again I saw her take out cigarettes and thrust them back into the packet without smoking them. She needed to touch them, be reassured that they were there. The roly-poly bitch would play with the packet, turning it over and over in her hands, moving it from one to the other, slipping it back into her pocket then out again. She was desperate to smoke and desperate not to.

She had more reason than most to quit the cancer sticks. She was asthmatic. The first couple of times I saw her pull the inhaler from her bag and draw deep on it I thought it was one of those nicotine inhalators that people use when they are trying to give up. Then I saw her heaving air back into her heavy lungs and knew what it was. Smoking and asthma. Smart combination, fatty.

Fiona Raedale was trying to give up. It struck me that I could help her give up for good.

I watched her. Carrying staff-discounted bags of shopping to her mother's. Scowling at people from her till to the bus stop to the bingo. Her life was limited and so were my opportunities.

There were times I wished I hadn't painted myself into a corner with the whole finger thing. It made life – and death – so much more difficult.

Killing Fiona Raedale, even with the method I had in mind, was not difficult. Strange to say maybe but killing her was easy.

Killing her and cutting off her little finger was a bit more difficult. Killing her, cutting off her little finger and getting away without anyone knowing anything about it was much, much more difficult.

My own fault of course.

The plan had required it. Demanded it. But Jesus Christ it made things complicated. I knew how to murder her. I knew a way that could make the front page of newspapers and yet I could be on the other side of Glasgow when it happened. She would die a horrible, shocking death and I could have any alibi I wanted in the unlikely event anyone asked me for it.

Oh I was clever as fuck. I could kill this woman almost by remote control.

I couldn't deny that the cleverness of that made me feel

a right smart arse. And yet I was way too clever and therefore nowhere near clever enough.

Because I had to be there. I had to be with her so that I could cut off that finger and dispatch it safely to Rachel Narey. Shit, shit, shit.

It was further complicated by the fact that I knew I had settled on the way to kill her and I couldn't be shifted from the thought. It suited her and it suited my purpose but it didn't make things any less difficult.

Once the method came to mind it stayed there. Lodged right at the front. I did consider other ways but I knew, right from the moment the thought popped into my head, I just knew. OK, maybe it was the tail wagging the dog but that was the way it had to be. I had spent long weeks playing with the plan in my head. Seeing avenues and every time coming up with a dead end. They were dead ends for Fiona Raedale that wouldn't work for me.

There was a hole in every plan, too many loose ends, too much risk. I had to be somewhere I could cut the finger off, somewhere without people around, somewhere without risk. But the places without risk were places without opportunity.

I could maybe get into her flat somehow but then maybe I would be seen and I'd definitely leave DNA. I could arrange it so she died while she sat at her ten items or less till but then couldn't get near her. I could chat her up, drop it into her drink but the finger, the bloody finger.

I had this vague thought of getting it into the asthma inhaler I had seen her use. That was clever and I liked it.

Getting it in there was doable, difficult but doable. But then how did I control when she used the inhaler? How did I control the situation so that I knew when she had used it? How did I make sure that I could then get to her, unseen or unnoticed and cut her fucking finger off and get away?

Same thought with the nicotine substitute I had seen her suck on. The stuff was in there, all I had to do was get more of it in there and she would be dead in no time. I could do that. I just couldn't clip her finger.

I thought about killing her and letting them think it was some awful but natural death. Then later, when her mother had been called and identified the body and no one had any reason to think otherwise, get access to Fiona Raedale's fat deceased person and snip the finger. Interesting but hospitals have cameras, lots of them, so hospital morgues will have cameras. It was a non-starter.

Then finally I toyed with the notion of not cutting off the finger. Of finding some other way of letting Rachel know. That went against every element of the plan except one. The part where I didn't get caught.

It was my plan though, no one else's. I could change it to suit me. I was in charge. I could do that. I would do that.

In fact I liked it. It would work. Ha. Rachel's face and fury came to mind and I laughed out loud. In the end I'd come to the conclusion that I was worrying too much. There was no way it wasn't going to be risky. The risk had to be embraced not feared.

I settled on it. The only question was where and when.

Work and weekly bingo were the only constants in Raedale's life but neither worked for me. Both were far too public and with far too many people. It would need to be one of the Friday nights out with the Tesco girls and they happened maybe three weeks out of four, depending, I guessed, on shift patterns.

On the first Friday after I had established a plan of action and readied myself, a bunch of them headed into town after work and went into Bar Budda on Sauchiehall Street. It was time.

I went into the Wetherspoons across the road, parked myself on a stool at a table by the window. I waited an hour with a pint in my hand and an eye on Budda. I gave them time to settle in and get a few drinks down their necks, gave it time for the place to fill up. If they left I'd see them, if they didn't I'd find them.

It wasn't hard to imagine fat Fiona sitting there moaning about the music, the heat, young people today and the price of drink, bitching about colleagues who weren't there and, as soon as their backs were turned, those who were. She'd have a face on her like a plate of mortal sins and her mouth pursed tighter than a midgie's chuff. She must have made great company.

I nursed my pint of shandy for the full hour I had promised myself, my eyes rarely straying from the door of Budda for more than a few seconds, whether looking at it directly or in the reflection of the window's neon glare facing towards Holland Street. Many more went in but neither Raedale or any of the shop girls left. She was there, my window of opportunity lying at her feet or clutched to her fearsome bosom.

The hour slipped past and I drained the last of the beer before leaving, crossing the road and going into Budda. The place was pleasingly mobbed and it took me a minute to see the Tesco crew crammed round a long table in the wooden pagoda-type effect to the back right.

Dark, busy, perfect.

I ordered another pint of shandy and took up a spot as near to them as I could without being openly in their view.

They were a typical works night out crowd. Loud, laughing, drunk and happy with one notable exception. Fat, frosty Fiona had a look of disdain that would have turned milk. I was sure she was only there so that the rest of them wouldn't be talking about her. It certainly couldn't have been because she wanted to enjoy herself.

Out of the corner of my eye I caught her waving her white handbag at them as a signal of some intent. She evidently wanted to go to the toilet.

I watched with interest as she began to squeeze her way out of the padded grey and purple seats, ungracefully extricating herself from the wedge that had been formed between a short blonde girl on one side and a spotty student-type on the other. They both got a glare, as if the lack of room was their fault and not her excess lard. As she made the last unsteady movement between seat and table, she put her half-open handbag on the tabletop for balance. Jackpot, I thought to myself. Penalty kick. Open goal.

Fiona Raedale was one podgy step out of the seat and towards the bar area when I staggered into her, knocking the bag from her hand and sending her spinning back onto the lap of the startled female student. I apologized, slurring it as best I could, hearing muffled giggles from the supermarket girls as Raedale fumed.

I knelt to the floor, apologizing over and over, and picked up the items that had spilled out of fat Fiona's handbag, stuffing them back in as quickly as I could. She grabbed the bag from me, embarrassment fuelling her naturally crabbit nature even further. Idiot, she rasped, checking that her purse was still where it should be. Righteous indignation masqueraded as steam coming out of her ears as she pushed past me and stormed towards the toilets.

I stood with my back to the Tesco crowd and shrugged apologetically to her retreating form before slouching out of the pub and back onto Sauchiehall Street.

That was it. Job done. All that was left to do was walk away.

And wait. And wonder.

I knew it would happen – except in the unlikely event that she noticed I had swapped her asthma inhaler for a seemingly identical one. It was just the where and the when that I couldn't be sure of.

I walked to the first corner and took a left up Dalhousie Street, turned right onto Hill Street and made for the side of the road that was in shadow. I kept going until I came to the corner of Rose Street and there, in the twenty yards of relative safety that afforded me, I changed.

I turned my jacket inside out, switching it from black to green. I took off the baseball cap that had been low on my head since I entered Budda. I tore off the dark wig that lurked beneath it. I straightened up to my natural height, a few inches taller than the way I'd been carrying myself.

It wasn't much maybe but I was confident it would be enough. The simple fact was that I was smarter than the people who may have seen me. The risk of knocking over that bag was one that had to be taken but I had known I needed extra insurance. If anyone had seen the guy that banged into Fiona Raedale and picked that bag back up, if anyone remembered him and connected him to what happened later then they would have remembered a shorter, dark-haired guy with several days of growth on his chin. Not me.

The wait and the wonder. The where and the when.

I was hoping it didn't happen in the pub although there was no doubt that there was a danger of that. The hassle and humiliation of being knocked over might have been enough to make her use the inhaler. It wouldn't be the end of the world if it happened there. Well, not mine anyway – it would definitely be the end of hers. The mass audience it would undoubtedly create would be a bonus, a spectacle like that would guarantee front-page news, but it would make it far too close to my being there. No, later would be better.

I walked on in the shadows, my mind full of the possibilities, when I heard the car racing towards me. It was the slamming of the brakes that alerted me more than the speed but it didn't matter either way. I had no time to react, no chance to run. Three men were out of the car in a flash, doors left open, engine still running.

They were on me before I could move. A dark shape came at me hard from the left and I was falling to the pavement. There was a moment of sweet calm, a vague feeling of feet against me then a long nothingness. Sleep came fast.

CHAPTER 42

When I came round I was unable to move or see. Sneaking consciousness without light is a strange experience.

I slowly became aware that my hands and legs were both tied. The little movement that I could make with my fingers confirmed I was lashed to a chair. My head was covered, not just my eyes. A hood, maybe a pillowcase.

I listened.

Nothing. No voices, no breathing, no movement. Then, from further away, maybe through a wall, I heard raised voices but could make nothing out.

Long, long periods of silence broken only by the occasional distant shout of complaint.

I was calm. Cold. Waiting for what had to come.

This wasn't part of the plan. Far from it. I'd deal with it though. So be it. Bring it on.

I slept on and off.

Much as I fought it, tiredness and even boredom washed over the adrenalin and I slipped away for a while. I woke now and again to hear offstage cries, reality and dreams mashing away time, snoozing through a nightmare that was almost certainly of my own making.

When a door slammed and people walked into the room, snapping me awake, I had no way of knowing how long I had sat tied to that chair but the aches in my bones and the lack of feeling in my fingers and limbs told me that it was long enough. I could see no light through whatever was tied over my head so it could have been night or day.

I stayed silent as I was grabbed then hauled, me and my chair pulled across the floor for some distance, one door then another closing behind us. I rocked to a halt, rough hands on my shoulders settling me. I breathed and waited again.

There were other people in that room. Not the ones who'd brought me there. Others almost certainly tied up like me. There was a raucous hubbub of voices, piping up angry, pleading and insistent. Something hard smacked against something else hard and the room fell silent.

'Nobody speaks. Not one word.'

Immediately a voice jumped up somewhere to my left.

'Fuck you!'

There was a swish of air, a crack and a roar of pain. After that no one spoke. Not one word.

We sat in silence for a few minutes. It probably wasn't as long as it seemed but someone was letting us stew, letting the anticipation grow.

Then out of the hush came the sound of feet across the wooden floor, echoing round what appeared to be a big, empty space. Three short steps and the person stopped. A few seconds later there was a gasp. The gasp was followed by the sound of a blow then more silence.

The feet moved again, three steps and stop. No gasp this time, a lesson learned. It happened another twice. Three steps and a wait.

The steps were getting closer, very close. He was on the move again, three steps and stop. Echo echo echo. He stopped right in front of me.

I had counted four seconds when the hood around my head was loosened and pulled off. I blinked at the light and saw Alec Kirkwood standing in front me, his eyes boring into mine. I made sure my face registered confusion more than shock, trying to give off the fear of an innocent man.

Of course it was Kirkwood. It could only have been one of two people and although Strathclyde polis could be capable of the odd bit of unlicensed heavy-handedness, this didn't really seem Narey's style. It had to be Kirkwood. No brainer. Had to be.

I looked left and right, seeing seven other bodies tied to chairs as I was, each with a hood over their head, each hood with a rope looped round them. Whoever we were, we weren't going to get to know the others. I was number five of seven ducks in a row. One of the ducks had a pool of piss at his feet. I caught a glance of a high window. Daylight.

Kirkwood put the hood back over my head, his eyes never leaving mine as the darkness closed over me again. He walked on, three short steps to the guy next to me. A wait then on to number six.

I wasn't scared. Maybe I would have been if it was only

285

me that had been hauled in there but the other hoods meant Kirkwood was on a fishing trip. A voice in my head told me that you can't go fishing for ducks, it was fishing or it was ducks, it couldn't be both. I told the voice to shut the fuck up.

If it was just me that was in there then I'd have been thinking that Ally McFarland had named me. I'd have been sure I was a dead man. Maybe I still wouldn't have been scared. Kirky couldn't kill a dead man, just torture him a bit. I could take that. Maybe I even deserved it.

Not scared, not for fear of what he could do to me anyway. Fear of being stopped, fear of not being able to finish what I'd started. Started so I'll finish. No passes.

Lots of footsteps now, three maybe four people on the move. They were heading away from me, back down the line, back to duck number one. There was a scrape of a chair, a muffled protest and a cry of pain then the footsteps were heading off in another direction, dragging a chair and an extra pair of feet with them.

A door shut and there was silence in the room. The noises came from further off, softened by wood and brick but unmistakably the sounds of accusing voices and strangled screams. No noise in our room though, the good little ducks were quiet as mice. We listened and we waited our turn. We heard a man scream really loudly.

Kirkwood was fishing. He'd rounded up seven suspects from his shortlist of Spud killers. Maybe we weren't even the first seven, maybe half of Glasgow had sat hooded in this room. I knew I'd asked too many questions, knew I'd pushed Ally to ask too much, knew that Kirky had looked deep into my eyes that day in the taxi office, knew my luck was on the run, knew he was coming for me, knew I was on his list. Knew I was not alone and that might just be my saving grace.

The feet came back into the room and hauled off another suspect on another chair and those of us that were left listened in distant silence, our ears straining to hear the fate of the departed. Judging by the noise that eventually came, his fate was not pleasant.

Fifteen minutes later and it was duck number three that was screaming loud and hard. I imagined Davie Stewart's twisted smile as he happily carried out Kirkwood's bidding. Eye? Ankle? Arse or knee? Take your pick, take a pick to it. Doing his worst, doing what he was best at. Suddenly the screaming stopped, the distant door opened and closed and I knew duck number four was shitting himself. He would have had absolutely no idea why he had been dragged here but he'd have had no doubt that he was next.

It seemed to take much, much longer until the near door opened for him though. Maybe it just seemed that way. Maybe the pain getting closer made time slow and stop like a watched kettle, like that boiling kettle that was poured over Hutton's balls. Einstein called it relativity. The sitting ducks called it torture.

Then the door was open and the feet rushed in, hauling number four away, ignoring his pleas and dragging him out of the room. He had been the only thing standing between me and what was to come and now he was gone. I missed him.

I listened for the shouts and the screams but instead the feet came back. Long before I expected it. Arms were on me, pulling at me, cutting at the straps that held me and pinning my arms tight to my side. I was being dragged away quickly, rushing towards that near door, leaving the chair behind. But I wasn't pulled into that room, wasn't propped up in front of Kirkwood. It was taking too long, they were dragging me too far.

Then I heard a crash of wood against a wall and felt wind on my face. I was outside. Then just for a moment or two I was being shoved. I flew through the air a few feet and landed with a shot of sudden pain as the side of my head hit metal. I was back in the van, bodies moving beside me, quiet moans and fear reverberating. I could smell blood.

Within minutes the transit door had opened and closed twice, two more bodies being thrown inside. The second of them landed on my right leg jarring my knee violently against the floor. The van was thrown into gear and with a screech it took off, chucking its cargo around in the back.

We drove no more than a few minutes then we screamed to a halt, the engine still running. The doors were opened and a body next to me was grabbed and thrown out. I heard it land on concrete. The doors slammed shut and the van moved off at speed. I reckoned maybe five minutes passed and it stopped once more, the engine again churning below us. The doors opened and my ankles were grabbed, my body was hauled along the floor, causing my head to crack off what was maybe someone's knee before I felt nothingness below me and dropped onto the ground.

I could feel grit and dirt against my arms as the feet moved around and away from me. A stamp on an accelerator and the van was gone. I lay still, not certain I was alone, not sure they had left me or were about to reverse the transit back over me.

I was still lying there when more feet raced towards me, making me brace myself for a kick or the crack of a baseball bat. Instead it was young voices, kids' voices, pure Glesga kids, scheme kids.

'Fuck's sake, man. Izzi deid? Dunno. Kick him. Naw don't. Ye mental? Get yer big brother. Talking aboot? Fuck's sake, man. Whose wis the van. Dunno. Fuck's sake, man.'

I pulled the hood from my face, scaring the shit out of the kids in doing so. It only took two seconds though before the bravado was back.

'Awrite, big man? Whit happened? Wizzit gangsters, man? Who done ye?'

I went mental at them. I needed them away from me as quick as possible so I could work out where I was, what had and hadn't happened to me and what was going to happen to me. I told them to fuck off, wore all my hate on my face and screamed at them. They backed off, knowing a headcase when they saw one, and retreated to the other side of the road where they felt safe to abuse me.

'Who you shouting at, ya prick? Gaun fuck off, ya muppet. Possil Fleeto, ya bass. Faw'in oot a van like a big wean. Fuck you, ya cunt. Gaun, get tae fuck.'

Possil. Cheers guys. I started walking down the road in search of the nearest bus stop, the jeers of the Fleeto ringing in my ear and a million questions battering the inside of my head.

I now knew where I was but I didn't know why I didn't get a beating, a cutting or worse. I didn't know why Kirky abandoned his line-up. Did someone confess? Surely not, not in a way he'd believe anyway. Some guy might have confessed to anything just to stop the pain but Kirkwood would have wanted details the poor mug couldn't provide. Couldn't have been that.

It was only after I'd got on board a 54 into Hope Street and went into the Pot Still where I sat myself in front of a large whisky and a television that I discovered I had saved myself. The word was serendipity.

CHAPTER 43

Fiona Raedale's mortal coil had been ripped from her as she sat at her till in Tesco. The where and the when. It hadn't been pretty. Losing control of your bodily functions and dying from an agonizing convulsive seizure while drenched in your own visceral lava rarely is. It could have happened in Bar Budda, in another pub, on a bus or in a taxi. In the lift of the multi if it was working or locked away in the safety of her own home. But as luck would have it, it was in front of three frozen meals, two pints of milk, a multi-pack of crisps and a bottle of Bell's.

The previous night I had swapped her inhaler for one I had prepared earlier. One with a little added something. Pure liquid nicotine is lethal stuff. One drop in the blood-stream will kill an average-sized adult in five minutes flat. It will take only slightly longer to kill a rhinoceros. It is virtually tasteless and virtually colourless and it is absolutely fucking deadly. The American National Poison Centre estimates that the lethal dose of liquid nicotine is 40–60 mg. A cigarette contains about 1 mg, so short of stuffing two or three packets of twenty into your mouth and swallowing the lot, it's not going to do the trick.

They use liquid nicotine as an anti-smoking measure, one that had worked particularly well in Fiona's case. A vial of liquid death, 100 mg in each, sits in those nifty little inhalators, released puff by harmless minuscule puff to fulfil the smoker's craving. I had carefully, very carefully, removed the vials of nicotine from two of them and placed their contents carefully, very carefully, inside a bog-standard inhaler, the same as the one I had seen her use.

She would have known right away that something was wrong, or at least different. But by then it would have been too late. Damage done.

Of course, it was just possible that she had some mecamylamine in her purse just for such an eventuality. A shot of that was the only thing that could save her but it wasn't likely to be found among her cigarettes and lipstick nor behind the Tesco pharmacy counter. Unless she had a hotline to a lab at Philip Morris or Imperial Tobacco then she had had it. The end, whenever and wherever it was to be, was always certain to be as messy as it would be quick.

Fiona Raedale lost control of her limbs, flopping to the floor in a big, fat, startled collapse. She suffered confusion and nausea but that was only the start. She soon lost management of her bowels and bladder, both discharging whatever they held in an abandoned flood of shit and piss. She vomited violently, emptying her guts till she wrenched up nothing but air. Then there was the terrible seizures, a final gasping convulsion before she slipped into a coma and sudden respiratory arrest.

It was a grotesque, undignified death – as any performed in front of a waiting queue of shoppers had to be. I felt some small measure of sympathy for the buyer of the frozen meals and sundry essentials, all the poor sods who endured the sight and stomach-churning stench, the cleaner dispatched from the juice aisle to deal with the mess. Still, eggs and omelettes, collateral damage and all that.

The real beauty of all this human ugliness is that liquid nicotine doesn't show up in a serum toxicology screening. If the cops or the coroner decided to go for a urine toxicology screen then they'd see it OK but maybe not suspect too much. A smoker like Fiona, stands to reason she'd have nicotine in her pee.

No, chances were that the awful demise of fat Fiona would have gone down as a tragedy, a mystery, a medical conundrum. Unless I told them otherwise.

And of course that's precisely what I did. The day before I had sent two first-class letters and on that Saturday morning they landed on two desks in Glasgow city centre. One letter to Rachel Narey, one to Keith Imrie. They might have removed her from being in charge of the investigation but they couldn't dictate who I made contact with. Two letters, no fingers in either. Instead both contained a till receipt from Tesco on Maryhill Road.

Imrie couldn't have known quite what he had but he certainly would have known immediately who it had come from and what it was likely to have meant. He was also armed with a slip of paper with a name and a phrase printed on it. 'Fiona Raedale. Pure liquid nicotine.'

Narey too would have recognized the envelope as soon as she saw it. It would have set off alarm bells the moment it dropped through the Stewart Street letterbox. Chances are that whoever brought it to her desk would already have patted it down and confirmed what their eyes had already told them, that there was no finger-shaped bulge. It would have been handed over with a confused, anticipatory shrug.

Maybe this Lewington guy would have known Rachel got the letter, maybe not. But either way it was her who would have got on to Tesco.

Narey was good. It wouldn't have taken her long. One phone call to the store to determine if any of their staff had gone missing, or worse. She would have been told of course that nothing had been reported. All was well. The receipt would have been sent immediately to the lab for fingerprint tests and whatever else they could get from it. That was the clever bit, my smart arse solution. I couldn't give her a finger so I gave her a fingerprint. I liked to think she would have appreciated that later.

Narey would have told the store manager to have a word with all his staff, urge caution, impress on them just how serious this was.

Imrie didn't phone her or Lewington but headed to the shop to snoop around on his own. The cops could wait, he wanted to be ahead of the game yet again. Had there been a murder, was there going to be one? His source had never let him down before. Whoever that source was, of course.

He'd still have been hanging around when the liquid nicotine kicked in and Raedale kicked off. He might even have seen it. He'd certainly have heard the commotion it must have caused and been there when Strathclyde's finest came rushing to the door with sirens blaring.

The cops wouldn't have been best pleased to see Imrie there before them. Not pleased at all. He'd have got an angry earful. He got a quote about his Cutter right enough, his story in the *Record* on the Monday confirmed that, but I was pretty sure Narey in particular also said a few things that couldn't be printed. She wouldn't have missed him.

She'd have found the soaked, stinking body of Fiona Raedale. She'd have known who any fingerprint on the till receipt from the Thursday was going to match up to. She'd have made sure they wrung every piece of evidence they could from that receipt. Every print, every bit of DNA, everything that might have passed for a clue.

I knew they'd have studied the CCTV tapes from the store, maybe as much as an hour or two before and after the 14.23 that was shown on the receipt. Everyone who entered and left. Looking for whoever might have purchased a six-pack of lager and a half bottle of whisky from Fiona Raedale's till in two separate transactions.

They wouldn't have seen me though because I was never there. Not that day at any rate. If they could have known then they might have seen a jaikie in a dirty, worn overcoat enter the shop about 14.09. They might have seen him leave about 14.24. Maybe if they concentrated on the exit time then they'd have spotted him as the buyer of the lager and the whisky. It still wouldn't have helped them much though.

I had found my alkie accomplice at a piece of waste-ground five minutes' walk away from Tesco. He wasn't hard to convince that he should help me. I gave him a tenner to buy the drink, making it quite clear that he had to buy from the till with the fat woman wearing a badge that said her name was Fiona. He had to buy the drinks separately so that he would have two receipts. When he brought the receipts back to me he could keep the drink and get another tenner for his trouble.

He was already pretty wasted on Buckfast and methadone when I went to him and he'd have been off his face within half an hour of me leaving. There was no way he could remember me even if the cops did track him down.

Anyway, I'd sworn him to secrecy under pain of reprisals and I knew he'd keep to his side of the bargain. He was full of bravado and Buckie but something about me frightened him. Maybe the jaikie could see things that others couldn't, maybe living on the streets just meant that he scared easily. Either way, he would stay drunk and silent.

The police knew. Imrie knew. Before long all of Glasgow and Scotland and beyond knew too. The Cutter had killed again.

The news couldn't keep. Imrie being there ensured that. There was no way that they wanted him to claim another scoop and Lewington was in front of TV cameras within an hour. No explanation of how they could be sure, no missing finger, no names, no pack drill. But confirmation all the same. Victim number six. Cue hysteria.

The news had travelled all the way to an empty house somewhere about five minutes from Possil where Alec Kirkwood held seven men in hoods and was halfway through extracting whatever he could from them. Killing Raedale by remote control, being miles away when it happened was supposed to be my alibi when Rachel inevitably came calling. But it turned out to be my alibi to Kirkwood.

I couldn't know if he'd got a phone call, heard from a rogue cop, heard it on the radio or had been watching Sky News. Didn't matter. All that mattered, all that saved me and a couple of others from extreme pain was that he found out.

The Cutter had struck again and it could not be any of the poor saps he had lined up tied to chairs. Whoever it was it wasn't any of them. We were kicked onto the streets without explanation and expected to be glad to be alive.

The next day I was visited at home by Arthur Penman, the accountant that fronted Kirky's takeover of the taxi business. I was told that it had been a mistake, an unfortunate understanding but that no more was to be said about it. Nothing said to anyone. I didn't have a job any more though, there had been a couple of redundancies, credit crunch and all that. An envelope was shoved into my hand containing twenty grand in cash. I didn't need to go in to pick up any of my stuff. My taxi-driving days were over.

CHAPTER 44

Daily Record
4 May 2010
EXCLUSIVE
CUTTER USED NICOTINE POISON
Record reveals method to cops
By Keith Imrie, Chief Reporter

The Cutter brutally killed victim number six using a deadly poison called pure liquid nicotine. The Daily Record can exclusively reveal that the callous serial killer murdered 47-year-old shop worker Fiona Raedale from Summerston using a huge dose of the lethal poison which can kill within minutes. The Tesco sales assistant died in the supermarket giant's Maryhill store on Saturday in full view of horrified customers.

The shop on Maryhill Road was closed for several hours after Ms Raedale died a horrible and very public death while sat at her till serving Saturday afternoon shoppers.

The Cutter has now killed six times. His victims are Glasgow lawyer Jonathan Carr (37), bookmaker Billy Hutchison (58), gangland underling Thomas Tierney (26), businessman Wallace Ogilvie (52), dentist Brian Sinclair (32) and Ms Raedale (pictured above).

Baffled police have no idea

how *The Cutter administered the deadly toxin to the shop worker. Unbelievably, officers leading the investigation did not even know that she had been poisoned until informed by the* Record!

Forensic scientists had been frantically analysing samples of the victim's blood and other vital fluids to establish a cause of death. However, one officer close to the investigation admitted that they had no clue as to how she was murdered – or even that she had been murdered.

Pure liquid nicotine is sometimes used in anti-smoking products but was given to the victim in such a high dosage that death was almost instant. Shocked shoppers watched as Ms Raedale vomited, and lost control of her bodily functions before dying in front of them in excruciating agony. Although deadly, liquid nicotine is incredibly difficult to detect and can easily be overlooked during forensic blood examinations. Strathclyde Police successfully ran tests for liquid nicotine after being advised to do so by the Record. *They have thanked us for our public assistance in this matter.*

We cannot reveal the source of our information but can say that it was from an informed party.

Startled shopper James McLenaghan (37) told of his horror at seeing Ms Raedale die.

'*It was terrible. The poor woman started moaning something awful then started shaking. She fell off her chair then there was stuff flooding everywhere. The smell was just horrendous. It only lasted a couple of minutes, maybe less. I was just a few feet away from her. Unbelievable. I know it sounds terrible but it was as if she had exploded.*

'*There were people screaming and nobody really knew what was going on. You could see she was dead though. It was obvious. I think a couple of people threw up just looking at her.*'

Another customer, Candice Ross (19), was in Ms Raedale's queue when she died.

'*It was unbelievable. Totally frightening. She just went into this sort of fit and she was throwing up and I think she must have messed herself as well. I was like, this can't be happening. I was just glad I didn't have my wee* girl with me. I wouldn't have liked her to see that. It was like something right out of a horror movie. I'll no be able to sleep for ages.

'I can't believe this has happened here. Everybody's been talking about The Cutter but you don't think it's going to happen on your own doorstep. You don't expect this kind of thing round here. I can't believe he was here and did this. It's totally scary.'

The murder of Ms Raedale is the first time that the killer has failed to carry out his trademark barbarous act of severing his victim's little finger. However, there is no doubt that it was The Cutter that killed her. Instead of sending police a chopped-off finger, the evil killer has sent a chilling and mocking message to bewildered detectives. The Record can exclusively reveal The Cutter posted a Tesco till receipt to DS Rachel Narey, the beleaguered officer who was formerly in charge of the case, and tests on the receipt revealed it bore a fingerprint belonging to Ms Raedale.

The murderer is clearly taunting police as he plays a twisted game of hide and seek with them. At the moment, there seems to be only one winner – the evil Cutter.

The police have established no link between The Cutter's victims and are convinced that he has killed indiscriminately. It is also understood that they have found no significant or useful forensic evidence that connects the murders.

DI Frank Lewington confirmed that Strathclyde Police are treating the murder as part of The Cutter investigation.

'We are in possession of information which leads us to believe that Ms Raedale may have been killed by the same person responsible for other murders currently under investigation. We are awaiting a full forensic report but until then we are treating Ms Raedale's death as highly suspicious. It will be investigated both on its own and also as part of the inquiry into five murders in the city.

'We urge anyone with any information about the death of Ms Raedale to contact the incident room at Stewart Street, their local police station or Crimestoppers. We know there is a widespread element of fear about this series of killings but we can assure people that everything that can be done is being done to apprehend the person or persons responsible.

'Finally, we would ask again that anyone with information about the death of Ms Raedale, or other deaths, should contact the incident room and not make contact with media outlets as this can seriously impair the police in their attempts to protect the people of Glasgow. This is an ongoing inquiry and it is vital that certain elements of the investigation be treated discreetly and not be put in the public domain before my officers have the opportunity to evaluate its worth.

'My door is always open, my telephone line is always manned. If anyone has pertinent information to this terrible case then I urge them to deliver it to me.'

CHAPTER 45

I sat at home with the television on. Not watching, not hearing a word. She sat to my left, not talking. See no evil, hear no evil, speak no evil.

My mind was on a lock-up garage in Springburn. Keith Imrie would be arriving there now. He'd be excited, maybe a bit scared. He'd be seeing his scoop, his reporter of the year award. He'd be reaching inside the box in the corner and fumbling for the brown envelope. It would be there, just as I'd promised him.

Later I wasn't sure how much of it I'd imagined or how much of it was the stuff I'd read in the papers or heard from the people who knew people. It was the talk of the steamie obviously.

Looking back it's as if it was all playing out in front of me in high-definition 34-inch plasma grotesque. I stared at that television and watched my play unfold, seeing it, remembering it, imagining it, feeling it.

Imrie arrived bang on cue at quarter past eight, just as the light was beginning to go on that cloudy May night.

He had parked up a street away and walked over to the lock-up, furtively looking around him in case he was being watched. Oh he knew the game all right, he could keep his sources sweet and discreet.

He pulled up the sliding door and slipped inside with just one backward glance at the falling gloom. Every step to the back of the garage took him a step nearer London, the metaphorical Fleet Street and a job on one of the national dailies.

He'd worked for this. It was his due. From council minutes and court reports in the early days, through tip-offs and lifts from local papers to crime tidbits and page leads, from hard days' nights drinking with arseholes and villains, keeping people sweet and keeping the whole thing discreet. He'd played the fucking game and it was his time now. He was the best there was in this wee pond and this was going to be his chance to show the big boys what he could do.

The game was the same wherever you played it. You just had to know when to kick arse and when to kiss it. When to slap someone on the back and when to stab them there. When to write the truth and when to write what suited you. Simple as. He knew the game inside out.

The Cutter stuff hadn't fallen into his lap as some of them said. Things didn't work like that. You make your own luck even if those jealous fucking idiots couldn't understand it. The Cutter could have picked any journalist in the city but he hadn't. He picked Keith Imrie because he was the best that weegieland had to offer. He'd worked for it and he'd earned it. Nothing at all to do with luck.

He made for the back right corner of the lock-up, just as instructed. The information had never been wrong before and nor would it have been. The muffled voice on the phone had never identified itself, the letters were always unsigned but he knew, of course he knew. It was straight from the horse's mouth. Everyone was desperate for a line on The Cutter and he had the best contact of them all. Of course he did.

The battered cardboard box was half-covered by an old carpet, as inconspicuous as it was insecure, the safety of its contents all but guaranteed by its unguarded shabbiness. Inside was his passport to Fleet Street. Sure, the big papers had moved out to Docklands and Broxbourne via Wapping but it would always be Fleet Street to him.

He reached under the carpet, keen not to actually touch the thing, and groped in the half-light for the envelope. Sure enough his fingers settled on it and with a satisfied smile he eased out the prize. A plain brown envelope, thinly bulging with hidden promises. All his.

Smug? So what. Show him a good loser and he'd show you a loser. Same goes for good winners. If the rest of the Glasgow meedja was looking on he'd give them a big Get It Right Up Ye to the lot of them. Come on down, the prize is right.

He carefully tipped the contents of the envelope onto the carpet draped over the box and eagerly examined his haul.

There was a glossy white business card. *Jonathan Carr. Salter, Fyfe and Bryce Solicitors. 1024 Bath Street.*

There was a newspaper cutting. Brian Sinclair's wedding announcement. Bingo.

There was a man's chunky gold necklace. Blingo.

There was a betting slip marked Hutchison's Independent Bookmakers, a till receipt from Tesco and a credit card in the name of Wallace R. Ogilvie.

House!

Fucking hell, it was even better than he'd hoped. His editor could kiss his golden arse. Never mind the series of front-page exclusives that this would serve up, it would get him so much pussy it was beyond belief.

Grisly Treasure Hoard From The Cutter's Lair. Open Says Me, *Record* Reporter Uncovers Killer's Cave. He could only think in headlines, could only see his name up in lights and in glorious 20-point byline.

He slipped the envelope and its prize papers into his inside jacket pocket, all except the chunky piece of man-bling which he put snugly into his trousers, enjoying the feeling of it rubbing against his golden balls. Fuck, he was the man.

He eased up the door to the lock-up and, with barely a glance to the waiting night, he left as he came, striding like a prince among papers back to the Saab convertible that would take him to London. He had gone all of five feet when he heard the footsteps behind him that sent his spider sense into overdrive and his sphincter shutting like a clam.

Despite every instinct telling him just to run, he spun to see what was behind him. As he took in the two very large men moving towards him, he heard more footsteps, this time from the direction he had been heading. He wanted to speak, to bluff it out, to talk his way out of it but no words would come. A boot from the guy nearest him crushed his golden balls and put him squealing onto his knees. He hadn't even begun to recover from that when something, a fist, a boot, a baseball bat, crashed into the side of his skull and he could taste his own blood as he sank onto the waiting concrete. His head rang, he'd bit his own tongue and his brains rattled against the side of his head.

Voices came at him as if someone was phoning him from inside a bathroom or underwater. Feet crashed against his knees and ankles, encouraging him to listen or stand. When he failed to do either he was hauled to his feet and his vision settled enough for him to recognize the face directly in front of his. Alec Kirkwood. Fuck.

Hands were rifling through his pockets, maybe Kirkwood's maybe not, finding and removing the envelope and then the necklace. Spud's necklace, he heard someone say. That revelation was followed by a punch to the stomach that blew away whatever little breath he had left. He was being held up like a rag doll.

We need to talk, wee man man man man. I've been waiting a while for this this this this. Kirkwood's words reverberated round his bruised skull.

It wasn't his show any longer. It was Alec Kirkwood's show. He didn't know how and he didn't know why but he knew his time had come and gone. His exclusive had gone. His reporter of the year award had gone. Fleet Street had gone.

Kirkwood held something up. The betting slip. He'd barely taken in what it was when a fist pummelled into his face, just under his right eye, almost certainly breaking his cheekbone. The pain was excruciating. He screamed.

When he dared look up he saw the lawyer's business card only inches from his eyes. It suddenly disappeared from his radar and was immediately replaced by Kirkwood's fist hammering into his left cheek. That hand had a ring on it, he could feel it rip into his skin and on into the bone. He wanted to pass out, throw up and die. Only the hands that were under his armpits allowed him to stay on his feet.

Did you kill Spud Tierney Tierney Tierney? Did you kill Spud you little bastard bastard? Did you kill them all?

Yes. He heard himself saying. Yes. Yes. Leave me.

Did you kill Spud? Yes, he slurred. Yes. Yes.

Did you kill them? Yes, he screamed. Yes.

Kirkwood was holding the necklace in front of him now, offering it up in front of his bloodied eyes as obvious proof of something. Then the fist came crashing into his mouth, breaking teeth and bursting his lips. A hand grabbed his throat and squeezed tight, forcing his mouth open in an instinctive reaction.

Something was being shoved into his broken mouth, being forced past the shards of teeth and rush of blood. The metal caught his taste buds and he knew it was the chunky bling. Alec Kirkwood was thrusting Tierney's necklace down his throat.

He gagged on it, fighting it with what little he had left. As he did he felt stings at his knees and hands, hot comforting stings that ran cool and fresh. The stings came again and again, sharp little reminders that he could feel more than one thing at a time. He could feel blood trickling across his skin, testimony to those sweet cool stings sliced by an unseen knife or knives. He could feel the chunk of the chain and savour its sour tang. He could feel the bile rising from his stomach and the chain sinking to meet it as dear life was strangled from him.

His last sight on earth was his right hand being yanked up and held in front of his face, its bloodied back streaked red, its fingers trembling and stark white. As his sight faded he saw a pair of gleaming secateurs close their grip round his pinkie, their deathly squeeze closing out his vision and his future. One clean cut and never-ending darkness. Bye bye Fleet Street, bye bye.

Kirkwood delivered a final kick to the dead reporter's bollocks, standing over him with bloodied knuckles, heavy breath and startled eyes, guilt and justice writ large over his face. There was no longer any pretence at sophistication, no businessman in a business suit. Here stood the animal who had fought his way out of Asher Street, the undomesticated version, the thug, the wild dog. From Maryhill to Castlemilk, from the Drum to Easterhouse they would know that if you messed with Alec Kirkwood or touched one of his then you would pay the price.

However, that final kick, that insult added to injury, had barely struck when the forecourt was flooded with light and sound and fury. Kirkwood's boot had registered its mark when it all kicked off.

The sounds of sirens and shouting announced the arrival of Strathclyde's finest.

Two birds, one stone. No turn unstoned.

My madness had method.

CHAPTER 46

The *Herald*. Friday, 15 May 2010. Page 1.
By Andrea Faulds

The serial killer who has been terrorizing Glasgow for over two years was yesterday named as being a well-known Scottish journalist. Keith Imrie, chief reporter with the Daily Record newspaper, has been identified by police as the man responsible for the six brutal murders which have shocked and horrified the city.

Imrie (32) died on Tuesday night as a result of an alleged attack which is in itself the subject of a report to the Procurator Fiscal. Police sources say they are no longer looking for anyone else in connection with the so-called Cutter killings.

It is believed that several pieces of evidence directly linking Imrie to the killings were found at the scene of his death. These included items belonging to The Cutter victims. Imrie's colleagues at the Daily Record are said to be startled at the news that he has been named as the killer. Members of staff at the newspaper's Central Quay offices have been banned from speaking to other media and today's early editions of the Record only referred to Imrie as being a journalist.

The 32-year-old rose to prominence by writing numerous exclusive reports on The Cutter case, frequently getting information ahead of other media outlets and, in many instances, before the police. He gained promotion to the position of chief reporter on the strength of his Cutter exclusives.

Imrie is said to have bragged to colleagues about his inside information, claiming that he had much better sources on The Cutter case than the police. Yesterday's revelations now give that boast a grisly ring of reality.

The dramatic turn of events has brought a sudden conclusion to more than two years of extraordinary tension in Glasgow as The Cutter claimed victim after victim, striking seemingly at random with police unable to establish any link between his prey. The killing spree made the city the unwanted centre of worldwide media attention, particularly when the barbaric nature of The Cutter's mutilation of his victims was revealed.

Ironically now, of course, it transpires that that revelation was made by The Cutter himself. Imrie was interviewed many times by news outlets from all parts of the world and colleagues have said how he revelled in the attention. At the time that was just taken to be the inevitable consequence of an ambitious journalist being placed in the spotlight but it is now being seen by many as a killer callously laughing at his pursuers and the families of his victims.

Imrie had been a reporter with the Daily Record for eight years. He was unmarried and lived in a two-bedroomed Victorian flat in Observatory Road in the city's fashionable west end. Yesterday neighbours there expressed their shock at the news but none were willing to publicly speak out about the deceased reporter.

One did say that he didn't mix a lot with others in his building but was pleasant when seen around the property. It was felt that the unsocial hours that came with his job was the reason that he often wasn't around and could be heard coming and going from his flat at odd hours of the night.

Chief Constable Andrew Chisholm said yesterday that while police inquiries were continuing, they did not expect that these would extend beyond Imrie. Mr Chisholm yesterday read out a prepared statement to waiting press.

'We are confident at this stage that Keith Imrie was the person responsible for the murders of Jonathan Carr, William Hutchison, Thomas Tierney, Wallace Ogilvie, Brian Sinclair and Fiona Raedale. We believe that he acted alone.

'We cannot give a definitive statement on Mr Imrie's guilt until exhaustive forensic work has been completed but we believe that will confirm that he was responsible for these brutal killings.

'This has been a terrible episode in Glasgow's criminal history but we believe that this episode is at an end. Strathclyde Police have worked tirelessly to bring the killer of these six people to justice. The identification of Mr Imrie as the person responsible for these heinous crimes was a victory for police intelligence, sheer hard work and a dedication to duty. The people of Glasgow, of Strathclyde and of Scotland can sleep safer in their beds knowing that this man is no longer a threat.

'There was some criticism of this force, perhaps understandable, through the course of the inquiry. However, I believe that today is the vindication of the efforts of my officers and everyone involved in this case.

'While it is regrettable that Mr Imrie is not to face trial, an issue sadly beyond the control of this force, it is nevertheless a relief to everyone that the so-called Cutter will never strike again. If, as we believe, Mr Imrie was responsible for these killings – and all the evidence that we have points in that direction – then his untimely death is the lesser of two evils in a case that has been heavy with evils.

'More details on the forensic evidence available to the investigation team will, of course, be made public in due course. Strathclyde Police would like to thank everyone who assisted in this investigation, one of the most difficult that the force has ever known. It was only with the assistance of various members of the public allied to the professionalism of serving officers that removed this threat from our midst.'

Detective Inspector Frank Lewington of Nottinghamshire Police, who assumed control of *The Cutter* investigation, said that all available information pointed to Imrie being the murderer.

'There is considerable evidence suggesting that Keith Imrie was the killer of Mr Carr, Mr Hutchison, Mr Tierney, Mr Ogilvie, Mr Sinclair and Ms Raedale. However, much of the evidence we currently have would perhaps be considered circumstantial by a judge. We shall now be endeavouring to establish firm forensic proof that he was the killer of these six people.

'While we have particular reason to believe that Imrie is the man responsible, we will continue to rule nothing out until we have completely determined the circumstances surrounding these murders.

'However, our message to the people of Glasgow is that they can sleep easier in their beds tonight. The threat from the so-called Cutter is at an end.'

Page 2: CUTTER TIMELINE
Page 3: IMRIE'S VICTIMS: FAMILIES SPEAK OUT

The *Herald*. Saturday, 16 May 2010. Page 4.
A well-known Glasgow businessman appeared in court yesterday charged with the murder of a 32-year-old man in the city on Tuesday. The Crown Office said Alexander Kirkwood (age 34) of Braidwood Gardens, Baillieston, appeared in private at Glasgow Sheriff Court charged with murder. He was also charged with attempting to pervert the course of justice. A spokeswoman said Kirkwood made no plea or declaration and was remanded in custody. She added that an application for bail had been made but had been denied.

The *Herald*. Friday, 22 May 2010. Page 1.
By Andrea Faulds.
Strathclyde Police have confirmed that extensive forensic evidence

proves beyond any reasonable doubt that Daily Record journalist Keith Imrie (32) was the killer of all six victims in The Cutter case.

DI Frank Lewington and DCI Lewis Robertson told a packed media conference that DNA, fingerprints and shoe imprints were among the evidence that definitively identified Imrie as the killer. All investigations into The Cutter murders have now ceased and the case is considered to be closed.

Imrie was named as the serial killer last week after his body was found outside a lock-up garage in Springburn. A man is to face trial over his death.

DI Lewington and DCI Robertson listed a number of items belonging to The Cutter's victims which were found both at the scene of Mr Imrie's death and his home in Glasgow's west end. These included a business card belonging to murdered solicitor Jonathan Carr, a betting slip from the premises of bookmaker William Hutchison and an ashtray taken from Mr Hutchison's flat. There was also a necklace belonging to drug dealer Thomas

Tierney, a supermarket shopping receipt from a till operated by Fiona Raedale and an asthmatic inhaler owned by her. There was a credit card in the name of murdered businessman Wallace Ogilvie and a running shoe belonging to dentist Brian Sinclair. DCI Robertson revealed there were also various photographic prints of homes, premises and favoured haunts of the victims. These were discovered inside Imrie's Observatory Road flat.

Detailed forensic evidence included a footprint found at the scene of the first murder, that of Mr Carr, which has been formally identified as being a match to a size seven Reebok trainer belonging to Imrie. Ridge markings on the shoe, recovered from the reporter's flat, were an exact match to a cast taken at the scene.

Even more damningly, DNA extracted from hairs found on the clothing of Brian Sinclair, the fifth victim, showed an exact match with Imrie. There is estimated to be, at worst, a one in 3.4 million chance that the hair was not Imrie's.

Imrie was also revealed to

have been caught on CCTV cameras in the Tesco supermarket on Maryhill Road where Fiona Raedale worked, just a short time before her death.

Most gruesome of all perhaps was the pair of secateurs found taped to the underside of Imrie's bed. The shears were famously used by The Cutter to clip off the right little finger of his victims. This trademark act was the killer's signature and was the first thing to alert police that they were chasing a serial killer. The secateurs found hidden in the west end flat were discovered to have DNA samples – said to be skin, tissue and blood – formally identified as belonging to Wallace Ogilvie and Brian Sinclair. It is believed that partial matches were made to three of the remaining victims on the basis of low copy DNA.

DI Lewington confirmed for the first time that Mr Sinclair was choked to death using a rolled-up newspaper. However he also made the startling revelation that the police have since learned that the newspaper used was the Daily Record and that the front-

page story was an article on The Cutter killings written by Keith Imrie. It is believed that the newspaper was removed from the scene or destroyed but that small fragments of it were recovered from Mr Sinclair's throat. Painstaking investigative work established the edition of the newspaper and then the story that it contained.

DI Lewington said that the fact that the newspaper had an article written by Imrie was in itself circumstantial but he had no doubt that it added to the body of evidence against him. He said that it also gave a 'frightening insight' into the egotistical mind of the killer.

'There is a huge catalogue of evidence against Keith Imrie, enough that we can disregard the particular newspaper that was used in terms of establishing guilt. However, this does go a long way to determining motive, something that has naturally proven difficult because of Imrie's death before we could have an opportunity to question him. That this man, a callous and brutal killer, felt driven to use his own story *as an instrument of murder gives us a frightening insight into his warped mind. Criminal psychologists have reported that they are in no doubt that this is an example of what they term Roman Emperor Syndrome, a man who believes he is lord of all he surveys. This was an incredibly egotistical man, someone who considered himself to hold the fortunes of others in his hands, to be judge, jury and executioner.*

'It was not enough that he killed a newly-married man with no apparent motive other than a thirst for blood, he had to taunt his victim and his pursuers in this manner. The psychologists believe that he was sending some twisted message that his pen was mightier than the sword, that he could kill by his words alone.

'There is complete confidence among Strathclyde Police that Keith Imrie was the serial killer known as The Cutter. It is vital that the physical information that was available to us was put to the utmost forensic examination

so that we could say with certainty to the people of Glasgow that the threat which they have so understandably feared is no longer present. The Cutter is dead.'

DS Rachel Narey, the officer formerly in charge of the investigation, said that the weight of forensic evidence was overwhelming.

'It is quite clear that with the amount and quality of physical evidence against Mr Imrie that there is no other conclusion for the force to draw other than that he committed the six murders.

'While it is not clear how he managed to carry out these killings unnoticed or what his motive might have been, the evidence found on his person and in his home clearly indicates his guilt. It is highly unusual for someone to kill without motive and with no connection to his victims. That obviously made this investigation extremely difficult for officers trying to apprehend the perpetrator of these murders.'

317

CHAPTER 47

Who'd have thought it? Hotshot reporter Keith Imrie a cold-blooded serial killer. They didn't see that one coming down at the old *Daily Record*. Must have fair put the editors and executives at Central Quay on their padded arses. Shame.

Well, maybe they should have thought a bit more carefully about the kind of person they hired. Perhaps they shouldn't have taken on the kind of evil cunt that would do a thing like that.

Most people think all journalists are low-life shit and fuck knows there's a lot of truth in that. Pushing out their lies and half-truths, selling their souls to sell stories. Writing shit that might not be entirely untrue but untrue enough so that by the time it appears in print it is a mile away from what is really going on. They know it and they simply don't give a fuck.

Not all of them. Only the ones that make it big. Wave a ticket for what used to be Fleet Street in front of their faces and some just can't say no. Greed, ambition and low moral fibre make a bad combination.

But I knew it wasn't like that for all of them. There were laws for a start. Ninety-nine per cent of what you read is completely true. Get them in court if it's not. Most of it is just what happens. If the news is bad you can't blame the messenger. I'd learned that.

The first time I saw Sarah's name in print, I screamed. Not in anger, not in rage, just in shock. The noise just came out of me. Couldn't stop it. I thought maybe it might be in the paper. Had prepared myself for that. But it was on page three. Didn't expect that.

Took the breath out of me. It just escaped. A wheezing gulp exploded out of me. It turned into a strangled scream after half a thought. I felt her mother's arms round me and that quelled the surprise a bit but it still hurt. Her name shouldn't have been in the paper, not unless it was for winning a prize or getting to university or being married or in some kind of celebration. Fuck's sake. That wasn't the fucking way it should have been. Not right. Wrong. On page three. So fucking wrong.

Felt weak. Should have seen it coming. Didn't.

Not all reporters though. A lot of them were genuinely decent. Or so they appeared anyway. Sure, some tried to pass themselves off as being on our side and then turned round and shat on us, but most were true to their kind words. There were people, reporters, who turned up at our place and talked to me and to her. They actually cared. Some cried. Genuinely cried and genuinely cared.

These people, the good guys, had kids of their own and were actually fucking angry, really enraged and infuriated, about what Ogilvie had done. I saw their eyes. They could have done what I was about to do. One guy, maybe mid-thirties, looked away as he talked to me. He looked out of our window and saw nothing, shook his head and said 'If it was me . . ., if it was my sons . . .' He shook his head again but he could have done it. I saw it in his eyes. One step, one fine line, one outrageous fucking horrible life-changing, mind-wrecking, drive-you-fucking-crazy happening and he was where I was. Didn't wish anyone to be where I was. God forbid. Not God. Too late for that but forbid it anyway. Couldn't wish it on anyone.

The good journalists, they were sort of reassuring. Nearly gave me some kind of comfort, nearly gave me belief in the decency of man. But not enough.

Because all it took to defeat the few good men was one arsehole.

Well fuck the arseholes. Well fuck Keith Imrie.

The *Record*'s hotshot was a prince among arseholes. A king amongst cunts. He had been the worst of the worst. He had asked and he had received.

What sort of father wouldn't do anything for his daughter?

Before I drove out to Milngavie to kill Jonathan Carr, I thought of Keith Imrie. I saw his face in my rear-view mirror and I smiled at him. I smirked at him.

Because I knew what he didn't. Shit, I knew lots of things he didn't. I knew that I hadn't only changed the tyres on my car. I'd changed my shoes too. The car's shoes, my shoes. If you are going to do something, then do it right.

When I walked up to Jonathan Carr, when I swung that car jack, when I cracked his head against the side of the Audi TT, when I taped his mouth and superglued his nostrils and when I snuffed out his life, I walked in Imrie's footsteps. Walk a mile in another's man's moccasins before you criticize him says an old Native American saying. Fair enough. I certainly wanted to criticize Imrie and so much more. Wearing his shoes was the least that I could do.

So the prints that I left on the soft ground near the Audi were Keith Imrie's size seven trainers, borrowed from his flat, rather than my own size eights. Tough tittie, Keith. I wore the same pair when I went into the woods at Inchinnan after Brian Sinclair. Trampled all over the ground there. Left plenty of prints. Left no doubt that the same guy that killed Carr killed Sinclair.

For the record, no pun intended, I didn't like killing Sinclair. That was wrong. Had to be done but it was wrong. Wrong. Seemed a nice guy. Not a bad guy. Had to be done.

Imrie. Imrie's feet ran all over Inchinnan woods.

His hairs were found on Brian Sinclair's clothing too. Proper bastard. Proper puzzle. It had taken ages to pick the hairs off the collar of one of Imrie's jackets. Took a bit less time to place them carefully on Sinclair. You don't realize just how small hairs are. Imrie's were fairish blonde as well so they were finer, thinner, harder to pick off. Bastard to get them all off that poncey cord jacket. Worth it though.

Every single strand of hair was worth it. They say there

are about a hundred thousand hairs on a human head. It would have been worth picking off every one of them, one by one, to nail that bastard. One by fucking one.

The secateurs. Oh, aye, the secateurs.

I'd taped them under his bed after I was done with them. No longer any use to me. Not for cutting anyway.

I was almost tempted to kiss them, which would have been of no use whatsoever but I felt the urge to do it. The thought of kissing all the crap that had accumulated on the secateurs could have made me boak but I was stronger than that. Fuck, I'd killed six people. I was hardly squeamish. Still. Not exactly nice and, more to the point, certainly wouldn't have been smart to transfer DNA on to them after all that care.

Of course there was a chance that Imrie would have found the secateurs there but it wasn't very likely. He didn't seem the type to go dusting under the bed.

Same reason he wouldn't have found the photographs I left or the camera I took them with. They were well enough hidden to escape the attentions of a lazy reporter but would easily be found by cops looking for evidence of a serial killer. They were printouts of photographs but they did the job. Getting them printed from a chemist or on a digital machine would have been stupid.

Carr's Audi, Billy Hutchison's bookies and his flat, Ogilvie's offices and his Mondeo, the Tesco where Raedale worked and Sinclair's dental practice and his house. Each and every photograph taken carefully and surreptitiously. Each and every one of them dated before the killings.

I'd carried out a factory wipe of my computer after printing them. I'd wiped everything at regular intervals in the sure knowledge that the cops would come calling.

The secateurs, the photos, the trainers, the DNA, the odds and ends liberated from the dead. No one needed to worry about opportunity and motive when so much evidence was handed to them on a plate. Not every competent cop would accept the bleeding obvious but that didn't matter now. It was done. It was true. The newspapers said so.

Imrie was easy. Too greedy, too ambitious, too eager for the next headline. He couldn't wait to see his name on the front page again under another exclusive. When I contacted him to tell him the brown envelope was waiting for him in the lock-up he nearly wet himself with excitement. He tried to be super cool but he was desperate to get his hands on it.

He didn't stop to think what it meant, that someone else had been murdered, that another innocent life had been snatched away. Nor did he pause to worry about the moral quicksand he was swimming in. Imrie knew who I was. No one could have been capable of giving him that information other than the killer. The real killer.

He made it far too easy for me.

Alec Kirkwood was different. He had all sorts of questions that I wouldn't answer. He demanded to know who I was and how I knew what I was telling him. He swore and he threatened. He wanted to know why the timing was so important. Said he'd be there when it suited him not me. I made it clear though. If he wanted the man who had killed Spud Tierney and the others then he had to be at the address I gave him at the time I gave him. No argument. It had to be then or he wouldn't get him. Did he want him? He did.

The people who answered the hotline in Lewington's incident room wanted him too. Wanted him enough not to ask too many questions other than the pertinent ones. The where and the when. They didn't ask the why. I was told my call would be treated in the strictest confidence and that I may be eligible for a reward. My voice was muffled and disguised when I called all three of them. They all got what they wanted.

Of course I thought about calling Narey, giving the prize to her rather than Lewington. But Rachel was too smart. She would have given a gift horse a dental examination and an X-ray. If she was to have been there when Lewington got Kirkwood got Imrie then it had to have been at Lewington's invitation.

The party was arranged. The invitations had been sent. Jelly and ice cream for all.

Irony. I'd been an uninvited guest in Imrie's flat in Observatory Road for nearly three years. I knew his shifts, knew his patterns, his movements. I knew the layout of that flat like I knew my own house. I could find my way round his flat in total darkness, taking no more than a few minutes to get used to the lack of light and being able to navigate by the streetlight alone.

I had followed him and watched him just as I had tracked the others. I knew Keith Imrie better than he knew himself. It had taken two months before I got my chance. So many pubs, so many restaurants and cafes, cinemas and theatres. I followed that shallow, morally bankrupt bastard from east to west, north to south. Finally one Saturday afternoon in Tennent's Bar on Byres Road, the opportunity was there.

The pub was packed, loud and jumping with football fans, crazy with simmering hatred. Imrie was off his face drunk and so were the people he was with. I was near enough to stone cold sober to make no difference. It was the easiest thing in the world to take his key from his jacket pocket. Goal to Rangers and an open goal for me.

I was out of the pub, in and out of the key-cutting bar and back into Tennent's before he knew it had gone. I slipped the key back into his jacket and finished my pint. I watched Imrie for a while, burning my eyes into him, resisting the urge to punch his head in. It would wait. It would be better.

After that I could get into his flat when it suited me. I waited another month before I first went there, until I was sure he hadn't realized his key had been taken, sure that he'd be working and not coming home any time soon. His work made it all too easy. Imrie could be relied upon to be out of his flat when everyone else was asleep or otherwise occupied. That was handy.

He wasn't too bright either. You'd think if you were going to have a flat in the west end you would get an alarm fitted. You really couldn't be too careful. Some very dodgy people about.

I didn't go there often. Just when I needed or when it

suited. Maybe just five times in all. To take stuff and to leave stuff. He was too stupid to even notice I had been. But then I'd always known he was stupid. Stupid and arrogant and cold and heartless and mercenary and deceitful and dishonest.

When he wrote those words about my Sarah I wanted to kill him. There and then I wanted to strangle him to death with my bare hands. I wanted to cut off his fingers and rip out his throat. Wanted to destroy the liar and the tools of his lying.

How could he do that?

I wanted him to suffer like I had. Wanted him to know what it was like. He couldn't have written what he did if he had known my pain. He couldn't have written those words if he was a decent human being.

'*Erratic behaviour*'.

'*Mucking around*'.

'*Unfortunate accident*'.

Maybe another person wouldn't have reacted the way I did. But they are not me and I am not them. When Keith Imrie wrote that article he may as well have signed his own death warrant.

Of course I couldn't have been sure what would happen to Imrie when I set out to frame him but there was no regret. Kirkwood's unwelcome appearance in my plans gave me opportunity. I already had all the motive I needed.

How could he do that?

Her fault. He as good as said so. That hideous interview with Wallace Ogilvie's wife. Defending the indefensible.

It was much later that I learned of Imrie's motives, the grubby motives of a grubby little man. He didn't know Ogilvie but knew someone that knew him very well. A contact of Imrie's inside the council was a friend and close business associate of Ogilvie's. This contact fed Imrie tip-offs, told him about contracts up for grabs and who was doing what to get them. Told him about the movers and shakers and what they were up to. Who was shagging who, who was bribing who, who owed who and why. Supplied him with enough information to allow a struggling hack to get out of the court and council circuit and onto the front page.

Such information always comes at a price though. A favour owed, a debt due, a soul sold. That is how Wallace Ogilvie drunken murderer became painted as a pillar of the community, a man who did so much for charity and made one small error of judgement, paying a terrible price for the actions of a wayward girl.

Daily Record. Thursday, 7 February 2004. Page 7.
Wife defends convicted fundraiser
By Keith Imrie, Chief Reporter

THE WIFE of Wallace Ogilvie, the prominent businessman facing jail for his involvement in a tragic accident which claimed the life of a young girl, has spoken out in defence of her husband. Marjorie Ogilvie has told of her husband's anguish after he was found guilty of being over the legal blood alcohol limit when his car struck 11-year-old pedestrian Sarah Reynolds in August last year.

Mr Ogilvie was also found guilty of death by dangerous driving. Sheriff Robert Burke has *deferred sentence awaiting background reports.*

'My husband is most definitely not the type to drink and drive,' she said. *'Wallace frequently attends business lunches so some measure of entertainment is inevitable but he is not irresponsible. He might have a glass of wine or perhaps a whisky to be sociable. It is part of his job. But he wouldn't have more than that. I think someone must have spiked his drink or perhaps the barman poured the wrong measure by mistake.*

'My husband is an important member of this community and does substantial work for charity. It is very unfair that he is being prosecuted, I would go as far as to say persecuted, over this unfortunate accident.

'My heart goes out to the family of this young girl but I do have to wonder why they are so insistent on this being dragged through the courts. I feel that it is probably a feeling of guilt on their part that is making them do it.

'We are parents too and we know that you cannot watch them 24 hours a day. However we would certainly not have let ours run wild and unsupervised at that age. Perhaps her parents are wondering whether their daughter would still be alive if she had been brought up better and taught the simple rules of road safety.'

It is understood that Mr Ogilvie, who had held a clean driving licence for 27 years, had little chance to avoid hitting the girl who was in the middle of the road. The Daily Record spoke to a witness to the accident who preferred to remain anonymous.

'It was a terrible thing. The girl ran into the road and the car didn't have a chance to stop. I think she was mucking around with her friends. Some of the kids round here are a bit wild. The girl was killed right away. The poor guy driving the car was distraught but he couldn't have done anything about it.'

Ronald Cooke, spokesman for the Motorist's Association, said that drivers were increasingly paying a heavy price for the 'erratic behaviour' of pedestrians.

'Clearly we cannot condone drink driving,' he said. *'But there is also a responsibility on other road users to avoid accidents. Motorists*

have a right to expect pedestrians to obey the laws of the road.

'We have seen incidents where children and young adults have blatantly put their own lives at risk with their erratic behaviour. They are also endangering the lives of drivers and putting them in positions where accidents cannot be avoided.'

Mrs Ogilvie said that her husband was anxious to avoid a jail sentence, as it would seriously hinder his charity work.

'Wallace does so much good work for local children's charities and it would break his heart not to be able to continue with that.

He is not worried about prison for his own sake but he has projects which are at a vital stage and he is so worried that they will fail without him. There is so much money at stake and it would be terrible if the children missed out.

'We are hopeful that the judge will use common sense and impose perhaps a community service order. That would allow Wallace to devote even more time to helping people and surely that would be of more benefit to everyone.'

The family of Sarah Reynolds were unavailable for comment.

My daughter did not run into the road. My daughter was crossing the road carefully. My daughter was not wild. My daughter was very well behaved.

Wallace Ogilvie was drunk. Wallace Ogilvie was more than twice the drink-driving limit. Wallace Ogilvie was driving at over 40 mph in a 30 mph zone. Wallace Ogilvie was a murderer. Wallace Ogilvie murdered my daughter. Wallace Ogilvie ended up spending one year in prison.

There was no anonymous witness. Keith Imrie made that up. I listened to every word spoken by every witness who was in court. None of them would have said anything close to that.

Ronald Cooke did not say all those things. I spoke to Ronald Cooke. Keith Imrie misquoted him.

We were not unavailable for comment. We very much wanted to comment.

His words, his weasel words, kept coming back to me. Like angry, hurtful, stabbing reminders. Salt in my open wounds.

Poor guy.

Erratic behaviour.

Bit wild.

Unsupervised.

Heavy price.

Accident.

Charity work.

Spiked his drink.

Break his heart.

Mucking around.

Guilt.

Persecuted.

Unfortunate accident.

The words were like arrows. Like grenades. Like bear traps. Like a kick in the balls when you are lying beaten on the ground.

Keith Imrie was a liar. Keith Imrie defiled my daughter's memory. Keith Imrie could not do that. Couldn't do that and get away with it. What kind of reporter would write a thing like that about a dead girl? What sort of father wouldn't do anything for his daughter? Screw your eyes wide shut and make a wish. Do anything to bring her back. Anything.

CHAPTER 48

Ingram Street on a cool, damp morning in May. Tourists wrapped up in jumpers and waterproofs, locals dressed in T-shirts. Cars crashing through puddles, pedestrians jumping. Buses spewing out exhaust fumes, a sharp wind chasing litter down the street. People hurrying to nowhere. A nowhere paved with dog shit, chewing gum and paper bags from Greggs.

Glasgow unchanged.

The Cutter had gone away and in two minutes flat it was as if he had never been there. And maybe he never had.

I still walked among them, untouched, unknown, uncaught. Blown past them in the wind, only seen out of the corner of a bleary eye, half-glimpsed, soon forgotten. There was a cup final coming on the telly and no time to talk about a man who was no longer there. Part of me wanted to stop someone, all of them, and tell them it was me. I did it. I was the one. I wanted to scream it out because the way it was, it just didn't work.

Revenge, even when served cold, doesn't taste as sweet as you hoped. A sour taste left in my mouth and a deep-seated certainty of something missing. A hollow, aching lack of satisfaction.

Wanted to tell everyone, couldn't tell anyone. That would have been sure to spoil it all. The best-laid plans would have gang very agley. Imrie would be seen as innocent when he was as guilty as the most grievous sin. And worse, much worse, I would have ruined my wee girl's memory. Her dad was a taxi driver. Not a killer, never that.

It rattled inside me, like a key in a biscuit tin, clanging against the few remnants of conscience. A man who wants to scream out his darkest secret to the world will never know peace.

Ingram Street on a cool, damp morning. Accusing looks from those who knew nothing, brushing by their empty stares, pushing past their pointing fingers and pointed indifference. Either they were ghosts or I was. How could they not see? How could they fail to notice my guilt, fail to hear my silent screaming?

I was ready for them though. When they saw me for what I was and what I had done, I had all the answers that were necessary. They couldn't fail to understand. The parents among them would appreciate it for sure. They would have done the same as me. Maybe not all of them but some, the driven and the guilty.

But they could never know. My wee girl's dad had to be whiter than white. She deserved a dad like that. Like Jack the Ripper fading back into the mist of old London town,

I had to get away with it. Job done. The screaming had to stay silent. The rage had to simmer inside me.

Jack got away with it. The single most famous serial killer in history yet still unknown. Outstanding. Some people thought they knew who Jack was but they didn't. They couldn't know. Outstanding.

Ditching the taxi and walking to clear my head wasn't working. A head so full of things was going to take a long time to clear. I'd need to walk to Hell and back not just the length of the Merchant City. The high, stone-blasted buildings were already closing in on me. I was so wrapped and trapped in their prison walls that I didn't notice her. I had walked two steps past before she stepped out of the shadow of the shop front and called out my name. It stopped me in my tracks. Nearly stopped my heart too. In the time it took me to turn round I had rearranged my face.

She was dressed in the dark suit I'd seen her wear for a television interview. Her hair tied back, white blouse crisp. Very businesslike. She was looking at me for a reaction. She wasn't getting one.

'DS Narey. Doing some shopping?'

'Sort of, yes. I'm on the hunt for something special. Something I've been looking for for a while.'

'Oh well. Best of luck.'

I was tempted to turn and go at that but it wouldn't have got me anywhere. She would have followed. That was the way she was.

'Aren't you going to ask me what I'm hunting for?'

'Why would I do that?'

CRAIG ROBERTSON

'Thought you might be curious.'

I held her gaze for a while. Weighing options. Making decisions.

'I'm curious why you are playing games, DS Narey. If you want to tell me something then tell me. If you want to ask me something then ask me. Stop messing me about.'

She smiled. Smiled as if she had scored a point.

'I know how it works. I've been doing this for a while.'

She left that hanging there. Still smiling. Trying to make me think she knew something. She knew nothing. Some people thought they knew who Jack was but they didn't. They couldn't know.

After an age, she spoke.

'Why would you think I was messing you about?'

'Well, for a start, you are doing it again now.'

'Am I?'

'Fuck off, DS Narey. Where is your fat friend DC Whatsisname anyway?'

'Day off. We don't go shopping together.'

'So are you working, shopping or hunting?'

'Bit of all three. We never rest.'

I could feel it inside me. The rattling key, the aching lack of satisfaction, the thing that was missing, all wrapped in the need to get away with it. Wanted to tell her, couldn't tell her. Silent screaming.

'What do you want from me?'

'The truth.'

Tell her. A child's voice came at me. My wee girl's voice. Tell her. No. Tell her. No. Can't. Ruin everything.

You want to. I know but I can't. Clang, clang, conscience, clang.

No.

'You can't handle the truth. That's the line from the film, isn't it?'

'Oh, I can handle the truth. That's not the problem. The problem is when people want to unburden themselves of the truth but don't.'

She is right, said my wee girl. Tell her. No. No. No.

'No fucking games, DS Narey. If you are still on about me killing Wallace Ogilvie then your information is out of date. Don't you read the papers?'

She was smiling at me again. Rattled me and knew it.

'Well, I never mentioned you murdering Ogilvie. Or anyone else. But seeing as you mentioned it . . . Yes, I read the papers. Don't believe everything I read in them though. Told you that before.'

Still smiling.

Me saying nothing. Thinking. Deliberating.

'For example. I have to wonder how Keith Imrie would have the first clue how to electrocute someone. Or how he could have got to Baillieston to kill Spud Tierney just half an hour after his shift at the *Record* finished. Or why he would have been so stupid as to go to the Tesco when Fiona Raedale died. And I really have to wonder why some of the stuff we found in Imrie's flat like the business card, the betting slip and the ashtray didn't have his fingerprints on them.'

'No idea.'

'That's it? The best that you can do? No idea?'

'Not my job to explain what you can't, DS Narey. What the fuck do I know about that scumbag and what he could or couldn't have done?'

'Scumbag?'

Step too far. Think.

'Yeah, scumbag. He murdered six people. Whole country knows it.'

She looked doubtful.

'Well, the papers say it. That's true enough.'

'Strathclyde Polis too. The rest of your lot have no doubt. Seemed quite pleased with themselves. No doubt whatsoever.'

'Between you and me?' She had lowered her voice in mock conspiracy. 'Some of my colleagues are fucking idiots. Believe what suits them.'

That hung between us. So did the voices that said yes and no to me. To give her what she wanted, to run, to finish it. She knew nothing. She couldn't know.

'We have been through this, DS Narey. Nothing to do with me. You have followed me. You have interrogated my wife. You have searched my house. You have taken my computer away. Nothing to do with me.'

'Oh aye. Your computer. Funny thing that. Nothing had been installed or downloaded onto your PC any longer than six months ago yet it was four years old. Never use it much till recently?'

Pause. Just a heartbeat.

'I had a couple of viruses. Had to wipe the computer to get rid of them.'

'That must have been very inconvenient.'

'It happens. Didn't lose anything important.'

'Ah you never know what you've got till it's gone. Never know what's important.'

This bitch was starting to annoy me.

She never took her eyes off mine. Never was going to take her eyes off me.

'This is fucking harassment.' I was shouting now. Anger was justified in an innocent man.

'I've told you till I am sick of it. I am not a fucking serial killer. The man who was responsible is dead. Everyone accepts that except you.'

'Yes, convenient that, wasn't it? That Imrie wasn't able to deny being the random killer of six innocent people. Well, five innocent people and Wallace Ogilvie.'

Yes, very convenient, DS Narey. Fuck you. Fuck you. Silent screaming at full blast. Fuck you.

'Fuck you!' I was shouting again. 'It has nothing to do with me if it was convenient for anyone else or inconvenient for you. Leave me alone and go and catch some criminals. That's what you are paid for.'

She smiled. I so wanted to wipe that smile off her pretty face.

'You're right. That is what I'm paid for. Although some of them I'd happily catch for nothing.'

She let that hang there. Challenging me. She knew nothing. She couldn't know.

'Go do it then. Come talk to me again when you have something to say.'

'I'll do that.'

'Fine. Now fuck off.'

She looked at me. Those hard brown eyes burrowing into me. She knew something that she couldn't know.

Then with one last smile, she gave a slight nod, spun on her heels and left me standing there.

As I watched her back disappear into the Merchant City shadows, I knew what had to be done. There was no choice.

Sweet Rachel was too close, too smart, too persistent.

There had to be one more death.

CHAPTER 49

There was a note on the kitchen table saying she would be home by five. Dinner in the fridge if I couldn't wait. Have it together if I could hang on.

I could wait. I wanted to wait.

All those times that I did anything and everything to avoid sitting here sharing a meal or, worse, a conversation. Now I wanted nothing more than to be here when she came in and to sit with her.

Still didn't want to talk about Sarah. Still didn't want to talk about drunk drivers. Still didn't want to talk about Wallace Ogilvie. Still didn't want to talk about the so-called Cutter. Didn't want to reopen ugly old wounds. Wanted to heal some.

All those times I couldn't talk. About those things or any other. Just couldn't bear sitting there, being alive. So guilty to be breathing when I failed to protect the one person I was supposed to. That was my job, my duty and I failed.

Had always wanted to suffer that guilt alone. Much easier that way.

My own pain was hard enough to bear without having to endure hers too. Didn't want her pain adding to or detracting from mine. Enough was enough.

Tonight was different. Needed to speak with her. Needed the time together.

The front door opened at five to five and my heart jumped at the sound of it. Eight strides and she would be in the kitchen. The squeak of the door handle. Turning so slowly. In.

She seemed surprised to see me there. More surprised to see me get out of my chair and head for the fridge.

'Not eaten yet?' she asked.

'Thought I'd wait.'

'Oh. Right. Well, I'll put it on then.'

'It's OK. I'm getting it. Sit down. You've had a long day.'

She slipped her coat off without taking her eyes off me. Wary almost. Hung it on the back of the door with barely a glance at the hook.

I could feel her looking at me as I put the casserole dish in the oven, ready-heated. Knew she was watching me and wondering.

I collected two plates from the cupboard on the wall and fetched cutlery from the drawer. All the time she said nothing. Just watched.

I sat the plates in front of her and took my seat. I didn't know what I was going to say but I knew I was going to speak first. She deserved that to happen at least once in seven years. Wasn't easy for me, old habits. This was an effort. Had to hurry or she would talk. Wanted this done right. I spoke.

'How did your day go?'

She smiled slowly.

'My day?'

'Yeah, your meeting with the traffic police. How was it?'

'It . . . it went really well.'

'How er, how many of your group went along?'

'There was about eight of us.'

I was thinking that maybe meant four but didn't say so. Calling her a liar wasn't where I wanted to go.

'Right. Good turnout.'

It wasn't much but it was enough. She was encouraged to tell me about her whole day and the day before. I listened and asked a couple of questions.

We were still talking about her campaign when the dinner was ready. Maybe it was the break while I served up but she shifted the subject. I guess the campaign had put her halfway there.

'We were talking about him today. The superintendent knew who I was. Knew all about him and what happened . . .'

I interrupted.

'So did you get the answer you wanted from the cops?'

'What?'

'About the random tests near schools.'

'They, well, they said they would have to get back to us. Again. Said they'd need to talk to the schools. But the superintendent who knew about him said . . .'

'I guess they have to make sure the schools are onside or else it isn't going to work. Don't you think?'

She either took the hint or else was just happy to launch into a discussion about safety outside schools. She was off and running and it was fully fifteen minutes before she mentioned the killer. Or rather, before she talked about Keith Imrie.

'I always hated that man for the story he wrote,' she said out of nowhere. 'But oh my God, I never thought . . .' her voice trailed off.

Couldn't have this conversation. Not tonight. Had to keep those voices out. Had to switch it.

'Newspapers. Can't trust anyone in them. Did that guy from the *Herald* ever get back to you about the zero alcohol campaign?'

I knew she couldn't resist that. A particular bee in her bonnet.

'No, he hasn't. I need to phone him again because he . . .'

It was enough. Cheap tactic but necessary. Couldn't have her going down that road. The gnawing was back in my stomach and I couldn't feed it further. Needed it to be calm. Needed it to be different.

I listened and manoeuvred. Kept her away from anything that would inflame either of us. All the time resisting the urge that ate away at me. Telling myself I was in control. It was done. It was all but over. One more move. Couldn't think about that. Control it.

She kept talking as I cleared the plates and filled the dishwasher. Had to change the subject again. Her campaign was the lesser of the possible evils but it was bound to bring talk of Ogilvie and Imrie round again. Wanted more peace than that could possibly offer.

I leapt at an unlikely tangent and brought up our first holiday in Corfu when she was pregnant but didn't yet know. We'd stayed in a tiny studio halfway up a dirt track but thought it was the height of luxury. She remembered us hiring a moped and me crashing it with her on the back. If we'd known she was carrying Sarah then we'd never have been on it. No harm done though.

We had sat in the town square and watched them playing cricket in blistering heat, sipping a beer and holding hands. We did the Zorba dance in the middle of a restaurant and I was terrible at it.

She laughed at the memory of my dancing and I saw something different in her. Something from a long time ago. The girl that I met in college and took to the Barrowlands to see Teenage Fanclub. The girl that was pregnant less than a year after we met. The best mum, a good-looking, funny, warm person. I'd almost forgotten her. It wasn't just that I'd stopped looking for that girl, it was also that she'd gone away. She left on the same day Sarah did.

We eased onto the couch as we spoke but not parked on it like bookends as we usually were. Together. I'd moved nearer the middle and she took the hint and slipped in next to me. We must have looked like normal people.

She cuddled into me, a warmth that neither of us had felt for a long time. Mainly my fault. No, mainly Wallace Ogilvie's fault. Hate flared in me again. Revenge served up but still I raged. She felt it, lifting her head off me to see what was up. I eased her back down, a squeeze of her shoulder to say it was OK.

Needed to keep a lid on it. Had to bury it back inside me. My screaming had to stop for now.

I squeezed her again, more to comfort me than her but she didn't need to know that. Her soap opera was on the television and she was enjoying the fact I was actually watching it with her. That we were together.

I realized how long it had been since I even touched someone. Something about it didn't feel right because my hands had been other places, done other things. My dirty hands were liars. Holding her as if they had done nothing wrong, as if they had the right to soothe and comfort.

I'd stopped touching her because I was dead inside. Continued not to do it because I was unworthy of it. Hands that could never be washed clean.

Stop thinking. Leave it.

Just hold her.

She was enjoying it, burying her head into my shoulder as if she had missed it. She seemed at some kind of peace. The voice jumped into my head telling me that she had peace because she was glad I had killed Wallace Ogilvie.

Let it go. Shut it out.

I stared beyond her head, above the TV, into the past and the dark. Pulled her closer and felt that she liked it.

We sat like that, her in my arms until she dropped off to a sleep fuelled by contentment as much as pills. When I knew she had drifted off, I kissed her forehead and ran my fingers through her hair, whispering apologies and explanations to her as she slept. Murmuring my regrets. And things I didn't regret.

I told her I loved her.

I should really have carried her upstairs and put her to bed. Undressed her and tucked her in, left her safe there, snug in thoughts of Sarah. Instead I eased out from under her, careful not to wake her.

I liked seeing her there, something approaching happy. She cosied into the arm of the couch as if it was me, suddenly looking years younger. Not younger than she was but younger than she had become.

I stood at the open door and looked at her for a while, not thinking anything in particular, just looking. I released the door handle and stepped back into the room long enough to kiss her on the lips. She stirred briefly, somewhere deep inside her, a trace of a smile appearing on her face.

That was more reward than I was due.

It was time to go out. Time for that one final death.

CHAPTER 50

Cineworld in Renfrew Street is the tallest cinema in the world. In 2004 it was voted the least favourite building in Glasgow. Twenty-two escalators. Two hundred and three feet high. Sixty-one point nine metres down.

The view from the ledge at the top was quite spectacular if you took the time to look. Due east and yards below was the Royal Concert Hall, so close you could almost jump to it if you had a mind. A crazy mind.

North and east across the interchange was the Park Inn, red-bricked, modern and ugly.

Further east was the expanse of Buchanan bus station, people flooding in and out from across the city and across Scotland. Tiny scurrying, hurrying people.

Further north. Past the *Herald* where STV used to be, past the passport office and *The Sunday Post*. On and up where Tennent's brewery sat up on the hill, firing out smoke and beer. And smells that could keep a jaikie drunk for a week.

Behind and to the west snaked Sauchiehall Street. Its

end was below me now where it marched into the pedestrianized semicircle in front of the concert hall. The other end was a mile away. Halfway down was where Thomas Tierney cut across my path and became nothing more than a number.

South sailed the rivers of West Nile Street, Renfield Street, Buchanan Street and Hope Street, all flooding to the Clyde and carrying the flotsam and jetsam of humanity along with them. An irresistible force of nature in the raw.

South of the cinema was where the city centre proper began. A tight-packed grid, rigidly and regimentally laid out, barely a curve or a gap to break the lines. Businesses and retail, double yellow lines and one-way streets. A warren of trade and industry.

To my left Queen Street station was bellowing out its presence. Further south you could just make out the sounds of Central roaring its reply.

Glasgow was so small from up there. So insignificant. So many people. Thousands of ants rushing to and fro in search of their next disappointment.

Lift your head if you dared and you could see as far as the weather would allow. North to the Campsies, south to East Kilbride, west to the airport at Paisley, east to Coatbridge. Up above the roofs and houses, you could see heaven and you could see hell.

East past Celtic Park and beyond to the wilds of Shettleston and Baillieston where Tierney died in a pool of blood. You could see it all.

North and west to Maryhill where Raedale died in her

own mess at her Tesco till and Billy Hutchison fried at the flick of a switch.

West and over the river to Inchinnan where Brian Sinclair, whose only crime was to have been married and happy, had choked on The Cutter's story.

Due north to Port Dundas Business Park where Wallace Ogilvie froze to death at least seven years too late. Much further north still to Milngavie where Jonathan Carr was glued tight and breathed no more.

City of death. City of devils and angels. All laid out before me like a body on a mortuary slab, grey and grim.

You could see it all from the tallest cinema in the world.

It was very windy at the top, quite dangerous really. Looking round and down and beyond was enough to make your head spin. They should be more careful about that emergency exit door on the thirteenth floor that leads to the repair crew's stairwell. Anyone could make their way up there. It would take a good few minutes before an alarm was heard and staff could get to the roof, even if they knew where to look and what to look for. There is no way they could be quick enough to stop what was going to happen.

One final death. It's the way it had to be. Nothing random about it though. It was more of a crashing inevitability.

I think I knew that from the moment that Detective Sergeant Rachel Narey first held my gaze and looked inside me, it could have turned out no other way. Call it fatalism or fate. Free will and random acts all lead to the same inevitable end.

That end was nigh.

It was no big deal. Just confirmation of something.

I'd been dead for nearly seven years. My headstone should have read, 'Died 5 August 2003. The same day as his much loved daughter Sarah. RIP.'

Rest in peace? Maybe.

Maybe now.

It was Confucius who said it first and best. Before you embark on a journey of revenge, dig two graves, one for yourself.

I dug my graves a long time ago.

When the first sod of earth was cut to make a hole in the ground for a sweet eleven-year-old princess then I picked up my spade. I dug for Wallace Ogilvie and I dug for Keith Imrie. Most of all I dug for me. I died the day she died. My eternity in hell began that day.

No big deal. Just one final, inevitable death after so many. Just making the outside match the inside. Pairing up the physical with the metaphysical. Bringing an end to all the shite. Call it selfish if you like. Call it putting things right but there is always a price to pay. You reap what you sow and my reaper was grim.

The grave I'd dug for myself was not a frightening place for me. I welcomed it now. I'd come to realize that it was the only way I could ever find the peace I craved.

It was right, too. It was right and it was time. It wasn't about salvation, redemption or penitence. Those were high moral stations that were way out of my reach and I wasn't going to wrap my reasoning in them. Salvation is supposed to be about escaping the bondages of sin but there are some sins you can't run away from even if you wanted to. I could feel no sorrow, no remorse or shame, no urge to repent. I was empty. All out of everything, even anger, even hate.

I had hated Wallace Ogilvie for taking what was mine and I had wanted my revenge. That was gone too.

What I was going to do was not about any of that. It was an end, the only kind of closure that could ever be open to me. There could never be a living closure. No living, breathing peace of mind. This was the only way I could find a kind of peace.

I'd done what I'd promised, to her and to myself and now I could end it.

A journey starts with a single step and it ends with one too. Confucius was only half right. I took one step. That was all it needed.

A step towards a strange kind of peace. One step. The ground came to me after that. From two hundred and three feet it called to me from the slabs on Renfrew Street.

From chewing-gum-stained concrete to fresh air at the top of the cinema. Hardly poetry but it would do the job. Tallest cinema in the world, you know. A long way up. A long way down.

Long enough to think thoughts of Sarah. Of Carr and Tierney. Of Billy Hutchison and Brian Sinclair. Of Raedale, Imrie, Kirkwood and Narey. Of Ally McFarland.

I thought of guilt and responsibility. Of power and punishment. Of justice and judgement. Of wishes and vengeance. Of deals in the dark with the Devil.

I thought of Wallace Ogilvie. He had killed my princess

and now he was killing me. No. He'd killed me then but he wasn't killing me now. This was my choice, my time.

I thought of her too. My wife. My only shame. I hadn't thought of her enough in a long time. Her pain was numbed by pills and denial but it was no less than mine. Maybe it was only then, when it was far too late that I realized how much I was throwing more fuel on her pyre. Too late, couldn't go back.

There is a Disney cartoon, an old Mickey Mouse one from the 1930s or so. Mickey is in the countryside, walking along a hilltop whistling away to himself and taking in the view. He's not looking where he's going though and doesn't see the big gap in the hill that's just ahead of him. We see it. We see it and we know what's going to happen.

Mickey steps out into fresh air and keeps walking. But he doesn't fall. The laws of cartoon science dictate that because he doesn't realize that there is nothing underneath him then he doesn't plunge down the gap.

He has to look eventually though, has to realize. And when he does then his feet begin to go. Mickey fast-pedals his feet on nothing and, under the same animation laws, it manages to hold him up for a bit. But he has to fall, no other way.

Same with me.

All that had been holding me up was hate.

And in the final seconds, as the shout from the pavement became a full-blooded, deafening roar, I hated myself more than anyone else.

It was good that there was no way back, no Mickey

Mouse pedalling on nothingness. There had been enough of that.

You don't always get what you deserve in this world but sometimes you get more than you should. If that bothered me then it wasn't going to do so for long.

I didn't want redemption, didn't need penitence, didn't deserve salvation. I wanted to see my wee girl again.

I was smiling. Maybe for the first time in seven years. As concrete roared up at me louder and louder, I smiled.

Because there was hope in the God that I didn't believe in. The God that let me down and had torn me in two had become my only hope of mending. He promised an afterlife, the resurrection and the renewal of creation. The God that I didn't believe in held out the prospect of an eternal peace. All I had to do was believe in the unbelievable.

If there was the slightest chance that I could meet her again by believing then I could not turn it down. I could not resist. What sort of father would not do anything for his daughter?

As I fell I made the deal. I believed. I fell and I believed. I went to my Lord with a smile on my face and hope in my heart. I was going to meet my wee girl again.

I closed my eyes and screwed them shut so tight that it hurt. I had kept my promise, remembered my vow. *Our father, which art in heaven, hallowed be thy name.*

I smiled. It was done, ended, sorted. *Thy Kingdom come, thy will be done on earth as it is in heaven.*

Glasgow rushed by me and I knew I had done the right

thing, knew my good works were taking me to her and to my strange peace. *Give us this day our daily bread.*

My guilt and theirs were things of the past. No hatred left, no guilt, no blame. *And forgive us our debts as we forgive our debtors.*

All that was left was a scrap of hope wrapped in belief and disbelief. A journey beginning and ending with a single step on a path of misguided righteousness. *And lead us not into temptation but deliver us from evil.*

Somewhere, a big black dog barked, a woman screamed in her sleep, a policewoman expressed doubt and a baby girl cried.

For thine is the kingdom, the power and the glory.

Terra firma came rushing, firmly and finally.

For ever. Amen.

Simon & Schuster proudly presents

the fantastically taut and gripping new thriller from

CRAIG ROBERTSON

set on the mean streets of Glasgow

Available to read in trade paperback in June 2011

Turn the page for a sneak preview . . .

CHAPTER 1

It was raining. Of course it was raining, it was Glasgow. It didn't get to be the dear, green place without more than its share of rain.

The hundreds of hunched, angry shapes who were lined up in a disorderly queue outside Blochairn Market were getting pissed on and pissed off.

Pitches were allocated on a first come, first served basis and so people made sure they got there early. Some of them had been queuing since four in the morning. It was now just after seven – although to Tony Winter it still felt like the middle of the night – and these people had probably been crabbit even before they were told they had to leave their stall and get back outside the gates because some inconsiderate fucker had got himself stabbed.

Tony lifted his camera and took a quick shot of the entrance to the market. Scene setting. Not strictly procedure but it was always his way. It was the way Metinides did it and if it was good enough for the Mexican then it worked for him.

The carbooters were all facing the entrance, some back in their cars and others pacing about on foot like mental bears in a zoo. It meant he was able to take a shot of them from behind without risking getting his head kicked in. Rows of cars and vans that had been stacked full to the gunnels with everything under the sun. Views out of rear windows still blocked with boxes and piles of clothes, impatient people crammed between paste tables and plastic sheeting. Bottled-up humanity, simmering in the rain and not giving a fuck for the poor bastard that was dead, just desperate to get back inside and flog second hand shoes and remnants of make-up.

The Sunday car boot at Blochairn, minutes north of the city centre, is the biggest in Scotland and one of the biggest in Europe. You can buy everything from nearly-complete jigsaws to designer coats, second-hand books to antique jewellery and everything in between. You wouldn't believe what people will buy. It's only when you see someone counting out loose change to buy a cardigan that should have been chucked out years ago that you realise how hard up some people are.

He'd been before and seen two women fighting over threadbare dishtowels selling for ten pence each. There was probably a decade of grease and dirt on the towels but it was that or nothing for the women that wanted them. One person's rubbish is another's only choice. This was real poverty. Okay, maybe it could be eased by buying a few less packets of fags or less booze but that was the way it was and who was he to judge? Harrods wasn't really an option.

Cars would roll up to the market entrance from the early hours and they'd sit in the dark and wait for opening time, steaming up windscreens with half-hearted expectancy. They'd be there no time at all before torches would be shone at them and there would be a knock at the window. Sharp faces and searching eyes would reach in from the dark. What you selling? You shifting mobile phones? Buy them off you. You selling gold? How much you looking for for it?

Time comes and they roll inside and set up: clothes on wire hangers, ornaments and toys on wobbly tables, money in biscuit tins. Sales start long before the punters arrive, carbooters buying from each other in strange middle of the night deals.

The idea is to sell everything they bring as fast as they can and get out again. Not this day though. This day, one of those miserable September mornings doing a passable impression of a nasty December afternoon, was different. Two cops stood in front of the newly-relocked gates at Blochairn, others were at work inside and Winter was about to join them.

He nodded at Sandy Murray and Jim Boyle, the two PCs on the gate, as he passed them and headed into the market.

'Awrite Winter? Another day, another dead body.' Boyle made the same crack every time he saw him.

'Word of warning, Tony. That crabbit cunt Addison is in a bad mood. As usual.' Murray and Addison had never seen eye to eye and the DI had booted the constable's arse on a couple of occasions. Chances were Addison wasn't as grumpy as they were making out. It was just the same old, same old.

The covered bit of Blochairn was built in a T-shape. The regular stallholders had already been setting up either side of the upright and along the topline of the T while the casual carbooters had mainly been left outside to take their chances with the Scottish weather.

The body was waiting for Winter at the back. Up the vertical of the T and along past the end of the topline. The early morning wake-up call had already told him much of what he needed to know.

A lifeless heap in a dark puddle of blood, a knife wound to the heart. Found by a woman who had gone in search of carrier bags to keep the rain off teapots. The dead man was a number, a statistic. He might as well have had 'cliché' scrawled in blood on his forehead. Getting yourself stabbed to death in Glasgow showed a spectacular lack of originality.

The guy was a number but they already knew his name. As the chip wrappers would put it, he was known to the police. Sammy Ross, two-bit drug dealer, professional low life. Now a no life. He had become a statistic. It's no way for anyone to end up, but when you deal in drugs then it's almost a lifestyle choice.

It was only September but this was already fatal stabbing number 46 in Glasgow. There had been too many non-fatal ones to count. Tony had personally photographed fourteen of the previous forty-five and it was becoming very dull. Number 15 was likely to be no more interesting than the rest. He needed more.

It wasn't his job to do so but off the top of his head he could think of a dozen reasons why someone might have killed Sammy Ross. You didn't work with cops all day without learning something.

Someone might have wanted to pay less. Someone might have wanted to pay nothing. Maybe Sammy was cutting his heroin with too much sugar or powdered milk. Maybe Sammy had been selling worming pills as ecstasy tabs again. Maybe he had made promises he couldn't keep.

He could have been shagging someone he shouldn't have. He might not have been shagging someone he should. He could have owed money, he might have been defending a pal, he could have been done for the cash in his pocket.

Maybe he just looked at someone the wrong way. Maybe he just supported the wrong football team. In Glasgow there was no end of ways to get yourself stabbed. It didn't matter. Sammy Ross was a statistic and he was Tony's mess to photograph that morning. Happy days.

There he was. Stabbing 46, lying empty having leaked his life at the foot of DI Derek Addison. Addy had his hands thrust into the pockets of his raincoat, studying Ross with all the interest of someone finding shit under his shoe. Only September but it had already been a long year. Winter focused the camera on the two men – one live, one dead – and fired off a couple of shots. Scene two. The rapid clack-clack-clack of the motor made Addison whirl round angrily.

'Where the fuck have you been, Tony? Some of us have been here for half an hour. And stop taking my fucking picture.'

Winter knew he didn't really mean it. Addy was just as pissed off at being there in the rain as he was.

'Ah fuck off,' he fired back. 'Some of us don't have a flashing light and a car that goes nee-naw. Sammy Ross, I presume?'

'You been watching CSI again? Aye, Sherlock. One dead drug dealer with regulation stab wounds. Hurry up and take his photo. I'm starving.'

'You're always starving.'

Police photographers didn't always talk to cops this way, especially not detective inspectors, but Tony had earned the right over countless pints and drunken nights. He knew where Addy's bodies were buried. So to speak.

Addison was starving, as per normal, but the thought of food was doing nothing for Tony. His head throbbed from the effects of the night before and his body was rebelling at being hauled out of a warm, shared bed to come to this shithole. He couldn't help thinking that she was still in there, curled up soft, smooth and cosy where he'd left her. Every splash of teardrops from the Glasgow heavens was taunting him, reminding him how much he'd rather be tucked in behind her, nudging her awake with tunes of morning glory.

Instead he was in the rain with a dead man. A dull dead man. And the worst of it? Nobody would give a toss. Short of maybe Sammy's mammy – and even that was doubtful given what a waste of space he was - no-one would care that he was lying in a pool of his own. No-one had time to be bothered. Not about Sammy at any rate. The next body would be along any minute. There would only be time to roll Ross out of the gutter to make way for the next scumbag that had drawn a target on his own chest and had to be immortalised on digital.

Pick up a Sunday paper any week and you'll likely find a couple of paragraphs on someone stabbed to death. Two paragraphs. That's all it was worth. Somebody's wean knifed into oblivion and all they could be arsed giving it was half a dozen lines. Said it all.

Winter could see on their faces that everyone else on site was as scunnered with stabbing 46 as he was. Scumbag stabbed by scumbag. City is one scumbag less. Only another few thousand to go. Case closed.

Uniforms: fed up with it. The DI: fed up with it. Campbell Baxter, the senior scene examiner: clearly fed up with it.

It didn't mean that any of them wouldn't do their job. Sammy Ross would get the same duty of care and attention as the rest. He would be measured up, dusted down, forensically examined and given a good wash before going to a hole in the ground or the burny fire.

In the unlikely event that there would be witnesses then they would be questioned; doors would be knocked on; known associates would be talked to. Maybe, just maybe, the cops would find out who shanked the dealer. Maybe, just maybe, the great Glasgow public would give a monkey's if they did.

There were probably worse places to be early on a wet, miserable Sunday than a damp corner of Blochairn but right at that moment Winter was buggered if he could think of any. The natives at the gate were getting restless and Tony imagined he could hear the sound of pitchforks being sharpened as they planned an attack. Mon to fuck. Hurry the fuck up. What's keeping you? A deid body that's what, haud your horses.

Little splashes of rain were falling into the burgundy pool that Sammy had drowned in, making waves that fucked up any blood splatter calculations that Two Soups Baxter would try to make. Not that it mattered much.

None of it made much difference. Tony had just seen it too many times. Fucking stabbings. This city was going to hell in a hurry. You were twice as likely to be murdered in Glasgow as in London. There was more chance of you getting stabbed in the no mean city than in the worst areas of Los Angeles or Moscow. It kept you in work if your job was to photograph the leftovers.

He'd been doing just that for four years and this moment, the point where he was about to look at the body for the first time, was always the same. From day one to this, it hadn't changed. Excited and scared, fifty-fifty. What he was scared of was also exactly what he wanted to see. And part of the reason he was scared of it was because he knew just how much he wanted to see it.

Tony could kid himself all he wanted about how dull another stabbing was but he was still interested in the business end of that shitty, miserable morning. It was what got him out of bed whether he liked it or not.

The thing is that being there, in the moment before the flowers and the football tops mourn another victim, when blood still runs hot in a body that has given up its ghost, is a strange privilege. You can see much of what the person had been and some of what they might have been if the city hadn't cut them down. It was a moment that messed with his head every time.

You saw them caught in the very moment that they were claimed. He was already feeling the ache to see and to photograph the expression on Sammy Ross's face as much as the wound in his belly. He knew that made him a bit of a sick fucker but it was his itch.

There was a Gaelic word that he loved. Winter only knew a handful of words and phrases, the obvious ones like *uisge beatha* and *slainthe*, whisky and cheers. In fact when he thought about it, the words that he knew in the Gaelic either said a lot about his drinking or about Scotland. Apart from words about boozing, he could count to five – *aon, da dha, tri, ceithir, coig* – and trot out *ceud mile failte*, a hundred thousand welcomes. His favourite though was *sgriob*. An old boy from Skye named Lachie, who used to drink in the Lismore, taught him it.

It means the itchiness, the tingle of anticipation that comes upon the upper lip just before taking a sip of whisky. Brilliant. The Eskimos may have a hundred different words for snow but trust the Gaels to have a word for that.

Another old teuchter later told him that you had to say *sgriob drama* or *sgriob dibhe* for it to refer specifically to whisky or else it just meant a scratch or scrape. Old Lachie was full of shit right enough but Tony preferred to believe he was right on this one.

Everyone had an itch and this was Tony's. *Sgriob* death. The hot, smooth, soft woman that was lying curled up in his warm bed once called it necrophotographilia. It wasn't sexual though. Not that. Cheeky cow, he thought.

Every bit as much as he was tired of death, sick of it, he couldn't help looking. Working in Glasgow is a daily car crash and he was a professional rubbernecker. He knew he was making himself wait. Prolonging the *sgriob*. Savouring the final seconds before he looked, wondering if Sammy boy would be scared or shocked, outraged or questioning. Would that stab wound be angry or clinical, lunatic or clean? How much blood and where?

The first dead body he ever saw was the first one he photographed. Day one on photo cop duty and called out to a car smash on the M80 just north of Muirhead. A woman no more than 25 had gone head-first through the windscreen. No seat belt, no chance. Silly bitch, really.

He'd been told what had happened on his way to the crash and his stomach was already doing somersaults. He nearly threw up when he saw her lying in a shroud of broken glass in front of her Renault Clio. A smart silver car with a pair of pink hanging dice that she had vaulted past on her hurry through the glass.

The cop on the scene said she must have managed to duck her head forward because there was barely a scratch on her face. The top of her skull was smashed and the steering wheel had wrecked her chest but her face was all but unmarked. She had this clear look of determination, had been doing all she could to stay alive and protect herself. Everything, that is, apart from putting her seatbelt on in the first place.

Tony took one photo. Knelt a few feet away from her, snapped one then was backing away towards the barrier when the uniform came over and hissed in his ear. Asked him what the fuck he thought he was doing. Told him he had to photo the woman from every possible angle, make sure there was no doubt whatsoever as to position, trauma, depth, scale, everything and then when he had done that he had to photograph tyre depths, skid distances, glass shatter, all approaching junctions, everything. Winter had known all that, of course, but every bit of his training had gone through his arse when he saw the woman lying on the road.

The cop dragged his head into gear and he did what he was supposed to. But he didn't stop there. Beyond the caved skull and the battered torso, the glass pattern and the skid signature, he photographed the look of business on the face of the uniformed polis that covered her up and the frightened stare of the witness who couldn't tear his eyes away from her.

Looking back, he wondered at the nerve of tucking his own Canon SLR away in his bag beside the digital Nikon that the department provided but was glad that he did. Something about the grain of the black and white film gave it a feel that he liked. More importantly the shots weren't on the official memory card.

Avril Duncanson, exhibit one. He didn't suppose he would ever forget her name if he did a million jobs. Anyway, her photographs were in his collection so there was always something there to remind him. As if it was needed. Some things you never forget. Close your eyes and they are hiding there behind your lids.

Tony snapped backed to the dreich reality of Blochairn and realised that Two Soups was huffing about him getting on with it, pushing for him to get his photographs done so that the examiners could get in about the body. He was a miserable old sod; easily Tony's least favourite of the six forensics that could have been on scene. If the lovely Cat Fitzpatrick was at one end of the scale then Two Soups was definitely at the other. He was a pain in the arse. Old school type who had this hatred of amateur forensics, particularly cops, who had learned all they knew from the rush of telly programmes on the subject.

But sadly for Baxter, photography always comes first at a crime scene, recording everything as is before the forensic gets in to touch anything and old Two Soups never liked that. It meant his time was dictated to and that wasn't the way he thought it should be. Monkeys with cameras ought not to take precedence over highly-trained scientists, or something like that. This morning he was clearly pissed off that Tony hadn't been on site earlier. He didn't say anything, just glowered. Well he could get to fuck. Winter only had one chance to record this scene and he wasn't going to rush it even if it was just yet another stabbing.

He lined up a full-length shot of the body and focused – in more ways than one. Two Soups was shut out and so was the rest of the world. It was just him and Sammy Ross.

He took in the look on the face below him for the first

time. Resignation. Total defeat. Not shock, though. Sammy Ross had seen this coming. Now he had this thousand-yard stare into infinity and it didn't look as if he liked what he saw.

Tony did though. For all its ugliness, it was a thing of beauty.

Rigor mortis had begun to kick in, so he must have been dead for a few hours. The knees that had given way as he buckled and fell were already locked. One arm bent under him, clutching at the hole in his chest, the other twisted at his side where he had tried to break his fall. No chance of breaking a fall like that though – it descended straight into Hell.

The burgundy blood-spill soaked his jeans and drenched his light blue t-shirt but was already drying on both. His skin was alabaster pale and his lips kissed with blue.

It was a deep incision. Through the torn, bloodied scraps of cotton, Tony could see the ripped skin where the knife had been stuck. An initial entry wound then it rose sharply up the chest tearing skin as it went. The killer had stuck it in then twisted the knife before pushing it up deeper and deadlier, seeking out vital organs to destroy. Been there, seen it, bought the t-shirt.

Whoever did it had used a knife before. In Glasgow, that narrowed it down to maybe a quarter of the male population between 12 and 25.

He focused on the wound. It was almost big enough to reach inside and grab those punctured organs, enough room to get in and search for the spirit that was no longer there.

The skin was split and smiling up at him, the treasures behind already starting to fester without the beat of life to sustain them.

Focus. Shoot. Every detail, from every angle. So tempting to lift the t-shirt and see the full extent of the damage but that was strictly forbidden. Look but don't touch. Record but don't interfere. Observe but don't violate. Chronicle but don't contaminate. He focused, he shot, he looked.

Designer trainers, at least £120 the pair. Hideous, flash shoes in black and gold that screamed price tag. The Burberry cap that had tumbled off his lank, unkempt hair and lay by the side of his sleeping head. The navy blue Ben Sherman jacket sprayed with his own blood and the Tag Heuer that was smashed on his wrist but still ticked even though his heart had stopped. It all said money. It all said bad taste. It all said trash with cash.

His blue-purple lips said no. His eyes said please. A rabbit caught in the headlights of his own destiny, a victim of what he did and of the city that spawned him. Bastard child of greed and poverty.

All that was laid out in the broken body before him, writ large in the wound in his middle and on his freeze-frame face. Sammy was a picture all right.

This was why Winter took photographs. To show it how it was, every wart, every insult, every injury, because every city is defined just as much by its ugly wounds as its architecture. He'd always imagined that if you cut Glasgow's gutterbelly, you'd see it run blue and green with bitterness but with as much hope as there was bile. It was a great city where terrible things happened, things that should never be ignored but should be captured forever.

His job had taken him to dark places that most civilians never go, seeing bloody puddles where life used to be, recording the moment before the mourners descended. All life was there, sitting cosy right next to death.

That was the bit that always got to him, just how close they sit next to each other. A split second, a nanosecond, an angstrom from one to the next. And he was there to ensure that that precise moment, where life turns to death and hope turns to shit, is always recorded right there on their face. Recorded forever by a Nikon FM 2 and a Canon EOS-1D.

A thing of beauty really.

CHAPTER 2

'If I remember right then Sammy boy is from Garngad or maybe Royston, east end for sure.'

The voice came from behind Winter and dragged him out of his dwam. It was Addison.

'He's 32, 33, something like that. Old to be still knocking it out on the street. Sure-fire sign he was going nowhere fast. Kind of bam that pushes out coke, heroin, jellies, ecstasy, dope, uppers, downers, steroids; whatever the junkies want, this cunt would stuff it down their throat, in their arm or up their nose.'

Addison was angry and it was obvious in his voice. He'd seen way too much of this shit.

'Just a foot soldier in Malky Quinn's army of bastards,' he went on. 'Funny how Malky and his like never end up lying stabbed in the rain. It's always the Sammy Rosses that get it. One of Malky's boys . . . brilliant. Means trouble for someone. Probably means trouble for everyone. Fuck sake, it's not even eight o' clock and the day's already turned to shit. I want a bacon roll.'

Winter had finished his photographs but hadn't stopped looking. He was irritated at Addy for shaking him out of it but when he caught the snappy look on Two Soups' face then maybe it was just as well. The fat old bastard looked fit to burst. Winter ignored his glare.

'You ever stop thinking about your stomach, Addy,' he said as he stood up. 'No wonder you are such a fat bastard.'

The DI was six foot four and a skinny sod, his height just making him look even thinner.

He was just about to come back with a smart arse remark of his own when his DS, a haunted looking guy with dirty fair hair name of Colin Monteith wandered up towing a human skelf wearing trackies, a heavy white jacket and the obligatory baseball cap. Junkie ned. Monteith must have had the uniformed boys talking to the walking dead that were anywhere near the market at that time of the morning. Though if any of *them* had ever known anything, chances were they had already forgotten. Addison rolled his eyes as if to say, jeez, this better be good.

Monteith told the skelf to stay put and came up to where the pair were standing.

'Might have a live one, Addy. This guy was dossing in the market but he actually knows what day it is so I'd say he's worth a wee word. Says he heard noises that sound like it was our man meeting his maker.'

'Knows what day it is?' Tony butted in. 'Does that qualify him for some award scheme? Junkie of the month maybe.' Monteith fired him a dark look that said keep the fuck out of it. Christ, take a joke man, thought Tony.

'I'll have a word,' said Addy with a sigh. 'He might be as near to compos mentis as we are going to get from the zoomers round here. Bring him over.'

The skelf was brought and Winter toyed with some phrase about Addison not going to the addict so the addict had to come to Addy. It was just a stabbing; he had to keep himself amused somehow.

The inspector's lanky frame towered over the under-nourished user, leaving him in no doubt who was in charge. The skelf looked up at Addison uncomfortably, shifting from foot to foot.

'So, you heard noises?' It was as much a statement as a question. 'Tell me about them.'

'It's like ah telt the other polis. I'd been sleeping. It was still dark o' clock. Know what I mean, man?'

Addy looked like he was resisting the temptation to tell him to get on with it but settled for a nod instead. 'Aye well, it wis still pure dark an ah heard voices. Arguing, man. But no that loud. It went on for a bit then there wis this bit eh a mad scream that stopped quick an ah heard the guy hit the deck.'

'What did you hear after that?'

'Nothing, man.'

'Nothing? Anyone walking away, anyone running? Anyone crying for help? A car starting, maybe a motorbike? Something hitting the ground after being thrown away?'

'No. Well, aye. Someone walking away. I'd say he wisnae running, kinda slow like he was maybe dragging something. Naebody crying for help though. Would say he was well deid.'

'And what did you do? Call the police like a good citizen?'

'No way, man. Sorry, but no way. I was jist laying low in case the guy came back. Nae point in me getting offed as well. I might have fell asleep again. No sure. Next thing I know the place is full of polis.'

'Did you see the person that did it? Height, hair colour, anything?

'It wis dark man, telt ye. Anyways, didnae lift ma heid tae look. Just listened.'

'What did you mean when you said he was dragging something? Carrying something with him?'

'Mibbes. Ah've nae idea. Carrying, dragging. Mibbes.'

Addison shook his head despairingly then nodded Monteith back in to take the junkie away and finish taking notes.

'Tell him anything and everything you remember and don't go booking any foreign holidays for any time soon.'

'Aye very funny. Any chance of a few quid for coming forward?'

'Sure. See the officer at the cash desk on your way back out the market. Mind and duck in case there are any pigs flying past. Fuck off.'

The skelf's comeback about pigs died on his lips and he slunk off with Monteith's meaty paw on his arm.

'Sunday, bloody Sunday,' moaned Addison. 'Hurry up and finish photographing that muppet and bring your camera with you,' he told Winter. 'There's a van down the street that does good grub even though most of the folk who go to it are too shit-faced to know the difference. You can photograph me eating two bacon rolls. Brown sauce on it and a cup of coffee. You're paying.'

Tony didn't bother asking why. Just as Addison didn't bother asking why he'd been photographing the dealer's body with his Canon EOS-1D as well as the standard issue Nikon FM 2. The same reason Addison didn't ask why Winter had sneaked a shot of the haunted look on the skelf's face as he stared down at Sammy's corpse. Addison was one of only two cops who knew about Tony's collection. He'd even said the snapper should stage an exhibition but that was usually when he was pished.

Suddenly, Two Soups barged in between them, asking if they were quite finished. Big mistake. He could pull that shit with Winter but not with Addison.

'Mr Baxter,' he glared down at the fat forensic and growled. 'I was interviewing possibly the only witness to whoever killed this guy. Tony Winter was photographing the body. Both of these tasks are vital to this investigation and it was imperative that they be done without delay. The body, on the other hand, isn't going anywhere. I take it you have no fucking problem with that?'

Two Soups blinked at some disbelief in being spoken to that way and struggled for a reply. He finally found some words but the DI wasn't for hearing them.

'Well I was just...'

'Fine. I'm glad you agree. We are both finished so now you and the lab monkeys can begin your equally invaluable work. Winter has footprints to photograph and I've got stallholders to interview. We won't keep you.'

With that Addy took Tony by the arm and led him away from Baxter and the body, leaving Two Soups spluttering a noise of discontent behind them before calling his forensic soldiers to the battlefield.

'That man is an arsehole,' said Addison with a grin on his face.

'Where are these footprints?' Winter asked him.

'Two pairs of them together on soft ground near a wall on the north side. Suggestion is that it could be our man Sammy and whoever came in with him because they were heading in the direction of where Ross was found before they were lost on tarmac.'

'So if they are on the north side, why are we heading this way?' asked Tony with a quiet laugh.

'Because I want bacon rolls and you are buying. Jesus Christ, do you never listen to anything I say? Two uniforms have got the area secure and covered over, the footprints can wait but my stomach won't.' Addison drove his hands deep into his pockets as he led Winter towards the van in search of sustenance. 'How many times are we expected to do this?' he moaned. 'If I'd wanted to sweep the rubbish off the street I'd have joined the council bin squad. At least I'd have been back in my fucking bed by now.'

Bed. She'd still be lying there, thought Tony, and probably sprawled over onto his side of it by now. Addy was still whinging but all he could think of was her body. A dead dealer and a bacon roll didn't really cut it in comparison.

It was less than a five-minute walk to the van. A dark-haired fat guy who was far cheerier than anyone had a right to be at that time in the morning was serving two teenagers as they arrived. The pair immediately spotted Addison for polis and couldn't wait to get their grub and leave. Their hurried departure didn't bother either Addy or Winter. If there was a soul in Glasgow whose conscience wasn't bothered by the sight of a cop then chances were it was another cop. It was water off a duck's back to them.

'Four bacon rolls, Charlie,' Addison said to the fat man.

'Three,' Tony corrected him.

'Four,' he repeated. 'I'll have your other one if you don't want it.

'Brown sauce, Mr Addison?' asked Charlie

'Does the Pope shit in the woods? Of course, brown sauce.'

Addy turned his collar to the morning chill and took in the smell of pork and fat and beef coming from the van's grill.

'This place should have a Michelin star,' he said to Winter. Then, 'What time did you start this morning, Charlie?'

'Half six. Think your boys and girls were already at the market by the time I turned up if that's what you were thinking.'

'It was. Who was on before you?'

'Jimmy Frize. He'd been on since eleven last night. Never mentioned anything out of the ordinary. Usual shit.'

'Drunks and druggies?'

'Does a bear wear a big hat?'

'Aye, aye. Where can I get hold of Jimmy?'

Charlie wrote Frize's number on a piece of paper and handed it over to Addy who had already scoffed his two rolls even though Tony had only managed half of one.

'Another roll, Mr Addison? On the van.'

'You trying to bribe a police officer, Charlie? Aye, go on then.'

'No as if you are going to put on any weight, is it? Put a slice of black pudding in there too, Mr A. Ah know how you're partial.'

'Plenty of brown sauce, Charlie.'

Addy started on his extra roll as they turned their backs on the van and ambled back towards Blochairn, the debris of a good night out still kicking at their feet.

Like its people, Glasgow looked at its gallus best on a Saturday night and at its worst on a Sunday morning. Empty Buckie bottles, vomit and broken windows. Scotland with style? This was the Glasgow they didn't put in the glossy ads. It was a ten-minute drive from Princes Square and the designer shops on Buchanan Street but it was a world away. And then again it wasn't. It was all Glesga, this was just the bit they didn't shout about.

Two seagulls fought over the cold remains of a fish supper dropped or thrown away by a drunk. The wind and rain made an empty can of Irn Bru scoot along the gutter.

'Fuck this,' complained Addison. 'There are times I fucking hate Scotland and it's usually when it's raining. Which is most of the time. Having to scrape a dealer off the floor of the market sure isn't doing much for my mood either.'

'Ah cheer up big man,' Winter laughed. 'Maybe by the time we get back, that twat Monteith will have solved the case and we'll know the secret of the mysterious death of Sammy Ross.'

Addison snarled.

'Sammy Ross? Waste of fucking space, waste of fucking time. He's just fucking paperwork.'

The DI's phone rang and he swore as he transferred the remains of his roll from one hand to the other, digging his mobile out of his jacket pocket. Swallowing food down, he held it to his ear and grunted a hello.

'Yes? Yes, sir . . . You're fucking joking me . . . No sir, I don't suppose you are. Sorry . . . Shit. Okay, I'll be there in half an hour.'

Winter was stuck between trying to not to smirk at his friend and worried about what he'd been told.

'What's up?'

Addison shook his head wearily. 'This town will be the fucking death of me. They've pulled a body out of the Clyde near the Squinty Bridge. Looks like she was a hooker. Some bastard's strangled the poor bitch.'

Winter tried to conceal the look that wanted to flitter over his face, a look that would register somewhere between disgust and excitement.

'We finishing up here before we go?'

'*We're* not going,' replied Addison. 'Just me. Monteith can run the show here but forensics are already photographing the body so you're not needed. And don't even bother arguing, it's out of my hands.'

'Fucksake,' blurted out Winter. 'They pull you off one fucking murder for another. Why, because it's more important? Yet they don't want to fucking photograph it properly!'

Addison smiled gleefully at his friend's irritation. 'You

know how it is, wee man. Everything's got its place in the scheme of things. Some scumbag getting stabbed on a Saturday night is worth about the same as an A in Scrabble but a murdered prossie is a J. And photographs of deid bodies are the same whether they are taken by you or a trained monkey.'

Tony knew that his mate was winding him up but, despite himself, he bit. 'Fuck you. Fuck right off and stick your letter J up your A for arse.'

Addison laughed loudly. 'Nice comeback, wee man. And so eloquently put. And now if you'll excuse me, I've got to go. I've got a date with a young lady.